Christine Marion Fraser is one of Scotland's top selling authors with world-wide readership and translations into many foreign languages. Second youngest of a large family, she soon learned independence during childhood years spent in the post-war Govan district of Glasgow. At the age of ten she contracted a rare illness which landed her in a wheelchair and virtually ended her formal education. From early years, Christine had been an avid storyteller; her first novel *Rhanna* was published in 1978.

Christine Marion Fraser lives with her husband in an old Scottish manse on the shores of the Kyles of Bute, Argyllshire.

Praise for Christine Marion Fraser

'Christine Marion Fraser weaves an intriguing story in which the characters are alive against a spellbinding background'

Yorkshire Herald

'Fraser writes with a great depth of feeling and has the knack of making her characters come alive. She paints beautiful pictures of the countryside and their changing seasons'

Aberdeen Express

'Full-blooded romance, a strong, authentic setting'

The Scotsman

'An author who has won a huge audience for her warm, absorbing tales of ordinary folk'

Annabel

'Christine Marion Fraser writes characters so real they almost leap out of the pages . . . you would swear she must have grown up with them'

Sun

A Rhanna Mystery

Christine Marion Fraser

CORONET BOOKS
Hodder & Stoughton

First published in Great Britain in 1996 by HarperCollins*Publishers* 1997
First published in paperback in Great Britain by
HarperCollins*Publishers* 1997

This edition published in 2002 by Hodder & Stoughton
A division of Hodder Headline
A Coronet paperback

A CIP catalogue record for this title
is available from the British Library

ISBN 0 340 82410 7

Printed and bound in Great Britain by
Mackays of Chatham, plc

Hodder & Stoughton
A division of Hodder Headline
338 Euston Road
London NW1 3BH

To Frank Gallagher,
Who made the dial of the golden sun,
To tell me of the dawning of a day that's just begun,
Who brings to me the laughter, of music and stories shared,
And all the treasures springing from a friendship, never spared.

With thanks to Ken
for all the numerous cups of coffee,
when I was back once again on Rhanna.

C.M.F.

Abbey ruins
Dunuaigh
Cave
Croynachan
Sgurr na Gill
Burnbreddie House
Sgurr nan Gabhar
Mo
Dhachaidh
Dov
Pas
NIGG
Sgurr nan Ruadh
Slochmhor
Murdy's
House
M
R of RHANNA
Tigh na Cladach
Burg Bay
Manse
Loch
Tenez
Schoolhouse
Todd the
Shod
Cro
Bea
Kirk
PORTCULL
Sgor Creags
Caves
Port Rum Point
Ranald's
Boats

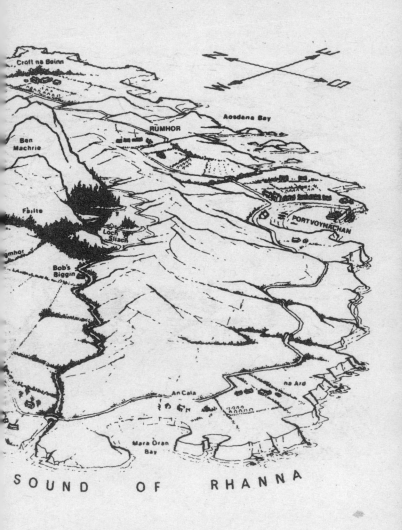

Croft na Beinn

Aosdana Bay

RÙMHOR

Ben Machrie

Failte

Loch Sliach

PORTVOYNACHAN

Bob's Biggin

gmhor

na Ard

An Cala

Mara Òran Bay

S O U N D   O F   R H A N N A

Part One

SPRING 1968

Chapter One

Fergus felt uneasy. He had emerged from a restless sleep and now he lay in the darkness of the room, wide awake and alert, his eyes on the grey oblong of the window. The March night was black outside. Normally he could see the rugged outlines of Sgurr nan Ruadh etched against the sky but now there was nothing, just the night and the blackness and this strange feeling of foreboding in the pit of his belly.

Taking a deep breath he made himself relax. The door of the bedroom was partially open; from the hall he could hear the faint ticking of the grandmother clock. It was a tranquil sound, one that he had known from childhood. The clock had been in the family for generations.

'A grand old lady,' his father had affectionately called it, and though Fergus himself would never have openly voiced such a sentiment he thought of it that way: the grand and tireless old lady who had stood sentinel in the hall all these years, the heartbeat of the house, the matriarch who had dictated the household routine for so many McKenzies.

It was a sound that was both soothing and compelling. One minute he felt lulled by it, the next he found himself counting the ticks. Tick-tock, tick-tock. His lids were growing heavy. Wryly he smiled to himself in the darkness. Other people counted sheep; he counted clock beats, maybe because, as a farmer, he'd had enough of counting sheep to last him a lifetime.

The house was peaceful and quiet around him, the big feather bed was warm and comfortable, there was no reason in the world why he shouldn't just allow himself to drift off. But he fought against it. Something out there was disturbing him. He strained his ears, listening; there was nothing unusual to be heard, only the sigh of lonely places, the voice of silence on the hills, the River Fallan rushing over the stones.

Throwing back the covers he padded quietly over to the window and looked out. A blanket of swirling mist covered the island; in the distance the beam of the Rhanna light filtered faintly through the haar; the mournful tones of the fog horn came eerily through the darkness.

There was nothing to be seen of the village of Portcull, nor of the Sound of Rhanna beyond. Down below, the ghostly grey shapes of the trees were still and silent, the pale glitter of hoar frost on the roadside verges the only vestige of brightness in the landscape. Menace seemed to lurk in the branches, melancholy crept amongst the twisted trunks... he felt threatened and oddly apprehensive.

He shuddered and tried to shake off his mood. He wasn't the sort of man to indulge in fanciful imaginings. Trees were trees, shadows were shadows, it wouldn't be night without them...

Straining his eyes Fergus peered downwards... and his heart lurched into his throat! Something had moved down there in the bushes, one of the shadows had detached itself from the rest, a being of the night, shuffling furtively towards the house ... He blinked his eyes and looked again. There was nothing, all was as it had been, not a branch moving or stirring.

If anybody was out there, he reasoned, it would most likely be old Dodie, the island eccentric, who had, for most of his life, wandered the hills and glens of Rhanna at all hours of the day and night. Yet Dodie was more settled these days, ever since the laird had moved him from his lonely cottage in the hills down to Croft Beag on the edge of the village. Dodie had never been more contented, his cow and his hens round about him, his garden to tend, Mairi McKinnon in the neighbouring croft, only too willing to see to all his little home comforts. Even so, the wanderlust was in his blood and would be till the day he dropped. If the mood took him he quite simply upped and went. No matter the hour, off he would go a'roaming, his huge, wellington-clad feet fairly covering the miles, his greasy black coat flapping in the wind.

But on a freezing cold March night? With barely a glimmer of light to show him the way?

Fergus decided he'd better go and investigate. Pushing his feet into his slippers he threw his dressing-gown round his shoulders and stole soundlessly downstairs.

The kitchen was warm and comforting, the fire had been damped with dross before bedtime and under the crackling of black cinders its heart was starting to glow. At Fergus's intrusion into the room a floppy,

5

indistinct shape half rose from the rug and Fergus laughed.

'It's only me, lazybones,' he said softly, affectionately rubbing the dog's ears. Last summer he had rescued the animal from the river, all tied up in a sack and left to drown. It had only been a pup then, big-boned and eager, an incongruous mixture of genes, jet black in colour with a soft spotted nose and a distinctive Border collie tail, recognisable labrador features, curly spaniel ears and 'God knows what else,' Bob the Shepherd had said with disgust when first he had clapped eyes on the beast. 'It's like one o' they comic creatures they have in the circus. It will be no good at all as a working dog and will likely just spend its life lazing around at the fireside.'

'Definitely a fifty-seven variety,' Kirsteen had said when her husband brought home his find, 'what else can we call him but Heinz?'

'Ach, you can call it all the fancy names o' the day,' Bob had spat disdainfully. 'It won't do a bit o' good. Why else do you think it was thrown in the river? It will become just an ornament on the rug, it has the look o' a lazy bugger about it already.'

Bob had never had time for 'lapdogs' as he put it. Neither had Fergus for that matter, but this dog was different; he'd had a traumatic start in life. Almost from the moment he had been fished out of the water he had shown a deep and lasting gratitude to his rescuer. As soon as he had recovered from his experiences he attached himself very firmly to Fergus and wouldn't let go.

Where Fergus went Heinz followed, watching every

6

move with his huge mournful eyes. When Fergus sat he sat, when Fergus moved he moved. He was like a shadow, faithful and loyal, even when Fergus was exasperated by his lack of prowess in all things useful and roared at him to go home. Because Bob had been right, Heinz *was* useless with sheep, and he was no good at all in the fields. Instead he liked to round up the hens in the yard and tease the cats in the barn and quite early on he displayed a terrible weakness for a game of football with the youngsters who came to visit Laigmhor.

He was marvellous with children and old people, but other than that he was 'a lazy good for nothing' in Bob's own triumphant words. Undoubtedly he adored the fireside and all the comforts of home and was effusive in his appreciation when Kirsteen set down tasty meals for his enjoyment.

Bob was soon proved wrong about one thing, though. Much to his annoyance Heinz was not destined to be a lapdog. As an ungainly pup he had only just fitted Kirsteen's knee, and deep had been his contentment in those precious few weeks, cosily dreaming and snoozing the evenings away. But when he was just six months old he had soon wakened to the reality that he had become much too big even for the biggest basket, and with many mighty sighs and moans he'd had to make do with the hearthrug.

One thing was certain however. At Laigmhor he had found a home for life. Everyone who met him loved him. He wooed and won all-comers to the house and in so doing allowed another of his little failings to become apparent: he would never even make a good

7

watchdog. He was alert to the everyday sounds round about him, such as a knock on the door or a chicken roosting on a windowsill, the rattle of the letterbox or footsteps on the path, otherwise he was at peace with the world and loved everybody. The only time he displayed any aggressive tendencies was if anybody showed signs of threatening behaviour towards Fergus, his god. If, in his master's presence, a voice was raised or a stick brandished, no matter how innocently, up Heinz would jump and the rumbles would start deep down somewhere in his massive lungs, growing in strength till his whole body trembled with the might and force of his feelings.

'Ay, I'll say that for him,' Bob admitted grudgingly, 'even if he's no' got much else in his head he's got your interests at heart, man. I have no doubt he'd kill anybody that looked near you and wi' those great buggering teeth o' his he'd make a good job o' it too.'

'I hope Bob's right.' Fergus smiled dourly to himself as Heinz responded to his fondling with a great show of stretching and moaning. He was vastly content and delighted to see his master at this unusually early hour of the morning, and it was obvious that nothing out of the way had disturbed him.

Seizing a torch from a hook on the wall Fergus went to the door and opening it he went outside, recoiling a little as the freezing foggy air penetrated his thin clothing. He went all round the house, shining the torch into nooks and crannies, checking the nearby outhouses to make sure nothing or no one was lurking there.

Heinz, feeling he ought to be on duty, reluctantly

left the warmth of the kitchen and followed in Fergus's wake, sniffing at every bush as he went, licking at the little mound of frost that had gathered on his inquisitive nose.

Hearing the stealthy padding at his back Fergus swung round and laughed in relief at the sight of his dog looming through the mist, unconcernedly lifting his leg at his favourite watering post – a gnarled old broom bush at the side of the path.

'Come on,' Fergus led the way back to the house, 'there's nothing here, back to bed wi' you, lad, as if you need to be told.'

Kirsteen stirred and murmured in her sleep when Fergus climbed back into bed and snuggled down beside her. His feet were like ice, she was as warm as toast, and he couldn't resist moving closer to the enticing heat of her body. She was soft and yielding and smelled faintly of new baked bread and apple blossom soap. The passing years hadn't lessened their desire for one another; last night he had made love to her with a fierceness that had taken her breath away.

In a few hours, weather permitting, she was going away from him, her little case all neatly packed and ready on a chair near the bed.

Doctor Lachlan's wife Phebie was going to Glasgow to nurse an old aunt who had just been discharged from hospital after a gall bladder operation.

'Why don't you come with me?' Phebie had said to Kirsteen, her rosy face sparkling at the thought. 'You haven't had a holiday in years and could be doing wi' a break. Aunt Minnie's a nice old soul, a widow wi' plenty o' money, thanks to having had a husband who was a bank manager. She's a bit grippy mind, doesn't believe in letting anything go to waste, she's also a bittie eccentric and fussy but a great character for all that. She lives in a lovely flat in the west end, near the botanic gardens. I won't have to be at her beck and call all the time and you and me could have a fine time in the Glasgow shops. She's got bags o' room and will be only too pleased to have company.'

But Kirsteen had hummed and hawed. She hadn't left the island in years, she wasn't too sure if she would like being in a town, Fergus needed her, he would be like a helpless bairn without her, there was far too much to do at Laigmhor, the lambing season was coming on; she couldn't possibly just up and leave everything and everybody to their own devices.

'Nonsense!' Shona, Fergus's daughter, had said briskly when she heard all this. 'If by everybody you mean Father you needn't worry your head about him. I'll make sure he's fed and watered and has everything he needs. He isn't a baby, you know, and Phebie's right, you do need a holiday, you're getting to be like Mirabelle was, with all your fussing and smothering!'

'Smothering! Well, I like that!' Kirsteen had gasped. 'I've never smothered anybody in my life . . .' she had glared at Shona contemplatively '. . . until now, that is!'

Shona had laughed unrepentingly. 'Alright, make that mothering. You do mother Father, and you do fuss over him. I'm just up the road at Mo Dhachaidh and I can easily pop in to make his meals, and if that isn't enough I'll even bring the bairns down here and

10

stay with him for as long as need be, Niall won't mind, I'm sure.'

But Niall had minded. When he learned of his wife's plans his face had turned red and his brown eyes had glittered. 'Hey, hang on,' he had protested, 'what about me? Your one and only husband? Where do I fit into all this?'

'Och, don't foul your breeks,' Shona had replied with a toss of her red head, 'we can manage between us just this once. Kirsteen has helped us out plenty in the past. It's time we did something for her for a change. Anyway, it probably won't come to me actually having to stay at Laigmhor, I only really said that to please Kirsteen. Father's perfectly capable of biding on his own for a while. After all, Phebie's leaving *your* father to fend for himself.'

'He has Elspeth to see to him,' Niall said quickly.

Shona smiled. 'Elspeth's head is too full o' Captain Mac these days for her to bother with anyone else, but I take your point. Ruth will be only too happy, I'm sure, to help me look after you while I'm looking after Father and Tina won't mind helping to look after Father while I'm looking after you.'

All this sounded rather confusing. Niall blinked and grimaced, Shona followed suit, then they looked at one another and burst out laughing, all their little differences forgotton in the daftness of the moment.

After that it was all settled; Kirsteen capitulated to all the persuasive tongues, the assurances that nothing would suffer in her absence. She was now quite looking forward to going with Phebie to Glasgow, but still she worried about leaving Fergus and spent the days leading up to her departure cleaning the house and cooking large quantities of the kind of foods that wouldn't easily perish.

'It will just go to waste,' Fergus told her patiently. 'Don't forget, the electrics haven't come to Rhanna yet and I'm thinking that the freezer you bought last year will rot away before we're able to wire it up.'

'We don't need a freezer, I've made things that will keep.' She had shooed him out of the kitchen at that point and after that he had held his tongue because he knew it would be useless to argue further.

The evening prior to her departure she had baked batches of scones, bread, and pastries and had tumbled into bed exhausted, though she hadn't been too tired to respond to his persuasive mouth, or to the demands of his body moulding itself to hers.

Now she was like a contented kitten, curled up and cosy, though when she became aware of his cold knees at her back she murmured sleepily, 'Is everything alright, Fergus? You're like ice. What have you been up to?'

'Nothing, go back to sleep.' Tenderly he kissed the crisp curls at the nape of her neck. A strange sensation of insecurity seized him. He didn't want her to leave him, her place was here with him, she had hardly left his side in all their years of marriage. The children were all grown up with lives of their own to lead, Kirsteen was the only one left to him and now even she was going away . . .

The heat of her body beat into his; he took a deep breath and allowed himself to relax against her. In minutes they were both asleep, held fast to one another in love, warmth, and trust.

Chapter Two

At ten-thirty next morning Lachlan's rickety little car drew up at Laigmhor's door and sounded its horn. It was a very distinctive sort of horn, with a tone to it that was reminiscent of a cockerel with a sore throat.

Laigmhor's cockerel hated it. Every time he heard it he set himself up in direct competition to it and this morning was no exception. Lifting his beak to the heavens he let rip, his crows growing louder in volume, higher in pitch, till the entire hen-run echoed with the raucous screeching. This excited the geese and the hens a great deal and they too added their contribution in support of King Cock, cackling and gaggling at the tops of their voices.

'Christ! Would you listen to that!' Fergus scraped back his chair from the table where he had been having his mid-morning break, and going to the door he thrust his feet into his boots. 'I'll thraw that bloody cock's neck if I get a hold o' him!'

'Fergie, Fergie.' Kirsteen drew him to her and held him close. 'It isn't the cockerel, is it? It's because I'm going away and you're trying to hide your feelings in angry words.'

Gently she kissed him and pushed a lock of dark hair back from his brow. 'Say you'll miss me, darling man. I know you, you don't like to let your emotions show but I think – just this once – you ought to tell me you love me and say you can't wait for me to get back.'

'Steady on,' he said gruffly, 'you aren't even away yet so how can I tell if I'll miss you or not?'

'Fergie,' she said softly, 'come on now. Don't send me away without a single loving word.'

Fergus hesitated. In truth he was feeling rather annoyed with himself for taking Kirsteen's departure so much to heart. He hadn't expected to feel like this but now that the moment of goodbye had come he felt that she was deserting him for some obscure relative of Phebie's who couldn't possibly mean anything to her.

He glanced at Kirsteen's face. She was biting her lip and watching him anxiously and – he had to admit it – she did look tired and in need of a break. 'Alright,' he conceded awkwardly, 'I'll miss you, isn't that enough?'

'If you're going to behave like that . . .'

She pulled away from him and he looked at her standing there. The passing years had not robbed her of the beauty that had so entranced him when first they had met. She was slim and smart in a blue suit that matched her eyes, her face was still finely honed, her skin had that lovely attractive glow that came from living in the dewy air of the Hebrides. She was his Kirsteen, so much a part of his life, so much a part of him . . .

'Kirsteen,' he murmured huskily and folded her to him to crush her mouth with his, 'you know fine well I'll miss you, every minute o' every day. I won't be able to settle till you get back. We belong to one another you

14

and me, it's been like that right from the start. I – I canny find the right words to tell you but always know – my life would be nothing without you.'

'Oh, Fergie!' The tears sprang to her eyes, and for a moment she was tempted to go outside and tell Phebie she couldn't go with her after all.

The car horn sounded again, the cockerel, the hens, and the geese set up a fresh cacophony of screeches, Heinz sat down and lifting his head bayed to the ceiling . . .

'Go.' Fergus pushed his wife gently towards the door. 'Go before we have the entire countryside down about our ears – and here, take this, enjoy yourself in the shops, you deserve it.'

He pressed a small wad of notes into her hand. She looked at it, the tears springing afresh. 'Oh, God, I don't want to leave you, I can't . . .'

Tucking her case under his arm he propelled her outside to the waiting car.

'Coming down with us to say goodbye?' Lachlan popped his head out of the window and gazed enquiringly up at Fergus.

From the back seat another head hove into view, one that belonged to Elspeth Morrison, Slochmhor's housekeeper. A grouse feather was sticking up out of her hat, and an unusual little flush burned high up on her cheekbones.

Elspeth had a very important mission on her mind that day. She was going down to the harbour to meet Captain Isaac McIntosh coming off the ferry. He had been to the island of Hanaay to spend a very belated New Year with his sister Nellie and Elspeth had missed him more than she could have thought possible. He and she were soon to be married and even now she could hardly believe that he actually wanted her for his wife, a widow woman of advanced years whose bitter tongue and sarcastic remarks were legendary on the island. But ever since Mac had come to lodge with her they had gotten to know one another very well indeed, much to the astonishment and curiosity of the entire island.

They had spent a marvellous Christmas together in Oban, shopping, sightseeing, exploring, walking hand in hand wherever they went, laughing, talking, or just being comfortably silent with one another. Elspeth had never known anything like it; the world for her had opened up and she had expanded with it. Mac's warmth, his frankness, his joy of living, transferred itself to her and she blossomed as she had never done in her life before.

Her marriage to her drunken sea-going husband, Hector, had been a farce. They had spent their time arguing and bawling at one another, and when he had died she had thought she would spend the rest of her life alone and lonely. Now there was Mac, and Elspeth had never been happier. She was well aware that the tongues were red hot with speculation and gossip, but she ignored it all and held her head high.

Fergus had scant patience with Elspeth, she had always irritated him with her knowing looks and her malicious innuendos, but worse than that was her air of smugness whenever anybody was in trouble and Fergus had no desire to share the back seat of Lachlan's old motor car with her.

'Thanks, man, but we've already said our goodbyes,' he hastened to say, a muscle working in his jaw when Elspeth stuck her sharp nose haughtily in the air.

Kirsteen squeezed his hand. 'I'll probably only stay in Glasgow for a week. I wish you would get the phone in, Fergie, everyone else has one.' She sounded wistful. 'I would have felt better, talking to you every night. You could maybe call me from Slochmhor or Mo Dhachaidh, but in any case I'll write. There's a steak pie in the larder for your dinner and a pan o' soup in the –'

Despite himself he laughed. 'Woman! Be gone wi' you! I'm not helpless and I won't fade away. Shona, Ruth, and Tina between them will see to that.'

The car door banged, her neat little head bobbed at a window, her face gazed out at him, her hand came up, and then she was gone from him in a cloud of exhaust fumes.

He stood watching the vehicle receding down the farm track and took a deep, rather shaky breath. The raw air flooded his lungs. The mist of the previous night having completely dispersed, it was a cold but beautiful morning; the slopes of Sgurr nan Ruadh were red with bracken, a cap of snow gleamed on its peak, and away in the distance the Sound of Rhanna was a dark blue ribbon against the paler blue of the sky.

Heinz gazed up at him. 'It's only you and me now, lad,' Fergus said quietly, and turning on his heel he walked back slowly to the empty house.

The harbour was quiet that morning, with only a handful of locals standing about watching the approach

17

of the steamer. By coincidence or design, Behag Beag, the Ex-Postmistress of Portcull, as she had entitled herself, was there beside Kate McKinnon, muffled to the eyebrows in scarves, a large black astrakhan hat pulled well down over her long ears, the collar of a moth-eaten fur coat enclosing the scraggy layers of her neck.

'It was my mother's coat,' she had told Mollie McDonald when first she had appeared in the garment. 'My father gave it to her on their second wedding anniversary and of course I came heir to it when she died . . .'

At this point her voice wavered a little but she certainly wasn't going to tell Mollie that her father had got the coat from a tink at the door in exchange for two shillings and a bag of meal. Her mother had never worn the coat, saying that it might have been stolen for all they knew, and what good was a fur coat anyway on an island where the womenfolk only ever went to kirk dressed in black and the only fur coats they had ever seen were attached to the sheepdogs. So the garment had been shoved to the back of a wardrobe, forgotten and neglected, till the recent cold snap had encouraged Behag to resurrect it.

'Of course, the moths have been at it,' she had explained glibly to Mollie, 'even though it's been well wrapped in camphor paper. But it's fine and warm for all that and I was never a body to bend to all that fashion nonsense.'

Mollie had eyed the coat and privately thought that it would have been best left to the tender mercies of the moths, but she was a kindly soul and said nothing,

18

not even when Behag eyed her own sensible tweed coat and said loftily, 'You could be doing wi' a change yourself, Mollie, 'tis all very well to be wearing the same things year. in and year out but as my own mother said to me, "If you leave poverty indoors and take pride with you the two will never go hand in hand in *this* family."

Behag had never fully understood what her mother's adage had meant, she still didn't understand, but it sounded good anyway and Mollie McDonald had certainly seemed impressed if her red face and astonished expression had been anything to go by.

Whatever Behag thought about pride, she certainly displayed very little of it when it came to nosing into other folks' activities. She was incensed with curiosity about Elspeth and Captain Mac and made use of every opportunity to poke and pry into their lives. Ever since the start of their 'affair', as she put it, instilling every sort of meaning into the word, she had made it her business to follow their every move. She had known full well that Mac was coming off the boat that morning and had contrived to be at the harbour in order to witness 'the reunion' at close quarters.

Now, the steamer had tied up, the passengers were disembarking, and Captain Mac was one of the first to come down the gangway. He made straight for Elspeth, his white hair tousled by the sea breezes, his big jolly nose glowing brighter than ever from the drams he had consumed with Tam McKinnon in the saloon bar. He and Elspeth greeted one another with restraint, conscious as they were of several pairs of eyes upon them.

19

'Behag's here,' Elspeth hissed into one of Mac's hairy lugs, ''specially to see us. You're surely no' going to let her down, Mac, she came for more than just a view o' the sea – and on such a cold morning too.'

Mac cottoned on quickly to her meaning – both of them took an absolute delight in tormenting the Ex-Postmistress of Portcull – and without ado he folded Elspeth into his big hearty embrace and kissed her soundly on the mouth, to be amply rewarded by an expression of sheer shock on Behag's face.

'Did you see that?' she gasped to Kate as Elspeth and Captain Mac went off arm in arm, choking back their laughter. 'Kissing and slavering for the whole world to see. It's bad enough for young folks to be doing that sort o' thing in public but at *their* time o' life – it's a disgrace!'

Kate looked thoughtfully in the direction of the receding pair. She was lost in her own train of thought and didn't pay much attention to Behag's comments. 'What good will the likes o' Elspeth be to a lusty great chiel like Isaac McIntosh?' she pondered with a devil-ish glint in her eyes. 'She's that scraggy and he's that big he would maybe break her in two if he climbed on top o' her.'

Behag's lips folded and she said coldly, 'There is no need to put it that plainly, Kate McKinnon, besides, they will surely no' be indulging in anything o' that nature at their age.'

Kate's eyes gleamed, she liked nothing better than to tease Behag. 'My, my, Behag, 'tis well seeing you are a spinster woman wi' naught in your head but pride and prudity. People do it at any age, the older the fiddle the better the tune! I myself have enjoyed it more as I got older. Tam used to just shake his breeks at me for another bairn to be on the way...' She grinned widely at the look of disgust on Behag's face. 'And talking o' the man, here he is now, all frisky and eager and maybe thinkin' o' taking me to bed for the rest o' the morning.'

As Tam approached, Behag flounced away in highest dudgeon, leaving Kate skirling with laughter as she took her husband's arm and marched him away homewards.

Lachlan was helping Phebie and Kirsteen to get their luggage out of the car, smiling a little when he felt the weight of his wife's case. 'Are you sure you're going to Aunt Minnie's?' he enquired, his brown eyes twinkling. 'Or have you and Kirsteen maybe cooked up something a bit more exotic between you? A cruise, for instance? Or a few weeks in the Bahamas while the rest o' us sneeze and sniffle and shiver our way through a freezing Scottish spring?'

'Chance would be a fine thing!' she replied with a giggle. 'If Aunt Minnie could bear to part wi' some o' her money, a cruise would be just the job, but she's aye been too mean for her own or anyone else's good!' Her plump face grew serious and grabbing his hand she said urgently, 'Oh, Lachy, are you sure you're going to manage without me? I don't like leaving you on your own like this.'

'I won't be on my own. The place will be jumping wi' visitors all anxious to see how I'm coping. I have no doubt that Fiona will pop in to make sure I am not

21

dying o' starvation, no' to mention Shona, and Tina and any number o' women fussing over me and spoiling me. And don't forget, there's always our Elspeth, all tight-lipped and serious and telling me that no self-respecting wife would ever go off and leave a poor hapless cratur' like me to fend for myself.'

Phebie laughed. 'I know, she's been giving me some poisonous looks lately but she's much too taken up wi' Mac these days to really bother her head about anything else.' Her eyes searched the harbour. 'Fiona isn't here, after saying she would be. Grant has a few days off at the moment so maybe she's too taken up with that to bother about her poor old mother. I hope she'll remember to look in on you.'

'Och, Phebie! Of course she'll remember! Stop fretting, I'll be fine, and I can always go to Laigmhor and drown my sorrows with Fergus over a game o' cards.'

Grabbing her to him he kissed her and slapped her on her well rounded bottom to send her on her way before giving Kirsteen a farewell kiss on the cheek. He stood watching as they boarded the boat and waved at them when they appeared at the rails.

'*Tha Breeah!*' Dodie came galloping up, shouting out his customary Gaelic greeting for 'It's a fine day' in his mournful voice. No matter the weather, Dodie always said the same thing, though on this sparkling blue March morning, with the sunlight silvering the sea and the wavelets lapping the long stretches of dazzling white sands, his words were perfectly justified.

As usual his clothes were pitifully inadequate to keep out the biting cold; his hands were blue, a large drip adhered precariously to the end of his nose and the tips of his ears were purple, yet despite all these obvious discomforts there was a spark of excitement in his dreamy grey-green eyes as he went on in a rush, 'I am waiting for Hector the Boat to see will he maybe take me out fishing wi' him.'

Dodie had always been a creature of the land, never of the sea. He was scared of everything pertaining to it, both real and imagined. Canty Tam had filled his head with tales of Green Water Witches, whose main aim in life was to lure unwary fishermen to their death beneath the waves. Then there were the Uisge Hags to contend with, dreadfully wicked beings who could change from ugly crones into beautiful mermaids for the sole purpose of capturing fishermen in their evil clutches and transporting them for their own use to the very depths of the ocean.

With all this in mind Dodie normally avoided contact with the sea, but Hector the Boat had recently pulled a muscle in his shoulder and was looking for an extra pair of cheap hands to help him haul in his lobster pots. Being possessed of a persuasive tongue he had somehow convinced Dodie that all the tales he had ever heard about sea monsters had been born of myth and legend, and that even if they did exist, it was only deep sea fishermen who ran the risk of close encounters.

'I thought you didn't like boats or the sea, Dodie,' said Lachlan with a frown. 'What's changed your mind now?'

For answer Dodie rubbed his stomach and rolled his eyes heavenward. 'Lobsters, fresh out the sea. Hector said if I helped him wi' his pots he would give me a whole one all to myself. Nothing finer wi' a boiled tattie and a bit turnip.'

Lachlan looked grim, 'And that's your payment for helping him? One lobster?'

Dodie nodded in a distracted fashion as he searched the harbour for a sign of Hector. A small boat put-tered into the bay and tied up alongside the old jetty. Hector's woollen-clad head came bobbing up the slimy stone steps. Cupping his hands to his mouth he yelled, 'Come along now, Dodie, the *Queen o' Scots* is ready and waiting for us!'

Hector had thought it a fine joke to name his tiny vessel in such a grand fashion, and even if it hadn't brought him much in the way of reflected glory, it had certainly caused a small sensation among the fisher-folk of Rhanna when he had christened it with a bottle of beer and had launched it amid much swaggering and boasting.

'Hector might no' be the full shilling,' old Jessie McKinnon had said at the time, voicing the general consensus of opinion, 'but he's all there just the same. The man would rob his grannie o' eggs and sell them back to her for a profit without batting an eye.'

Whatever his faults, Hector the Boat was a likeable rascal and he undoubtedly seemed to have Dodie under his sway if the old eccentric's new-found enthu-siasm for fishing was anything to go by.

Turning to Lachlan he puffed out his chest and said importantly, 'I will have to go, doctor, the *Queen o'*

Scots is here and Hector will maybe no' wait for me if I don't get a move on.'

Dodie still addressed Lachlan as 'Doctor', even though he had been retired for some years, and Lachlan couldn't help smiling as the old man took to his heels with gusto, the loose sole of one enormous wellington slip-slapping noisily on the stone flags of the quayside.

The steamer was leaving the harbour; as she sailed out into the open sea Phebie and Kirsteen soon became just dots at the rails. Lachlan stood watching till all he could see was the smoke from the funnels.

Fiona, his daughter, came running up, a tall young woman with a lively face and neatly bobbed glossy brown hair. 'Damn! I've missed it!' she panted. 'After saying to Mother I'd be here to see her off. Grant's keeping an eye on Ian and I meant to be on time but at the last minute old Jessie popped in for a blether and you know what she's like once she gets going. Her niece Barbara lives in the Midlands and has been ill for some time so Jessie is trying to get her to come to Blair Croft for a holiday.'

Lachlan nodded, 'Barbara McKinnon, I remember her, left the island to work in England and married a man by the name o' Benson. There's a whole bunch o' bairns, I believe, and Benson flew the coop when his wife became ill, leaving the family to fend for themselves.'

Fiona shook her head. 'I heard all about that, from Jessie herself of course . . .' She broke off to gaze at her father. He seemed a little forlorn, she thought, and just a tiny bit lost looking.

'Come on.' Linking her arm through his she pulled him away from the harbour and onto the road. 'A cup of tea is what you need, and maybe a nice hot scone absolutely smothered in bramble jam. Jessie brought some of each and once Grant gets his teeth into them there won't be anything left for anybody else. You and me will make merry first so just you relax and come with me whilst mother-cum-wife sails o'er the sea.'

He laughed; she was light-hearted and talkative and just the boost he needed in that strange moment of loneliness he had experienced when the steamer had sailed away taking Phebie with it.

Chapter Three

It was quiet in the house and after only a few minutes Fergus could bear it no longer. None of the usual faces were there that morning. Donald was in bed with flu, Davie McKinnon had a septic toe and 'couldny get his boots on', and Bob hadn't yet arrived, which wasn't like him as normally he was up with the lark and immersing himself in his work. It was a busy time of the year too, the early lambs were arriving and Bob liked to be out there in the fields, striding amongst the ewes with his dog at his heels.

Everything was strange and silent, both in and out of the house. The geese had marched down to the fields and were now grazing peaceably on the grasses, the hens were crooning contentedly in their run, and King Cock had crowed himself to a standstill and now stood balanced on one leg, thoughtfully eyeing the upturned backside of Granny Hen, the grand old lady of the hen-run who bossed the other hens unmercifully and pecked King Cock if he dared to come near her with anything other than honourable intentions.

Fergus glanced towards the road, hoping to see a sign of Shona, or Ruth or even Tina, who had promised to look in to see, 'Will you be needing a bittie help?'

He had scorned the idea of all these women fussing over him and had expected the feeling to last for some considerable time after Kirsteen's departure. Now here he was, Kirsteen just five minutes away, and already he felt bereft of human companionship.

Get a hold o' yourself, man, he told himself sternly, and striding over to the barn he yanked the door open and began forking cut turnips into a barrow which would later be scattered in the fields for the sheep.

Heinz, as usual, had followed his master and now lay sprawled on the straw-covered floor, languidly scratching one ear and yawning for all he was worth. Suddenly his ears pricked forward and he scrambled to his feet, a few long lopes taking him over to the stumpy wooden steps leading up to the hayloft. Excitedly he began whimpering and yelping and gazing upwards.

'Be quiet, boy!' snapped Fergus irritably, in no mood for Heinz and his games.

But the dog ignored the order. Whining and barking he clambered up into the hayloft to disappear from view, the sounds from his lungs growing in volume till with a sigh Fergus abandoned his task and strode over to see what all the fuss was about.

Heinz appeared, looking down from his lofty perch, bits of grassy debris adhering to his fur, his eyes big and bright in his lolling-tongued face.

'Get out o' there, lad!' Fergus scrambled up and made to grab the dog by the scruff of the neck, but Heinz neatly evaded the movement and bobbed out of sight once more, his short yelps and barks becoming more muffled as he burrowed his way through the loose hay.

'I'll kill you for this, you bugger!' roared Fergus as he went after the dog. He didn't have to go very far. Heinz was waiting for him, standing on top of a pile of sacks like the king of the jungle. Before his master could pour any more vitriol into his ears he turned his head to look over his shoulder in a dignified gesture that very effectively conveyed all that he was feeling.

Fergus looked over the dog's head. The sight that met his eyes took his breath away. A young girl in her early twenties lay sprawled in the hay. Her eyes were closed, she was dirty, ragged and unkempt; her hair was a mass of matted black ringlets, her skin pale and translucent in the rays of sunshine streaming in through the skylight. A large purple bruise on the side of her forehead stood out from the surrounding smooth skin like a medallion, and her legs and feet were scratched and bleeding through the rips in her stockings.

Fergus stared, 'Well, I'll be damned,' he swore softly, 'where in God's name did she spring from!'

Then he remembered last night, the darkness, the shadows, the feeling of foreboding that had seized him, the sensing that something or someone was out there, watching, waiting, before creeping furtively towards the house. It must have been *her*, this slip of a girl, seeking shelter from the night and the cold. But why was she out there in the first place? And who was she?

He asked himself these questions even as he fell on his knees beside her and applied his fingers to her neck to feel for a pulse. It was there alright, beating faintly but steadily. She was icy cold to the touch and with a sense of urgency he rose to his feet and hurried out of the barn to the house.

For once Heinz didn't follow but lay where he was, his soft muzzle on the girl's chest, his large, moist, mournful eyes holding an expression of anxiety beneath the furrowed canopy of his brows.

Seizing one of Kirsteen's own coats from the hall-stand Fergus ran back with it to the barn and in minutes was tucking the heavy woollen tweed folds round the girl's body. He sat back on his knees, staring at her, nonplussed as he wondered what to do next. Having lost one of his arms in an accident many years ago he knew he wouldn't be able to lift her on his own, except perhaps to throw her over his shoulders – not a very good idea bearing in mind that she might have other injuries he didn't know about.

He felt uneasy. Where the hell was Bob? He should be here! Unless of course he was at last past it and hadn't bothered to get out of his bed this morning. But no! Bob would never behave like that. He was a diligent worker and scorned idleness of any sort, especially in what he described as 'these soft young buggers you get mooching around nowadays!' No, no, Bob would have a good excuse for not being here, he'd better, or else! Fergus knitted his brows and scowled. Then he remembered Lachlan. He ought to be coming back from the harbour about now. He was a doctor, he would know what to do.

With a sigh of relief Fergus gladly vacated the barn and with Heinz once more at his heels he walked swiftly to the end of the farm track to await the approach of Lachlan in his little car.

* * *

Lachlan was feeling more cheerful as he drove slowly away from the smart new bungalow into which Fiona and her husband, Grant McKenzie, had recently moved. One of three, nestling into the lower slopes of Sgurr nan Ruadh close to Murdy McKinnon's tiny cottage, it was neat and bright and, along with its equivalents, regarded as a 'featureless box wi' funny wee chimneys' by Rhanna's older and more traditional inhabitants.

'I wouldny live in one if you paid me,' had sniffed old Annack Gow disapprovingly. 'You can hear yourself clattering about in them as if you were wearing clogs. They don't smell like real houses and forbye all that there are no wee corners to hide in.'

Her contemporaries knew what she meant. The houses they had lived in as children had been full of little corners, both in and out of the house; character had been built into every stone, and they had smelled of peat smoke and salt herring, not to mention all the other smells associated with self-sufficiency. Families had all lived under the one roof, grandparents, parents, children, looking after one another, sharing and caring, comforting each other in times of trouble, just being there in the home together in the long, dark nights of winter.

Things were different nowadays. Families no longer remained together, the children going their separate ways as soon as they were old enough, into houses of their own where they could live their own lives away from the watchful eyes of parents and grandparents.

Self-suffiency wasn't as important as it had once been. The steamers brought regular supplies to the islands and it was easy to take a trip over the water to the mainland shops. Mail order catalogues were part and parcel of everyday life and only a few of the womenfolk spun yarn into cloth, and then it was mainly to sell to the tourists.

There was no doubt about it, everything was easier all round, yet no matter how comfortable they might be, the hankerings for a past way of life remained with the old ones who liked nothing better than to gather together and reminisce about their youth, even though there were few among them who would honestly have wanted to return to a way of life that had often been hard.

Their lifestyle now was somewhere comfortably in between the past and the present. As long as they could get together with their cronies for a good gossip and a 'cosy wee cuppy' the world wasn't such a bad place to live in and though their offspring might not be under the same roof as them they were reassuringly close at hand if they were needed.

Houses in general retained the look of 'real houses', with proper chimneys, good thick walls, and roofs that were slated, pitched or corrugated, according to taste and finance. Peat smoke still spiralled from the chimneys to add its distinctive bouquet to the air and make town-bred visitors pause and wonder at the strange, evocative smell.

Television had not yet arrived on Rhanna. People had to make their own entertainment, as they had done for centuries, and the ceilidh still survived, with people visiting one another's houses for evenings of story and song.

But times were changing, there was no doubt of that. New buildings were gradually going up; a small council estate was presently being built near the village, and there was talk of a public convenience being erected at the harbour – 'the sooner the better' according to Ranald, who was heartily sick of people 'peeing up against his boatshed and rotting the wood'. The Portcull Hotel had recently had an extension added, the present owner, Duncan 'Bull Bull' McManus, declaring he had been 'bursting at the seams for the last few summers', which Todd the Shod had attributed to his trousers rather than to the proportions of his hotel.

These modest innovations didn't unduly spoil the appearance of the village nor made that much difference to the general way of life. The menfolk were glad of the extra work, the young folk enjoyed the extra activity, while the womenfolk attributed the changes to 'moving with the times' and hoped optimistically that a grammar school might one day be included in the curriculum so that their children wouldn't have to travel to the mainland in order to further their education.

It wasn't easy however to persuade some members of the older generation that everything was for the best and that the new houses would soon melt into the background and never be noticed.

'Rubbish!' maintained old Annack Gow, who was ninety and had been born in a blackhouse into which she often moved during the winter months because she claimed it was cosier than the 'modern hoosie'. 'They will aye be noticed for they are no more than

33

pieces o' flotsam wi' bits o' cement and spit holding them together. A puff o' wind will blow them down in no time!'

'Ay, you're right there, Annack,' agreed Jessie McKinnon, a fiercely independent spinster woman of seventy with a fresh rosy skin and a big hooked nose, who lived full time in a cottage with a thatched roof which was always needing to be repaired and was a 'damt nuisance' though her pride wouldn't allow her to admit the fact. 'I wouldn't part wi' my house for all o' they new ones put together. My walls are so thick a gale can be blowing outside and I am never the wiser.'

'Except when your roof blows off, Jessie,' interposed Tam McKinnon, who had lost count of the repairs he had made to the thatch of Blair Croft. 'But you're right enough in what you say,' he added quickly because Jessie's defence of her property could be formidable. 'They'll never build houses like yours again. The young ones will never know the joy o' these wee secret rooms that were built to hide the whisky stills from the customs mannie.' His eyes had gleamed, and he went into a muse as he remembered the day he had found an old pot still in Annack's byre, which he and his cronies had resurrected in order to brew a few casks of the bonny malt which had tasted all the better for being illegal.

'Here!' Jessie had barked, bringing Tam sharply out of his reverie, 'I hope you're no' suggesting that I have a whisky still in *my* house. All that died out wi' my father, may the Lord rest him, the rascal! In his day he was that busy making whisky he just let the croft fall down about his lugs and the only time he ever stopped was when he dropped. My mother – the Lord rest her too – couldn't wait to have the wee room sealed up and that way it has remained to this very day, as sure as God's my judge!'

Jessie, her old eyes growing misty, was getting carried away with self-righteousness, and shaking his head sorrowfully Tam had muttered a hasty, 'Ay, right enough now,' and gone smartly about his business.

Fiona McKenzie didn't give two figs about these opinions. She was young, she was modern, she was delighted with her new house and extremely proud of it. Fiona's home was Spic and Span with capital letters. She never left anything on a chair and if anyone else did it was whipped away in double quick time and deposited in its 'proper place' and woe betide the sinner who dared to leave any kitchen requisite on her 'best furniture'.

Lachlan enjoyed going there to play with his grandson on the shining floors, though he was always glad to return to the homely atmosphere of Slochmhor where spiders could spin their webs without them being too noticeable and it didn't seem to matter very much if a few books and newspapers were left on a chair or a cup on a sideboard.

But he had to admit, Fiona had a soft spot for spiders; from childhood she had been interested in all forms of animal life and had gone on to become a marine biologist. Nowadays she was more inclined to enjoy being a wife and a mother and Lachlan teased her about it, telling her she was becoming soft, to which she just laughed as they both knew full well she would never fully lose the tomboyish streak that had always been in her.

Lachlan looked around him with appreciation as he drove along the Glen Fallan road. Although he had lived on Rhanna for more years than he cared to remember he never ceased to be impressed by its wild beauty and lofty grandeur. On one side of him the Muir of Rhanna stretched away like a vast umber mattress; on the other, the patchwork fields of Laigmhor rose gently up to meet the russet foothills of Ben Machrie. In front of him the great bens sheared up, purple and blue, towering into the azure sky, enfolding gossamer trails of vapour into their lofty bosoms so that the corries were veiled and secretive looking.

The hill burns were glinting in the sunshine, grey fangs of wet rock 'slavered and spat into the ravines', as described by Tam when he was waxing lyrical after a dram too many in the Portcull Hotel. Little white blobs that were new lambs dotted the lower fields; on the roadside verges the daffodils were opening their yellow trumpets to the sun; hazel catkins hung suspended above the peaty brown water of the river; the dark green leaves of bluebells spiked the mossy earth and clumps of primroses peeped shyly through their winter covering of dead leaves.

Rhanna was a good place to be on a day like this, Lachlan decided as he eased *Banger McCoy* round a pothole. It was Fiona who had given the car its title, saying the noisy emissions from the exhaust pipe reminded her of an Irish aquaintance of hers who had almost exploded after dining recklessly on beer and baked beans.

As *Banger McCoy* progressed slowly homewards Lachlan deliberately eased his foot off the accelerator till the car was just crawling at a snail's pace. The further he drove the more he was becoming aware of what it would be like at Slochmhor without Phebie's cheerful presence. How quiet the house would be without her, how empty the rooms. He had always told her laughingly that a month or two on his own wouldn't go amiss, as then he could really get on with the book he was writing about his experiences as an island G.P.

He had started the book on his retiral in 1965. The islanders had given him a little portable typewriter to 'send him on his way' and he had positively bristled with enthusiasm at the idea of getting all his accumulated notes down on paper at last. But thinking and doing had proved to be two very different entities. His wastepaper bins had overflown with all his discarded efforts and there had been more little bonfires than usual in the back garden.

Then of course there were all the interruptions in a writer's day. Fiona was a regular visitor and how unnatural it would be if Ian Lachlan McKenzie, all of three and a half, was not permitted to see his very own grampa whom he adored and treated as his equal during lively games of hide and seek. If Shona and Niall came by, bringing their three children, the hide and seek could turn into a riot with the grown ups making more noise than their offspring, all of them vying with one another to see who could talk the loudest. Over and above all that, a regular stream of people 'just dropped in to see were you needing anything'. Strupaks and ceilidhs were part and parcel of daily life and what chance did an aspiring writer have with all that going on?

'With you away I'll have the place to myself for a while,' he had said, tongue in cheek, to Phebie. 'I'll maybe get my book finished – and – who knows, I might even start another one.'

'Finished!' she had retaliated pertly. 'You haven't even begun it yet! As for another, save that for the rest o' the pipe dreams.'

'You wait! Just you wait!' he had laughed, but now he wasn't too sure of how he would feel in an empty house with the silence and stillness all around him . . .

The sudden appearance of Fergus, standing in the middle of the road waving his one arm imperatively, an excited Heinz dancing around at his feet, brought Lachlan very effectively out of his daydreams as, amid much clanking and stuttering, he brought *Banger McCoy* to a wheezy halt.

'What the hell are you playing at, McKenzie!' he cried, sticking an indignant face out of the driver's window. 'I could have run you over just now!'

The gross overstatement brought a dour smile to Fergus's face. 'Driving at the pace you do?' he said sarcastically. 'I don't know why you bother wi' the damt motor! You would be quicker getting out and walking!'

'That's beside the point. You *were* standing plunk in the middle o' the road and I just might have injured you. Old McCoy doesn't always answer to the brakes and I myself was lost in a bit o' thought as I was coming along . . .'

'Never mind that now, man,' Fergus spoke brusquely, 'I want you to come along wi' me to my barn. I have something to show you.'

Lachlan was used to the other man and his imperious ways, which didn't mean to say he always took too kindly to them. He was about to open his mouth in protest, but Fergus was already away, striding through the gate and up the track in no uncertain manner.

'Bugger you, McKenzie,' Lachlan muttered as he manoeuvred *Banger McCoy* alongside the gate and got out. 'At least have the manners to wait for me, Fergus!' he shouted.

Impatiently Fergus halted and waited for Lachlan to catch up with him.

'Just what is it you want me to see?' demanded Lachlan, his brown eyes glinting a little.

'A woman!' Fergus hurled the words over his shoulder as he began walking quickly towards the barn.

'A woman?'

'Ay, an injured one. I hope you've got your bag.'

'Dammit, man! I retired years ago in case you've forgotten. I'm not in the habit o' carrying my doctor's bag around with me. I don't even know where it is. It's Megan you want. She's the doctor now.'

'She isn't here, you are,' was Fergus's succinct reply as he strode into the barn and became lost to view.

Lachlan clenched his fists and gritted his teeth. Taking a deep breath he fought down his annoyance at Fergus, curiosity getting the better of him despite himself. Kirsteen had only just turned her back and here was her husband, finding himself another woman

39

as if they grew on the ground like daisies! Lachlan grinned. He was getting to be like old Behag with his wicked thoughts ... The jet black bundle that was Heinz appeared at the barn door, as if urging the doctor to get a move on. Even the dog was at it, hurrying people, demanding attention, getting to be more and more like his master with every passing day.

So thought Lachlan wryly as he entered the portals of the big airy barn with its cobwebs and lancing beams of sunlight and mysterious corners where people could hide out for days if they so desired.

'Hurry up, Lachlan!' Fergus's voice floated down from the hayloft.

'I'm coming, man,' Lachlan called back as he climbed upwards to where an unknown young woman lay, one whose unusual arrival would titillate the island's curiosity for many weeks and months to come.

Chapter Four

Lachlan's hands were gentle as he made a thorough examination of the strange young woman in Fergus's hayloft. 'She's been in the water,' he said decidedly. 'Her clothes are damp and smell of salt and she's got sand in her shoes.'

'You made a good doctor but you might have made a better detective,' Fergus said with a short laugh. 'I never noticed any o' these things, I was too busy finding out if she was alive.'

'Years o' dealing wi' every sort o' situation taught me a lot. She's alive alright but suffering from exposure and possibly lack o' nourishment. There's no indication of internal injuries, the cuts are superficial and the bruise on her head isn't as bad as it looks. She must have come in here and knocked herself out on a rafter. There could be concussion so we'll have to get her into the house and into bed. I'll take her head, you take her legs.'

With Heinz leading the way they manhandled the girl down from the loft and over to the house. Although she was so slightly built, her helplessness made her seem a dead weight and both men were panting slightly by the time they had carried her upstairs and into the bright little attic room that had once been Shona's.

'Help me get her clothes off,' Lachlan directed as soon as they had deposited their burden on the bed.

'Her clothes?' Fergus looked taken aback.

'Ay, you heard me, she canny very well stay in these damp things or she'll get pneumonia.' As he was speaking he was removing the girl's dress, peeling off her undergarments, his hands deft and sure as he worked.

Fergus could only stare as the layers were removed. Soon the girl lay naked on the sheets, as vulnerable-looking as a young child. Her tumble of dark hair cascaded over the creamy-gold skin of her· shoulders, her breasts were small and perfect, her waist tiny, her hips narrow, her legs surprisingly long. She was utterly and breathtakingly feminine and Fergus became aware of a strange sensation of entrancement gripping him as he observed her lying so still and silent in the white bed.

'A nightdress, man!' Lachlan's voice made Fergus jump. 'Don't just stand there gaping. Surely you must have something we can put her in. Shona bides here on the odd occasion, she'll have some bits and pieces in her dresser.'

Fergus gave himself a mental shake and striding to the dresser he unearthed a blue nightdress and a woollen bedjacket which he quickly handed to Lachlan.

'Hot water bottles', Lachlan ordered, 'as many as you've got. We must get her body temperature up – and you could maybe bring an extra blanket or two while you're about it.'

'Yoo-hoo! Father!' Shona's voice floated upstairs. 'Are you in? I've brought some things for your lunch!'

42

At the sound of his daughter's voice relief washed over Fergus. She was cool and calm in emergencies, she had been a nurse, she would know what to do.

'Up here, Shona,' he called, 'in your old room! Hang on, I'm coming down.'

But before he could move Shona came bounding upstairs to appear in the doorway, breathlessly declaring, 'I've left the bairns with Niall, I knew you might be feeling a bit sorry for yourself so I –'

She stopped short at the sight that met her eyes, Lachlan bending over the bed in which reposed a strange young woman, one whose raven hair tumbled over the pillows and whose wild beauty was strikingly apparent even though her eyes were closed and she looked very pale. Shona let her breath go in a hiss. This was *her* room! That was *her* bed . . . and most disturbing of all, these were *her* night-things that the girl was wearing, the spares that were always kept in the top drawer of *her* dresser, wrapped in layers of perfumed tissue paper to keep them fresh smelling.

The three bears! The thought came ridiculously and humorously into her head. 'Who's been sleeping in *my* bed?' Ellie Dawn loved that story and adored saying those words in a deep grumbly voice. But this was no laughing matter! Not with Kirsteen newly away, sublimely unaware of what was happening as she sailed serenely over the sea on a much needed holiday, never dreaming that another woman was snugly ensconced in Laigmhor as if she had planned the whole thing!

A spark of annoyance shone in Shona's deep blue eyes. Turning to her father she was about to demand an explanation but Lachlan got there first, clarifying the situation in a few short sentences, ending with, 'You were a nurse, Shona, you know what's needed. Later we'll have to call Megan, she might suggest getting the lass into hospital, but for now we've got to do all we can to make her comfortable . . .'

Just then the girl in the bed stirred and laid a hand on Lachlan's arm. 'No, no, not hospital, please,' she begged in a husky whisper, fear in the great dark eyes that looked up at him. Glancing around the cosy room with its gold-coloured curtains and homely decor she went on, 'Let me stay here, in this room, I'll – I'll be safe here. Don't let anybody take me away.'

'Alright, lass,' Lachlan said in his quiet, reassuring voice, 'you're going to be fine, no one is going to take you away. Just you lie back and rest and let us do the worrying.'

A sigh of relief escaped the girl's lips, and sinking back into the pillows she closed her eyes and fell asleep like a trusting child who knew it was in good hands.

An odd little silence descended on the room. Fergus and Shona looked at one another then rather dazedly they descended the stairs to the kitchen where he tried to tell her what he knew about the mysterious stranger, which wasn't much since he himself knew so little about her.

'I'll get the hot bottles,' Shona turned to the stove where the kettle was keeping warm. She was lifting it down when the door opened to admit Bob with his sheepdog, Gaffer, at his heels. Gaffer liked to think he was boss around the place and he immediately

44

made for Heinz, whom he loved to try and bully. Soon the kitchen was ringing with the barking of dogs and the hissing of the cats from their safe perch atop the oven.

'Come away here, you bugger!' Bob roared at his dog, and grabbing him by the scruff of his neck he rushed him outside and shut him in the barn.

''Tis sorry I am for being late,' Bob apologised when he got back, looking sheepish and red about the ears as he spoke. 'I can only say it was due to circumstances beyond my control,' he added rather grandly.

'And what might they be?' Fergus demanded curtly. 'I could have been doing wi' you here this morning.'

Bob coughed and shuffled his feet. 'Ay, well you see, it was curtains.'

'Curtains!'

'The very thing. Grace gave her ankle a wee twist and canny walk very far for the time being. She sent word to see would I come over to her house wi' my van to take her to Blair Croft where Jessie McKinnon is running her up some curtains. Jessie's a dab hand at making things on thon wee treadle sewing machine o' hers and wanted to ask Grace what size she wanted.'

'But you could have stopped by here on the way down to tell me you would be late,' Fergus said with a frown.

'Ay, well, I was going to do just that but it was so cold this morning the damt van wouldny start. I had to get Croynachan to give me a push wi' her down the brae and once she got going I was feart to stop her in case she wouldny start again.'

45

'It's high time you had that van looked at,' Fergus admonished. 'You haven't had it serviced since you got the damt thing.'

'Ach, I will, I will,' Bob spoke carelessly. He had scant interest in machines of any kind and what went on under the bonnet of his van was as clear to him as mud. Giving Fergus a sidelong glance he went on, 'As I was just after saying, Jessie is making curtains for Grace but we had to go to my house first to measure out the sizes.'

'Ay, you've already mentioned the curtains,' Fergus spoke impatiently, his mind refusing to dwell on such mundane matters when there was so much else to occupy it.

But Shona was quick to grasp Bob's meaning. With sparkling eyes she turned to the old man and laughed. 'Your house, Bob, the one you bought when you had that win on the football pools and which has lain empty since Fiona and Grant moved into their bungalow?'

'Ay, the very one,' Bob agreed slyly. 'It is much too grand for me to bide in all by myself. I thought it best to remain up yonder in my biggin till the time was ripe.'

'In other words, you're trying to tell us that you and Grace have at last decided to get married and move into the new house together.'

Bob's blue eyes twinkled. 'There is no fooling you, Shona my lass, and you're right enough in what you say. As you know, when Old Joe died, me and Grace thought it wouldny be decent to get wed right away so we agreed to bide our time for a wee whilie. I was beginning to think she had forgotten all about our arrangement when out o' the blue she said to me all coy like, "I'm getting lonely again, Bob, I think 'tis high time we started making our wee plans for the future. It isn't right to be leaving that fine house o' yours empty for too long and we could do no better than start off wi' some nice new curtains."'

Shona let out a peal of laughter, while Fergus went to the sideboard. Withdrawing a bottle of whisky he held it up and said, 'This calls for a dram, and I don't mind telling you I could be doing wi' one after all the upsets o' the morning. Sit you down Bob and let me charge your glass. It will have to be quick mind, one o' us will have to go for Doctor Megan in case the lass upstairs is needing medical attention.'

'Lass upstairs?' Bob's grizzled brown face lit up with interest. His gnarled fist closed round his glass as he waited for Fergus to explain himself further.

'Pour one for me,' directed Shona, 'I'll just go upstairs first with the blankets and the bottles.'

She departed, leaving her father to tell Bob the latest happenings at Laigmhor. When she came down she was accompanied by Lachlan, who joined briefly in the celebrations before departing to Slochmhor to telephone for the doctor.

'Will we be having any dinner today at all?' Bob enquired anxiously. 'Jessie wanted Grace and me to bide at Blair Croft for a bite to eat – mealy herring it was too, one o' my favourites – but I said I had to get over here as everyone would be wondering where I was lost.'

'Don't fret yourself, Bob,' Shona told him with a

47

smile, 'you'll get fed alright and it's another o' your favourites, mince and tatties, made by my own fair hands this very morning and transported down here in a couple o' milk luggies.'

'Ach, you're a good lass, just,' Bob settled back in his chair with his dram, contentment on his craggy features as he waited for Shona to heat the mid-day meal.

Suddenly she turned from the stove and looked at her father. 'That girl, the one upstairs, does she have a name?'

'Ay, seemingly she whispered it to Lachlan when we left the room, he said it sounded like Fern something, he couldny quite catch it all but said he thought it was maybe Fern Lee.'

'Fern Lee! Whoever heard o' a name like that? It's straight out o' the theatre if you ask me.'

Fergus stared down at the contents in his glass. Shona was right, there was something terribly unreal about the name, just a shade too fancy for it to be true. Time would tell ... Throwing back his head he gulped down his drink ... and couldn't help wondering just what would emerge about the mysterious stranger in the course of the next few days. If she was still at Laigmhor by then! He hastened to tell himself this for he had gone hot and cold at the remembrance of the girl's undoubted beauty as she lay on the cool white bed – as naked and as vulnerable as the day she was born and looking just as innocent. Then the thought came to him: what would Kirsteen have to say about all this if she knew what was going on under her very own roof? But nothing was going on, he hastened

48

to reassure himself, and Kirsteen would be as she always was to anyone who was needing help: kind, sympathetic, and completely understanding . . .

Shona set down a steaming plate at his elbow. He looked up at her, and in her eyes he saw an expression of curiosity – as if she was wondering what was going on in his mind. Then she smiled at him and squeezed his shoulder in a reassuring gesture and he knew that she understood how unsettled he was feeling with Kirsteen away and his life turned suddenly upside down.

The water was clear and calm as Hector the Boat guided the *Queen o' Scots* round a point of land into a little bay known as Camus nan Uamh, which was Gaelic for Bay of the Caves. Here there was good lobster fishing and Hector got to work with his pots while Dodie sat in the stern, gazing in fascination down into the depths of the translucent water.

The Uisge Hags, the Green Water Witches, the Cackling Crones of the Sound, were far from his mind that morning. It was a glorious day; the water was turquoise, the sky a hazy blue; above the cliffs the seagulls were swooping and diving, their wings flashing white in the sun; the cry of a curlew came bubbling up from the shore; sharp imperative whistles arose from the oyster catchers as they probed amongst the rocks with their bright red beaks. It was all a vastly new experience for Dodie and he had all but forgotten his mistrust of the sea in this amazing experience of seeing Rhanna from such a completely different angle.

49

Getting into the boat had worried him a bit. It had wobbled and bucked and he had held back till Hector had grabbed him and yanked him unceremoniously aboard.

'Come on now, Dodie,' Hector had said soothingly, 'you'll enjoy it once you get used to it. There is nothing like the sea to take away a man's worries. I myself have done most o' my thinking whilst floating on the waves. Just think o' the boat as a cradle rocked by a mother's hand and you'll relax in no time.'

It was a lyrical way of speaking and lulled Dodie into silence as they left the harbour and headed east. Then he had looked up and seen all the familiar landmarks that he knew and after that there was no stopping him. He had pointed and exclaimed and grown very excited till Hector had taken the pipe from his mouth to tell him to, 'Shut up, you're frightening the fish,' whereupon Dodie had fallen silent, spell-bound by the sights and sounds they encountered as they puttered peacefully along.

When eventually Hector brought his boat to a halt and cut the engine, Dodie continued to be entranced by all that he saw and showed no signs of moving one finger for fear the *Queen o' Scots* would start to 'rear up and drown him'.

'It's no' a horse you're talking about,' Hector pointed out witheringly, 'it's a boat in case you didny notice and we didny come here to admire the scenery. You'd better get busy before your erse attaches itself to that seat so just you ease yourself round a bittie and get to work wi' these pots.'

Gingerly, Dodie did as he was told and was soon

50

engrossed in the task set before him, though he wasn't too busy to pause occasionally and examine the pieces of flotsam that were bobbing about in the water.

Dodie loved flotsam. In the course of his beach-combing sojourns he was forever finding things of interest washed in by the tide, some of which he would take home to use as bits of furniture or to make into gifts for those he considered to be suitably deserving. There was quite a lot of debris floating about that day in the Bay of the Caves and with one thing and another Dodie's attention was greatly taken up.

Hector, a satisfied smile on his face, puffed contentedly at his pipe as he sat back to observe Dodie working. Every so often he removed his pipe to aim a gob of spit overboard, or to give Dodie a bit of advice on the best way to handle the pots. It was very pleasant sitting there in the bay, the wavelets gently rocking the little craft, the sun growing warmer on his back as the morning progressed.

Hector's eyes idly panned the immediate vicinity, coming to rest on the caves that pitted the cliffs above the beach. The bigger ones were like cathedrals with fantastic columns of basalt rock that receded back from the mouth of each cave to disappear into yawning dark depths. In these vaults the seabirds drifted and screamed and raised their young, yet, despite their picturesque appearance, they could also be spectacularly wild places, especially in the high seas of winter or during the equinoxes when the tides washed right into the caves in heaving, foaming splendour.

There was one cavern in particular that had always fascinated Hector. It was known as An Coire, the kettle, the spout being a strange formation of hollow rock into which the sea forced itself at high tide and came spuming out of a blow-hole in the cliffs far above.

As a boy Hector had delighted in perching himself on a ledge inside the cave to watch the sea come thundering in and blowing itself out of the spout, falling like a great white curtain down the cliff face and back into the sea from whence it had come. It had been a dangerous game but he had known exactly which ledges were safe when the cave was filling up with water.

He gazed at An Coire now with affection, and his watery blue eyes grew dreamy as he remembered those far off, boyhood days when such adventures were part and parcel of his life . . .

He was startled out of his reverie by a movement inside the cave, where a shadowy, indistinct figure seemed to rise up out of nowhere and remain suspended for a few brief moments before it appeared to melt away as if it had never been. Hector gaped, his heart accelerated, and his pipe hung from his slackening mouth. All the hags of myth and folklore came leaping into his mind and for quite a few moments he was paralysed into complete and utter stillness with his eyes glued to the spot.

But nothing further happened to cause him alarm, all was as it had been; the seabirds wheeled and cried and glided, looking like fragments of windblown white paper against the black cliff face, the oyster catchers whistled, and the sandpipers darted. Gradually Hector calmed down, it had been nothing, just a trick of the light; so he convinced himself till a thin, wailing cry came floating out of the cave, sounding just like the hobgoblins that Hector's mother had warned him about when he was just knee high. In all of his life Hector had never heard a hobgoblin, talking, crying, or otherwise, but to him the eerie cry was exactly how he imagined a hobgoblin would sound and so startled was he that he let out a small strangulated scream of his own.

Dodie, immersed in his task, looked round enquiringly, and Hector quickly pulled himself together. It would never do to frighten the old eccentric at this stage in the game, not when he was just getting to grips with the art of lobster fishing.

'It's nothing, Dodie,' he said as calmly as his racing heart would allow. 'I burnt myself on my damt pipe, that's all, I'm just no' at myself since I pulled this muscle in my shoulder and I'm thinking it's maybe time we had a bite to eat . . .' He paused, surprised at his own loquacity, then he went on, gabbling a bit in his excitement, 'I have some sandwiches in my satchel and I know a good place we can go to eat them.'

'Ach, I like it fine here,' protested Dodie in disappointed tones, for he had been thoroughly enjoying the novelty of the morning and was loath to leave the new-found joys of Camus nan Uamh.

But Hector wasn't listening. He had started up his engine and opening the throttle to its full extent he endeavoured to put as much distance as possible between himself, the bay, and the Hobgoblin of An Coire.

Chapter Five

'Fern Lee!' Babbie exclaimed, as she and Doctor Megan Jenkins sat in Laigmhor's kitchen partaking of a strupak supplied by Shona, who had stayed on to 'supervise proceedings' after Bob and her father had departed to the fields. 'Sounds like a figment o' the imagination to me.'

'I know, that's what I said,' Shona nodded as she topped up Babbie's cup and passed the biscuits to Megan. 'Father seems to be taken in by her however, and while Lachlan was being very doctorish and cool about the whole thing I could tell he had fallen for her too.'

Babbie, who was the island nurse, pushed a hand through her mop of red hair and shook her head. 'She's young, she's a beauty, and she looks as if butter wouldn't melt in her mouth. I suppose any man might be excused for admiring her. The big question is, who is she, and where did she spring from? She has nothing on her in the way of identification so it looks as if we'll just have to wait till she is recovered enough to explain herself.'

'*If* she tells us,' Shona said meaningfully. 'She came round quick enough when Lachlan mentioned sending her to hospital. She seemed afraid o' the very idea, like she had something to hide. All she wanted was to stay up there, in *my* room, as if it was some sort of retreat.'

Megan looked thoughtful. 'I've carried out a thorough examination of her and have found nothing much except some bumps and bruises. The knock on her head might have caused a slight concussion but otherwise she seems alright and ought to be up and about in a few days.'

'Meanwhile, who's going to look after her?' Shona wanted to know. 'Father can't be expected to do that and I have my hands full with my own lot.'

As if in answer to their questions Tina put her head round the door, her plump face wreathing into smiles at the sight of the teapot on the table. 'Just what I am needing,' she said approvingly. 'I came to see was Fergus wanting anything but first I myself am in need o' a cuppy. It's a fair walk up from the village and no' a soul on the road to give me a lift.'

Plunking herself down at the table she poured herself a large mug of tea and helped herself to a scone oozing with butter and home-made jam. She bit into the tasty morsel with gusto, causing a dollop of jam to roll down her chin. 'My, my, would you look at the mess, I'm worse than a bairn,' she observed with mild dismay, mopping the jam from her face while she demolished the rest of the scone in two bites.

Only when she had drunk her tea did she become aware that everything was not as it should have been at Laigmhor. 'Doctor Megan,' she acknowledged in some surprise, 'and Nurse Babbie. Has Fergus o' the

55

Glen taken ill? If I'm mindin' right he was the picture o' health the last time I saw him.'

In her concern she began to fiddle with her hair, a habit of hers whenever she was upset about something. Fine, flyaway strands departed from their precarious anchorage, and with an impatient, 'Tch,' she removed the kirby grips and applied them to her teeth to open them before jabbing them rather viciously back into place.

'It isn't Fergus,' Megan began, 'it's somebody else.' She went on to explain to Tina about the girl in bed upstairs, ending, 'She'll need looking after for a day or two and we were just wondering who we could ask that would be capable enough to take on such a task.'

Tina, utterly enthralled by the doctor's description of the stranger, sat up straight and pushed out a bosom that had the appearance of a well-upholstered cushion. 'Look no further, doctor, I have been caring for people all of my life. First it was my very own Matthew and my bairns when they were little, then it was the minister before he became your husband, the fine good man that he is. And, as you know, I nursed my own dear Otto when he was dying, God rest him. Forbye all that I have Grandma Ann and Granda John to see to, and not forgetting any o' the others who are needing a bittie comfort in their old age.'

The other three women breathed sighs of relief. Tina was perfect for the job; she was sweet-tempered and placid and was never happier than when she was looking after some lame dog or other. Her 'own dear Otto', as she fondly referred to the big Austrian who had come to Rhanna seeking his roots, had left her five thousand pounds in his will but the money had never made any difference to Tina's way of life. Some of it she had gifted to her son and daughter, the rest she had banked, declaring laughingly that one day she would use it to go on a world cruise. After that she just carried on as before, 'doing' for whoever needed her.

'If you're sure you can spare the time, Tina...' Megan began, when the door opened once more to admit Elspeth, her sharp nose stung to a bright red hue which she immediately attributed to the 'bitter cold o' the wind' as not for one moment would she ascribe it to the 'welcome home' drams that she had just imbibed with Mac in the privacy of her own home.

'I just came by because I heard tell that Doctor Lachlan was here wi' his motor and I thought to save my legs the walk to Slochmhor.' She imparted this with alcohol-induced flippancy. Elspeth was not a regular visitor to Laigmhor, only appearing if she was specifically invited in by Kirsteen, a rare occurrence owing to her animosity towards Fergus. But curiosity was a driving force in her life and she wasn't going to miss out on the latest events to have befallen the McKenzies, Fergus or no Fergus. Her eyes roved round the room. 'I must say, I didny expect such a gathering o' wimmen. Fergus McKenzie is indeed a popular man.'

'That he is,' returned Megan coldly, because Elspeth never failed to annoy her with her references to 'Doctor Lachlan' as if he was still the practising doctor on the island and she was an interloper who had to be tolerated.

'Is he needing the doctor at all?' Elspeth fished relentlessly. 'And the nurse too? If so I am thinking he has taken ill at a bad time wi' Kirsteen just fresh away from home and never knowing what has happened to him.'

Shona, Megan, and Babbie glanced at one another. Elspeth, with her self-answered questions and hasty assumptions, was about the most infuriating creature that anyone could wish to meet and not one of them had any intentions of satisfying her inquisitive prying.

Tina, however, with her artless nature and tolerance of her fellow humans, had no such reservations. In two minutes flat she had spilled the beans, so to speak, and when Elspeth's spindly legs at last took her from the house she was agog with excitement and eager to pour the latest revelations about 'the goings on at Laigmhor' into the ears of anyone who would listen.

'You didn't offer her a lift,' Shona remarked to Megan with a mischievous grin.

'I'm going in the opposite direction,' Megan returned with an equally devilish smile. 'Besides, she doesn't need one, she has enough hot air in her to carry her to the moon if she so desired and that's where she just might end up if she makes more out of all this than is necessary. Scandals can materialise very easily on an island like Rhanna, and I should know what I'm talking about.'

Both Babbie and Shona turned red, knowing only too well the truth of the doctor's words, for she had been the subject of much speculation and hurtful rumour when she and Mark James, the minister, had

been sorting out their different problems before becoming man and wife.

'All this is bound to be talked about,' Babbie
hazarded, her green eyes flashing a little as occasionally she became annoyed with the virtuous air that
Megan had adopted since becoming the wife of Mark
James. She was nursing grievances, there was no
doubt of that, and in Babbie's book it would have
been better for everyone concerned if she was to bring
them right out into the open instead of just hinting at
them now and again.

Shona, sensing an impending disagreement between
the two, made haste to gather up her things and depart
the scene before she became involved in an argument.
With her fiery temper she had long ago learned it was
better to avoid trouble if at all possible, and with that in
mind she fairly flew up the road to her neglected
husband, children, and animals, who were awaiting her
at Mo Dhachaidh.

'Have you heard the latest?' Elspeth marched purposefully into Merry Mary's grocer shop and banged
her shopping bag on the counter. 'Fergus McKenzie
has a woman biding wi' him and I can tell you this for
a fact – she is not his wife!'

'Ach, we know full well that Kirsteen is away in
Glasgow, it is common knowledge – and who are you
to talk? Captain Mac lives wi' you and he is not your
husband.' Merry Mary spoke with some annoyance
since Elspeth, in her hurry to enter the shop, had left
the door swinging open, allowing a wicked draught to
swoop in and rattle the ancient blind at the window.

'Be shutting the door behind you, Elspeth!' she ordered sharply. 'The shop is cold enough as it is.'

'Och, keep your breeks on, Mary.' Aggie McKinnon, a young woman of ample proportions and an exceedingly good nature, ambled over and closed the door with a snap.

Merry Mary allowed a smile to split her homely features. 'In this weather I have no intentions o' taking them off – for anybody.'

'Ay, well, there's those on the island who might no' share your views.' Elspeth, choosing to ignore the remarks about herself and Captain Mac, spoke cryptically. 'It seems Fergus McKenzie found a young woman in his barn, half naked and half dead. He got Lachlan to help lift her into the house and in no time at all she was wrapped up in one o' Shona's spare goonies and tucked into bed.'

'And how did you come to know all this, Elspeth?' asked Aggie.

'I had reason to visit Laigmhor yesterday and there was Doctor Megan and the nurse in the kitchen, drinking tea wi' Shona, as cosy as you like and none o' them giving much away. But Tina was there too and she just couldny hold her tongue. It all came out, except of course the identity o' the woman. With the exception o' her name, none o' them seems to know who she is. As to where she came from, that's anybody's guess, she was soaked to the skin when they found her – and it wasn't caused by rain or anything normal like that – it was sea water!'

'There will be a simple explanation,' Barra McLean spoke up, her eyes flashing. Idle chit chat had always

60

worried her and she liked to try and be open-minded whenever possible.

'Nothing is simple where Fergus McKenzie is concerned,' pronounced Elspeth, gazing malevolently at a tin of peas which looked as if it had been lying in the shop since the year dot. 'He was aye a one for the wimmen, him and his brother both, ever since they were lads chasing after the girls in school.'

Her words were met with silence and, gathering up her bag without buying anything, Elspeth left the shop and made for the post office, hoping to find a bigger and more interested audience than the one she had just left.

As it was almost dinnertime there was quite a crowd in the post office, all wanting last minute 'messages', and Elspeth, her eyes flickering in satisfaction, went briskly inside. In two minutes flat she had delivered her bombshell and stood waiting for results, lips folded primly, hands clasped firmly over her stomach.

'Oh, ay, and before I forget . . .' she shot home the final bolt with the utmost enjoyment, '. . . her name is Fern Lee – and that's about the only thing anybody knows about her so far.'

'Fern Lee!' snorted Totie Little Donaldson, the postmistress. 'If that's the case then I'm the Queen o' Sheba! Fern Lee indeed!'

Old Sorcha, who had turned down her deaf aid to save the batteries, hastily turned it up again, causing it to emit a loud, penetrating whistle. 'Eh, what was that?' she demanded while everyone screwed up their faces and held onto their ears. 'Hernia did you say, Totie? Ay, well, you'll just have to learn to live wi' it.

61

I myself have had hernias and piles all my days and I'm still here to tell the tale.'

Hector the Boat was staring at Elspeth. 'Strange things are happening on the island,' he hazarded in a throaty whisper, his pupils darkening as he remembered all that he had heard and seen in the Bay of the Caves. He gulped and was about to say something but changed his mind. No one would believe his account of the Hobgoblin of An Coire. He had always made up ghost stories with a marine flavour and they would just think this was another of his tales.

'Here! It is just like one o' they whodunnits,' Ranald commented eagerly, his mind on the latest murder mystery he was reading.

'How could it be a whodunnit when nobody's done it yet? Somebody has to be murdered before questions can be asked.' Totie, who was of the opinion that Ranald read too much 'trash' for his own or anyone else's good, spoke scathingly.

'Ach, I didn't mean it that way,' Ranald remained unperturbed. 'It was the way she was found in McKenzie's barn, all nicely arranged in the hay like she was acting in a stage play. It could all be a trick.' He lowered his voice to sepulchral tones. 'She must have come on that night o' mist and fog, the kind o' night just ripe for high jinks o' all sorts. For all we know she maybe had it in her mind to lure Fergus back to the ocean wi' her.'

'Ay, and don't forget the sand in her socks,' Todd the Shod put in eagerly, 'and she smelled o' salt so she must have come up out o' the sea. She might be a mermaid who came ashore to look for a man.'

'Or she could be a Uisge Calliach,' Canty Tam looked stunned at the thought. 'Rising up out the waves in all her glory only to turn into a horrible witch as soon as she finds herself a man.'

'Very strange,' Hector the Boat repeated, shaking his head and shivering slightly.

'She'll be a woman wi' a past,' stated Behag with conviction.

'So are we all,' Kate said firmly.

'She'll maybe be one o' they nymphomaniacs you hear about.' Robbie never agreed with his sister Behag if he could at all help it, but his imagination had been fired with all the talk and now his tongue took over as he went on gleefully, 'You know, the type o' woman who spends her time ogling the men and taking her clothes off wi' a flourish.' As he finished speaking he glanced rather fearfully over his shoulder. He had left his wife, Barra, in Merry Mary's shop, but she could easily pop into the post office at any moment and woe betide him if she caught him indulging in tittle tattle.

'She'll be just another Jezebel,' sniffed Behag, 'and the island full o' them already.'

'Ay,' Kate glanced mischievously at Elspeth, 'there's some who take off their clothes and some who just hang out their underwear for all the world to see. We're still waiting for a simple explanation for that little adventure.'

Elspeth had the grace to blush. Last summer she had shocked the village by displaying the most luxuriant silk garments on her washing line, all for the sake of wreaking her revenge on those who had scorned her chances with a man after her husband had died. She had enjoyed that little episode thoroughly and had no intention of ever enlightening anybody about it, far less Kate.

'Some things will never be explained, Kate Mc-Kinnon,' she imparted with a disdainful sniff.

'Ay, she didn't come here to wash her dirty linen in public,' Ranald stated, looking very gratified by his own wit and by the laugh his words raised.

'Ach, all that is in the past,' said Mollie as she experienced an uncustomary pang of sympathy for the red-faced Elspeth. 'New things are happening all the time and this mystery woman o' Fergus's will keep us all guessing until we learn a bit more about her.'

Totie, with one eye on the clock, was dispensing stamps and pensions as fast as she could but her active mind had been busy ever since Elspeth had come into the premises and now she paused for a moment to say, 'We could run a competition if you like. If you all agree I'll make up two boxes, in one you put your name and who you think the woman is, in the other you put two shillings a guess. The nearest to the solution gets the winnings and I will only charge him or her five per cent o' the total amount collected.'

'You would be better to have it in my shop. The post office, being a government run body, is no place for gambling,' Holy Smoke, otherwise Sandy McKnight, the butcher, spoke up. He was a man of bedraggled appearance with straggly hair and a drooping moustache which failed to disguise his perpetually downcast mouth. To all intents and purposes he purported to be a man of the church, one who was quick to condemn the evils attached to drink and tobacco, though his puritan views had never carried much weight ever since Todd the Shod had spied him smoking behind a rock on the seashore. Everyone knew that he would do anything for money, no matter how small or how large the amount, and no one was surprised when he muscled in on Totie's suggestion.

'So!' Totie exploded. 'The holy man speaks! I will have you know, Mr McKnight, that I am as against gambling as the next law abiding citizen! It is a post office I am running, not a betting shop, and what I have in mind is only for a bit o' harmless fun.'

'Ay, ay,' nodded Todd, 'you spoke out o' turn there, Mr Smoke. Totie is no' the sort o' woman who would turn her premises into a den o' iniquity. In my opinion we should bide in her camp and do it in the post office where everything will be legal and binding,' he ended grandly while all around there came murmurs of agreement.

With a shrug of his thin shoulders Holy Smoke slunk out of the shop and Behag, who despised the butcher and all that he stood for, waited till the door had closed firmly behind him before she lent voice to her own feelings on the subject.

'I will not take part in vice!' she intoned primly. 'There is enough sin and corruption in this place without you adding to it, Mrs Donaldson. I would not give that man the satisfaction o' letting him see that I agree wi' him, but on this matter I have no choice.'

With that she fleered away outside – only to return fifteen minutes later when the post office was empty.

'How much did you say you were asking, Totie?' she enquired in a hushed whisper.

Totie's lips twitched, making the old woman squirm. 'What for, Behag?'

Behag's wizened cheeks grew red. She glowered at the postmistress.

'Fine you know I am talking about the competition, Mrs Donaldson.'

'Och that, why did you no' say so in the first place. Two shillings a try, in this box here, and a slip o' paper wi' your name and opinion in this other one.'

Behag took the piece of paper and retired furtively to a corner. She took a long time to jot down a few words and Totie, her eyes pointedly on the clock, said, 'Are you nearly finished, Behag?'

Behag came back to the counter and dropped the folded up slip of paper into the box with the same look of dignified importance she might have worn when placing her vote in a ballot box for a general election.

'There now, that wasn't so bad,' Totie said benevolently while Behag bristled. 'And I'm glad you came back, Behag, because I've been meaning to ask if you would mind taking over the post office for a day or two to let me and Doug have a wee break in Oban.'

Behag was most gratified, there was nothing she liked better than these little returns to 'her premises', though of course she never let Totie see how much they meant to her.

'I will be pleased to do so, Mrs Donaldson, just let me know when you are leaving,' she imparted in a flat voice. Very stiff and straight she made her exit, leaving Totie at the counter grinning from ear to ear like the Cheshire cat.

Chapter Six

It was peaceful sitting there in Slochmhor's parlour with the peats glowing warmly in the hearth and a bottle of whisky winking tantalisingly on a small table by the fender. Heinz had come to visit with his master and now lay rapturously on the rug, stretching his paws to the heat, tiny snorts and snores of contentment issuing from his throat as he dreamed the minutes away.

It was a scene of great comfort and homeliness, yet try as he would Fergus couldn't concentrate on the game of cards he was playing with Lachlan. Every few minutes his eyes strayed to the clock and he found himself trying not to shift too often in his seat for fear Lachlan would wonder at his restlessness.

Fergus himself didn't really know the answer to that, all he knew was this feeling of wanting to be home in his own house where he could, in his own words, 'Keep an eye on events,' the main event being of course the young mystery woman who had made such an unusual and unexpected arrival into his home and his life.

That afternoon she had rallied round, awakening from a deep sleep in such a violent manner that it had taken both him and Tina all their time to keep her in bed.

'How long have I been here?' she had shouted at

them, her eyes black and crazed in her white face. 'By all that's holy, I can't stay here! I'll have to be getting on my way. *He'll* be watching and waiting! I'll be too late! I know I'll be too late! Mary, Mother o' God, look upon me with kindness, don't let this happen, please oh please.'

She had rambled on, sobbing and praying. Her accent was Irish, soft and pleasing, except when her voice had risen to harshness and she had pleaded with them to let her go.

'But yesterday you wanted to bide in this room,' Fergus had told her in bewilderment. 'It was as if you were – hiding from someone and felt safe here.'

'Och, she wouldny know what she was saying at that stage,' Tina interposed calmly, 'she was ill and confused and her head was likely birling round in circles.'

'That's right,' the girl caught Tina's hand and held it tightly. 'You understand, you've got a good face, you'll let me go, I know you will.'

'Och, lass,' Tina had chided gently, 'you're no' fit to go anywhere, not for a wee whilie yet. You're in Mr McKenzie's house, he found you in his barn yesterday morning and here you have been since. Doctor Megan and Nurse Babbie have been keeping an eye on you and I myself have hardly left your side.'

The girl glanced from one face to the other. 'Mr and Mrs McKenzie?'

'Ach, no,' Tina giggled girlishly, 'he is Fergus McKenzie right enough, but his wife is away in Glasgow for a holiday. I'm Tina from the village down the road, and I'll be here for as long as you'll be needing me.'

After that Fergus hadn't been able to settle. Tina had become tired of his pacings and had chased him from the house, saying that she had plenty to keep her occupied, one of them being the preparation of hot water to give Fern a bath.

'The lass is in a fine state o' filth,' she had told him bluntly. 'She canny lie in that bed any longer, reeking o' sea and sweat, 'tis high time she had a good wash. We will all feel the better for it and I myself will know just where I stand once I get her up on her feets.'

Fergus, used to Tina's quaint way of expressing herself, didn't pursue the matter any further and leaving the house he took himself off rather half-heartedly to Slochmhor with Heinz at his heels.

Lachlan, despite his show of concentration with the cards, was feeling unsettled himself that evening. His mind kept straying to Phebie, wondering what she was doing, what she was saying, if she was perhaps missing him as much as he was missing her. The house had been lonely and strange ever since her departure from it and he couldn't help comparing the emptiness to the atmosphere of warmth and life when she was around. She would have come in with the cocoa about now, together with a plateful of new baked scones and hot buttered pancakes, and they would have sat together by the fire, going over the day's happenings, the latest gossip, family affairs, puffing a bit with pride as they discussed the day-to-day escapades of their grand-child, Ian Lachlan McKenzie.

A mighty sigh escaped Lachlan, then another. It had the same effect as of someone yawning in a roomful of people. His sighs found their echo in the man in the opposite chair and Lachlan glanced up sharply, thinking that his visitor was taking the rise out of him. But Fergus, his dark face bent to his handful of cards, was oblivious to anything but his own sense of unrest.

'You sound like a dog wi' the colic,' Lachlan observed with a wry smile. 'And I'm thinking we're both suffering from the same ailment. I think I would be right in saying you're missing Kirsteen, just as much as I'm missing Phebie.'

'No, no, it isn't that,' Fergus protested, a frown gathering on his brow. 'I'm just a bit preoccupied, that's all.'

'Och, come on, man! Why not admit it? We're just not used to being on our own. We've had our wives around us for most o' our lives and just canny stand it without them. We'll give them a ring to see how they're doing.' With that he got up and going to the phone he dialled Aunt Minnie's number. 'It's ringing,' he called to Fergus, 'you go first.'

Lachlan held out the instrument and gingerly Fergus took it. He had always objected to having a phone in his own house, saying that it was just a waste of good money. Kirsteen however knew that his real reasons were born of mistrust for an instrument 'with so many wires attached, anyone could listen to whatever you had to say into it'. His conversation with his wife was therefore stilted and unnatural and as brief as he could make it.

'Phebie's seeing to Aunt Minnie at the moment,' Kirsteen's voice crackled over the line. 'Tell Lachlan

70

she's been waiting to hear from him and will ring back in a few minutes.'

There was a short pause, as Fergus glowered into the mouthpiece, then her voice came again, warm, loving, affectionate, and he was immediately sorry for his surliness.

'I miss you, my darling,' she whispered. 'Are you alright and feeding yourself properly?'

'Ay,' he said huskily, 'don't worry about me, Shona and Tina between them are keeping me alive.'

'Has anything been happening while I've been away?'

For a few long moments he didn't answer; eternity seemed to pass. 'Nothing much,' he said at last. 'You only went away yesterday and this is Rhanna, don't forget, the island where time stands still, though of course if you'd like to hear the latest about Kate McKinnon's bunions and Jim Jim's piles I'd be glad to oblige.'

She laughed. 'I get your point, don't rub it in. Just remember, I'm thinking of you all the time and – I love you.'

'Love you too,' he mumbled and put the instrument carefully back in its cradle.

Lachlan immediately rounded on him. 'You didn't tell her about Fern!'

'I'd forgotten about her.'

'No you haven't! The truth is you can't stop thinking about her! I saw you wriggling about in your chair as if you'd ants in your pants, no doubt wishing you could get up and run back to her. Dammit, man, this puts me in an awkward position. Naturally I want to

71

mention the girl to Phebie. If I don't she'll think we've a conspiracy going between us.'

'Calm down,' Fergus grunted, 'the lass won't be here for very long. She'll be gone before Kirsteen comes back. Don't make such a fuss, it isn't important.'

Lachlan looked at him strangely. 'I wonder,' he muttered, then seeing the other man's set, determined chin, he shook his head. It was a look he knew well. It meant that McKenzie o' the Glen was not going to utter one more word on the subject. Lachlan knew from experience that it would be useless to air any more of his opinions at that point and seizing the whisky bottle he poured each of them a stiff dram before going to speak to Phebie on the phone when its persistent tones jangled through the air.

Soon after that Fergus took his leave and with a sigh Lachlan sat back in his chair to warm his glass between his palms and stare into the fire as he thought of Phebie's humorous account of the journey to Glasgow and her equally lighthearted report on her administrations to Aunt Minnie – 'A tough old bird with a tongue o' fire and claws o' steel. She's worse than Elspeth any day o' the week but I'm the boy for her and fine she knows it. Kirsteen's softer, but she'll learn. Take care, Lachy, darling, and don't forget to finish writing that book while I'm away!'

That parting shot made Lachlan squirm in his chair and cast his eyes heavenward. 'Devil of a woman!' he said aloud. 'How can I finish what I have hardly even begun? Give me strength, Lord, give me inspiration, but most of all, give me a magic pen that will do the whole jing bang for me in double quick time.'

'Amen to that!'

Startled out of his wits he spun round in his chair to see a slightly built, fair-haired girl, standing outwith the pool of light cast by the lamp.

'Ruth!' he cried. 'I didn't hear you coming in. You just appeared like a spook in the night.'

She giggled and shook her head. 'I knocked the door. When there was no answer I just walked in to find you muttering and praying up the lum and wishing impossible wishes.'

He looked at her, violet-eyed, flaxen-haired Ruth, whom he had delivered into the world some twenty-seven years ago. In many ways it was difficult to believe that she was no longer the little girl he remembered so well. With her doll-like fragility and expression of innocence she still retained the big-eyed air of solemnity that had been so much a stamp of her childhood. But she was tougher than she looked. Her early life with Morag Ruadh, her religious fanatic of a mother, had bred in her a resilience of spirit that could manifest itself very firmly and somewhat disquietingly when the need arose. She was also a determined and ambitious young being, having succeeded in becoming a popular novelist despite leading a full and busy life as the wife of Lorn McKenzie and the mother of two young children. Lachlan had always enjoyed chatting with her about her literary career and his voice was warm and welcoming as he invited her to draw a chair closer in to the fire.

'I didn't come to roast myself,' she laughed. 'Phebie told me you always have your cocoa about now and I came along to make it for you! The bairns are in bed, Lorn is having forty winks, so ... here I am.'

'That woman!' he cried. 'Anyone would think I was daft as well as helpless! As if I wasn't capable o' putting a kettle on the stove!'

'Ay, maybe that – but would you remember to put a light under it?' she teased. 'I'll make us both a cup then we can have a nice cosy wee blether about all the things you were praying for when I came in.'

She went off to the kitchen, reappearing in ten minutes with mugs of piping hot cocoa and a plate piled high with buttered oatcakes.

'You know, Ruth, you might just be the answer to my prayers,' he told her as they settled themselves round the fire. 'It was gey strange, the way you materialised out o' thin air when I was least expecting it. Just like a fairy godmother about to grant me three wishes.'

'I don't know about that,' she said with a giggle. 'I might be able to give you some advice though, if you tell me the reasons why you want that magic pen so badly.'

'To write a book, Ruth, the one I said I would write when I retired and had all the time I needed on my hands. It hasn't worked out that way at all and Phebie is beginning to think it was just a lot o' hot air.'

'Maybe you're aiming too high to start with,' Ruth said bluntly. 'I myself started off with short stories and articles before I even thought o' writing a novel. Why don't you try doing an article first and submit it to a newspaper or magazine? If they like it they might ask for more and you could take it from there. Walk before you run in other words.'

He looked at her and his brown eyes were alight with gratitude. 'Ruth, you're a genius! Why didn't I think o' that?'

'Because you aren't a genius – yet – but you will be, once you pick up that magic pen.'

They both burst out laughing and chinking their mugs together they wished one another health, happiness, and success.

Fergus stood for a moment at his own gate, wondering whether he should go inside or if it might be better to go for a walk in order to calm the coils of tension that were winding ever tighter in his belly.

He didn't know why he should feel like this. It wasn't like him to be so unsure of himself. He was cool, calm, collected, McKenzie o' the Glen, always in control, always the master of any event that chanced along. In just two short days everything had changed and he had changed with it.

That girl! That beautiful, young, witch of a girl had upset everything by coming to his house the way she had! Disrupting the routine, unsettling everyone, creating a situation that he had no desire to be entangled in. No doubt the tongues would already be wagging, the jungle drums steadily beating, from croft to cottage, village to village, port to port, till soon everyone on the island would know that Fergus McKenzie had a strange young woman living in the same house as himself and his wife not there to keep an eye on him. A muscle worked in Fergus's jaw. Let them talk! He had weathered worse storms. None of this was his doing. It was just something that had – happened.

The cool night air washed over him; he filled his lungs with it and gazed at the dark shapes of the hills standing clear against the night sky. In the distance the lights of Portcull winked and sparkled; he gazed beyond them to the silver-grey sheet that was the ocean and he thought about Kirsteen, how far away she seemed, how curt he had been with her on the phone.

'Mo cridhe,' he said softly, 'I'm sorry, I wanted to tell you – about her – but she'll be gone soon anyway and everything will be back to normal.'

Heinz was snuffling and sniffing in the bushes, lifting his leg with single-minded enthusiasm at various favourite watering posts. He was solid, real, and uncomplicated, and somehow he transferred some of his implacability to his master.

Fergus pulled back his shoulders and without further hesitation he opened the gate and strode purposefully across the yard to yank open the kitchen door and go inside, feeling as he did so that he was entering the portals of some strange house where dangerous destiny lurked amid an orchard of forbidden fruits.

Chapter Seven

The minute Fergus walked over the threshold he knew instantly that he should not have come home so early. The room smelled of steam and perfumed soap and was lit only by firelight which cast a soft, mysterious aura over everything.

In the centre of this ambience of light and shade and quietly dreaming shadows was Fern, newly emerged from her bath, the droplets of water that adhered to her body looking like a myriad dazzling pearls in the fire's glow. Fergus had never seen anyone so stunningly beautiful. There was about her a gypsy-like quality that seemed to enfold her in a mantle of colour; her thick wavy hair hung round her slender shoulders like a glossy blue-black curtain; her golden skin was satin smooth; her body willowy yet tantalisingly curvaceous; her dark eyes were luminous in her perfectly sculpted face; her mouth, though pale, was enticingly full and trembled just enough to make it look child-like and utterly innocent.

As Fergus stood there, drinking in this figure of entrancing loveliness, he experienced a rush of fierce longing. He wanted to crush that wonderful mouth to his, he ached to touch the satiny smoothness of her skin, he wanted nothing more than to hold her and run his fingers through those shining black ringlets of hair . . . he wanted . . .

His heart thumped, his legs felt weak . . . he knew that he had to get out of here, away from *her*, before . . .

'Fergus McKenzie! What are you doing back so soon? This is no place for a man to be at a time like this. You've caught me wi' my breeks down!'

He became aware then that Tina was also in the room, coming at him, or so it seemed to him, from some hidden corner, with her 'breeks' perfectly intact, though of course, knowing Tina, her words made absolute sense to him. She was hot and pink and puffing a bit; coils of baby-soft hair had escaped their anchorage on top of her head, kirby grips swaying gaily around her ears like little tribal ornaments.

Plunking herself very firmly between Fergus and the zinc tub, she surveyed him with mild annoyance and more than a tinge of embarrassment. 'You should have chapped the door,' she stressed, motioning behind her back for Fern to take the bathrobe she was holding. 'You know how long it takes to heat the water for a bath and the girl needed a good scrubbing. I myself was up to the eyes in soapsuds and running about daft trying to find something clean for her to wear. I never heard a thing till you just came barging in like a bull wi' the skitters.'

'It is my house, Tina,' he asserted himself breathlessly, 'and I think I have a right to come and go from it when I please.'

'That's as may be,' she conceded, while she prodded

a few hair grips back into her head, 'but you knew fine how busy I would be and surely to goodness you should have knocked before you came in.'

The lass in question had omitted to do anything with the garment that Tina had all but thrown at her. She just stood there with her back to the fire, surrounded enchantingly by its amber glow, staring at Fergus as if she was mesmerised.

'Enough o' this!' cried Tina in a burst of exasperation, glaring at the girl as if she would like her to disappear through the wall. 'Put that goonie on at once and make yourself decent or I'll take it and wrap it round your lugs wi' my very own hands!'

With a shrug the girl retrieved the robe from the floor and slipping her arms into the cosy folds she wrapped it round herself and tied it loosely round her waist. The colour of it was blue and it suited her to perfection. Her long hair flowed down her back, a million secrets seemed locked in her flashing dark eyes, while her tremulous mouth promised delights beyond compare.

Fergus felt there was more to this young woman than met the eye; she was hungry for affection and she was letting him know it. He couldn't tear his gaze away from her and she, interpreting the look in his burning black eyes, tossed her head a little and allowed the robe to fall open so that her shapely legs were revealed to him.

'It's one o' Kirsteen's own goonies,' Tina's voice, homely and practical, broke the spell of taut silence that had fallen over the room. 'I found it hanging behind the door. I hope you don't mind, Fergus?'

'No, no, of course I don't.' With an effort he brought himself back to reality, 'And I'm sure Kirsteen wouldn't either.'

'Right, I'll make us all some nice hot cocoa, then I'll have to be going. Eve will be wondering what in the world has happened to me and I promised Doctor Megan I would go over to the Manse in the morning to see to my usual duties.'

'No, you mustn't go!' Fergus, coming completely to his senses, took Tina's arm, and steering her out of Fern's earshot he said urgently, 'You can't leave me alone wi' – wi' her. The cailleachs would have a field day if anything o' the sort got to their ears and besides, she hasn't quite recovered from that knock she took and I – wouldn't know what to do wi' her.'

Tina's dimples showed. 'That wasny the impression I got just a few minutes ago ... I thought you were going to eat her the way you were gawping at her.'

His brow darkened. 'I just got a surprise, that's all, it isn't every day that a man finds a naked young woman in his own kitchen. Come on, Tina, you've got to help me. This will all get to Kirsteen's ears eventually and I've had enough woman trouble to be going on with.'

'Ach, alright,' she relented with one of her radiant smiles, 'I did say to Eve I might no' be home and no' to wait up for me. But only for tonight, mind, Grandma Ann and Granda John like me to be around the village to go their messages and the minister relies on me to keep house for him wi' himself and the doctor being such busy people.'

Fergus breathed a sigh of relief. 'Right, that's settled,

you get the cocoa while I go upstairs and tidy myself up a bit.'

Tina looked at him in surprise; the Fergus she knew didn't speak that way but she made no comment as he left the kitchen with the faithful Heinz very firmly at his heels.

A short while later, when they were all sitting round the fire partaking of supper, Fergus looked directly at Fern and said softly, 'Don't you think it's about time you told us a bit about yourself? So far we only know your name and that's all. I for one would like to know where you come from and why you showed up here at Laigmhor the way you did.'

A wary look came into the girl's great dark eyes and turning her head away she murmured in a low voice, 'Myself was cold and hungry and needing to find a bit o' shelter. I saw your house, I went into your barn and bumped my head on a rafter. That's all I can remember.'

'But why were you here on Rhanna in the first place?' Fergus persisted. 'Have you got family here? Were you coming to visit friends? People don't just arrive on an island in the middle o' the night with nowhere to go.'

'Please,' the girl shook her head, her tumble of hair falling about her face with devastating effect. Fergus was struck anew by her quality of gypsy-like beauty, by the unbidden thought that here was a wild thing, one who needed light and air and freedom, in order to function properly. 'Please don't be going on at me,' she continued in a pleading voice, 'I don't want to talk

81

about anything yet. I need time, just give me a bit o' that and I'll try and tell you everything there is to tell.'

'Och, poor lass, you're tired and upset and needing your bed,' Tina's voice was warm with sympathy. Bending down she placed on her feet the pair of battered slippers she had brought with her, before scliffing over to the sink to run a kettle of steaming water over the supper dishes. 'I'll just be filling you a nice hot bottle,' she told Fern, 'then we'll go upstairs together. I'm about dead on my feets from all the rushing about I've been doing today.'

Fergus had to hide a smile since Tina, 'born in a sleeping bag', according to Kate, had never been known to rush anywhere except once, when her daughter's son had entered the world, and in her excitement she hadn't known whether she was 'coming or going' and had omitted to 'don her breeks' for the doctor when she came even though it was a safe bet that neither the doctor nor anyone else would have cared if she had been wearing a fig leaf at the time!

Fern didn't answer Tina. She was gazing into the fire, lost in thought, her chin propped in her hand, her golden-skinned face pensive and sad as she absently stroked the head of a large tabby cat who had commandeered her knee. There was something very, very sensuous in the way she was fondling the animal; in fact, every move she made reminded Fergus of a creature of the wild; lithe, graceful, watchful.

With a sudden movement he got to his feet to damp the fire with dross and put the guard over it. 'I'm away to bed,' he announced as soon as his night jobs were finished. 'It's been a long day and in the morning we'll have to decide what to do about you, young lady.'

He gazed at Fern but she avoided his eyes. He was seized with the notion that there was a great deal she was hiding from him and he determined he would get her to speak about herself the next day. By hook or by crook he was going to uncover the mystery surrounding her even if he had to shake the truth out of her!

'We're coming too.' Tina seized the hot bottle and taking Fern's arm she guided her upstairs. 'I'm in the spare room,' she told the girl. 'If there's anything you need just let me know, though mind, you'll have an awful job waking me. Once I hit the pillow I'm dead and auld Nick himself could have his way wi' me and I'd be none the wiser.'

Fern smiled faintly at that, all three wished one another goodnight, and softly closed their respective doors.

For several minutes Fergus stood behind his own door, every fibre in him alert and churning. He stared at the bed, it looked vast and empty, and with a sigh he got undressed and slipped between the sheets.

It took him a long time to get to sleep, his mind just wouldn't be still. He thought about Kirsteen and wondered what she was doing. The bed was cold without her in it, snuggled up beside him, smelling of fresh air and roses, whispering in his ear the way she always did before falling asleep in his embrace. He wished she was here, longed to tell her how much he was missing her, how much he loved her.

A terrible sense of guilt gripped him. What would

she think of all this? A strange young woman in her house, bathing in her kitchen, wearing her bathrobe ... a young woman called Fern, tormenting him with her grace and her beauty and that wonderful body of hers. He remembered how she'd looked fresh out of the tub and he broke out in a sweat. Kirsteen must never find out about that! It would cause ructions and no mistake and it had been through no fault of his. How was he to know she'd take all that time to bathe herself? He had been at Lachlan's a good hour and had thought the bathtime ablutions would be over with by the time he got back. Tina should have locked the door, anyway! Anyone could have walked in on the same scene he had witnessed! To ease his conscience he conveniently forgot that people seldom locked their doors on Rhanna and that it had just been a matter of habit that had made Tina forget to bolt theirs.

He spent a good few minutes blaming Tina for what had happened, then he gave a groan and turning over he shut his eyes and willed himself to go to sleep.

Eventually he drifted into a light, uneasy slumber only to wake during the night, feeling that some sound had disturbed him. He strained his ears, listening. Was that a tiny furtive click that he heard? Followed by a faint rustling and creaking?

The moon was shining in the window, bathing the room with its ghostly light. Getting up he padded over to the door in his bare feet, recoiling a little as the cold from the wooden floorboards seeped into him. Opening the door a crack he peered out. Nothing stirred, nothing moved. Everything was dark and secretive in those dreaming night hours. All the doors on the landing were closed, all was quiet, except for a faint snorting and snoring coming from the spare room.

He smiled to himself. Tina was enjoying her repose, having obviously 'died' the minute she had hit the pillow, and a visitation from auld Nick himself would no doubt have been a waste of his time.

The grandmother clock in the hall began chiming out the hour. Fergus counted the strokes. Three-thirty. Just three-thirty! How would he ever get back to sleep now? He was wide awake – and he was freezing!

Softly he closed his door and went to the window just to make sure that no one was out there who hadn't any business to be. The whole of Rhanna seemed spread before him as he stood there, looking out. It was a calm clear night, the hills rising up starkly on either side of the glen, shearing up into a pewter-coloured sky where the stars winked and the moon cast its heavenly light over land and sea.

The undulating fields were filled with shadows; the trees that lined the riverbank looked like gnarled old men hunching their backs against the cold; the pale grey ribbon of the road snaked away into the distance and beyond all was the moon-silvered expanse of the Sound of Rhanna, ethereal and timeless in its cold, remote beauty.

Fergus stood at the window for a long time, drinking in the quiet splendour of the countryside. Only when he began to shiver did he crawl once more under the covers to curl himself into a tight ball and eventually drift off into a fitful sleep.

He was wakened a short time later, or so he imagined,

by someone shaking him. With a start he opened his eyes to see Tina gazing down at him with a worried expression on her plump, pleasant face. 'Fergus, 'tis sorry I am to wake you but it's Fern, she's gone. I looked into her room to see was she needing anything but the bed was as empty as my belly is before breakfast.'

Dazed with sleep, Fergus struggled to make sense of all this. 'Gone? By that do you mean – vanished? From the house?'

'Into thin air, from the room, from the house, from the planet. I've searched and searched everywhere and nary a sight o' her have I seen. Mind you, she's gone off wi' some o' the warm woollies Shona keeps in her wardrobe. I know them off by heart because I myself helped her to arrange them in their places no' so long ago.'

Fergus's mind began racing as he wondered where on earth the girl was and what she was up to. The noises he had heard in the night must have been made by her leaving her room, but why had she gone about it so stealthily? And why leave the house in the middle of the night when there was no possible means of getting off the island?

Then he remembered how anxious she'd been to get away from the house. How she had pleaded with both him and Tina to let her go, her referral to some man who would be 'waiting and watching' and that soon it would be 'too late'. It was obvious that she was a young woman with an unhappy past and it was equally obvious that she was living in fear of someone from that past life catching up with her.

Fergus was secretly relieved that Fern had gone. Her presence in his home had caused him too many dilemmas, both moral and physical. He told himself that he had done all he could for her and shrugged off the notion that he had perhaps been too hard on her with all those probing questions he had asked her last night.

'She wanted to go, Tina,' he said at last, 'nothing we could have said or done would have kept her here against her will.'

Tina emitted a great sigh and looked sad. In her concern over Fern she had made no attempt to tidy herself; her hair was straggling in sad little wisps about her ears; a lilac shawl that she was clutching round her neck looked as if it had suffered a serious disaster in a mangle; her slippers were on the wrong feet and looked as if they were walking away from one another when she moved to the window to peer outside. But her appearance was the last thing on her mind in those moments. 'Do you know what I think, Fergus?' she said pensively. 'I think the lass is running away from some evil, terrible creature who is out to get her and wreak some horrible revenge on her.'

Fergus glowered at her. He wasn't at his best first thing in the morning and Tina – in common with many of the other islanders – had a fertile imagination, and loved nothing better than to spin a good tale of blood and gore.

Throwing Fergus a coy, sidelong glance she went on, 'I was also after thinking that she is no' the snow white angel she would have us all believe. That doesn't mean to say that she is a bad lassie by any means, but wi' her looks she knows how to tempt the men and she is likely used to having them sniffing after her in droves. Maybe, in some way, she went too far wi' one o' them and he is out to get her blood. Yesterday, when she was begging us to let her go, she seemed shat scared and is maybe worried that this bloke, whoever he is, is out to murder her.'

'For God's sake, woman!' Fergus barked. 'Will you get out o' this room and let me put on my breeks if that's no' too much to ask! We'll talk about the girl later but first things first. Later on, if I can spare the time that is, I'll have a look around for her.'

Tina gazed at him with calculated sympathy. 'Ach my, this lass has certainly got us all going. I could see by the way you were looking at her last night you had a wee liking for her. She certainly flaunted herself at you, and wi' my experience o' men, I know fine that even the strongest have their weak points. It was enough to tempt the flesh o' any man, the way she stood there in her birthday suit for all the world to see . . .'

'*Tina!*' he roared, and that lady took herself slowly and majestically out of his sight but not before she paused briefly at the door to make her parting shot.

'We haven't heard the last o' Miss Fern Lee. She'll turn up again, as sure as I breathe – and wi' you having such a soft spot for her you'll be the first mannie she'll make for – you mark my words.'

Chapter Eight

'My, my,' Tina gave vent to an almighty yawn as she entered the butcher's premises, 'I just don't know what's wrong wi' me this morning. I have been asleep on my feets ever since I got up and found myself in a strange bed that wasny my own.'

'Oh, ay,' Holy Smoke placed a heavy intonation on the two simple words, 'a strange bed, eh? And you looking as if you hadn't slept a wink all night.'

Tina looked at him askance. There were times when the butcher man could rile even her and her tone was somewhat acid as she said with dignity, 'Och, you have a terrible bad mind on you for a holy man, Mr McKnight. If you must know, I spent the night at Laigmhor. Fergus o' the Glen asked would I stay to see to the lassie who is biding there, as he was a wee bittie worried about her. And now, after all the fuss, she just upped and went in the middle o' the night, nary a word to anyone, and himself not too sure what should be done about it.'

Almost before she had finished speaking she was pounced upon by the other customers in the shop.

'I knew it, I knew it!' cried Kate triumphantly. 'There's something fishy about that whole business. The girl just sneaked in from nowhere and now she's disappeared in a like manner. There's more to this than meets the eye and I for one would like to know what it is.'

'Are you talking about that lass o' McKenzie's?' Jim Jim was sitting in the shop. He was hard of hearing, and moulding one hairy lug into a wizened trumpet he cocked it to the main source of sound. 'You mean she just left him? Without a word o' thanks for his hospitality?'

'Ay, if you put it like that,' Tina agreed. Then, with a nervous glance over her shoulder, she went on to say melodramatically, 'If you ask me, I think she's on the run from the law. In fact . . .' Here she paused long enough for her words to sink in before going on, 'She might be a murderer for all we know. She was certainly in a terrible state when Fergus found her. She had blood on her clothes and . . .' she gazed around the shop . . . 'though some o' it was hers the rest might have belonged to somebody else.'

'That's what I said!' Ranald looked stunned. 'I wrote it all down when Totie suggested having that competition to guess who was the stranger. It's in the box!' In his excitement his voice was rising. 'And seeing as how I'm right I'll just go along to the post office this very minute and collect my winnings.'

'You'll do nothing o' the sort, Ranald McTavish,' Kate told him scathingly. 'Until we know for sure why the lass came here, the money stays where it is and that's final.'

Holy Smoke, not at all pleased at the interruption to business, deftly wrapped a pound of his best pork sausages in a scrap of grease-proof paper and handed the package to Kate with a flourish. Kate took the sausages and glowered at them. At least three of them had escaped their meagre covering and with a snort she pointed out this fact to the butcher.

'Ach, come on now, Kate,' he said in his high-pitched, whining voice. 'Surely it is the meat and no' the paper that counts. You have to admit you would never get links as good as mine anywhere else in the land.'

Kate sniffed disdainfully. 'Ach, you're nothing but a mean bodach and a blether to boot, Sandy McKnight! How would I know about shops in other lands? I have lived on this island most o' my life and have been forced to buy my meat where I could get it.'

'Forced! Forced!' Holy Smoke almost choked on the peppermint he was sucking to mask the tobacco on his breath. 'And here's me, working my fingers to the bone in an honest attempt to provide this island with the best possible produce there is.'

Bob, coming in at that moment, prevented a serious clash of personalities as both Kate and the butcher had been at loggerheads since the day they had met.

'A quarter pound o' wee beefies,' Bob requested, taking out his money to count it carefully as he spoke.

'A *quarter* pound?' Holy Smoke repeated with a frown on his mournful features. 'You surely must be mistaken, Bob. An amount like that wouldny decently feed a hungry mouse, far less a man o' your stature.'

'A quarter pound,' insisted Bob with dignity, 'and it is not for me, it is for Grace Donaldson's cat.'

'Her cat!' Holy Smoke was taken aback. His moustache drooped, and his eyes bulged. 'I don't make mince for cats! I only make the best for human consumption and it is an insult to suggest otherwise. How about a nice bit offal? I have plenty o' that and it's what folks usually buy for their animals.'

'Wee beefies,' Bob repeated with a dangerous glint in his blue eyes. 'And, if you don't mind, I'm in a hurry, and have no intention o' standing here arguing wi' you, Mr McKnight.'

Grumbling under his breath the butcher went to work the mincer, leaving Kate to smile at Bob and say curiously, 'I believe congratulations are in order, Bob. I am after hearing that you and Grace are going to wed yourselves to one another at last.'

'Ay, that would be correct,' Bob agreed with a guarded expression on his face. He had never been one for what he called 'shop talk' since, in his opinion, they were places where rumour was born and idle tongues 'ran away wi' themselves'.

'Ach, my,' Kate's eyes grew misty, 'when I think o' my poor old Joe, himself and Grace that happy in their own wee hoosie by the harbour. She is a good sowel, that she is, and made his last years tick sweetly for him. She will do the same wi' you, Bob, for she is a woman just born to keep house for a man. I myself wouldny dream o' taking on another husband after Tam. One o' him is enough for any woman in any one lifetime, though I wouldny change him even if I could. Mind you, I would never tell him that, his head's as big as a football as it is.'

'Well, I myself would not say no to another Matthew in my life.' Tina, who had been carefully examining the strings of black puddings hanging in the window, spoke up. 'He and me were just made for one another and while we had our differences we aye respected each other's opinions.' She gave vent to a lofty sigh. 'If I could have another exactly like him it would be beautiful just, but I know I will never meet his like again. There was only one Matthew as far as I am concerned and now he is dead there is no' another could take his place.'

At that point Holy Smoke served Bob with his 'wee beefies', a meagre amount of money was exchanged, and the old shepherd departed the shop with dignity.

'Why can he no' ask for minced beef like everyone else?' grumbled the butcher. 'Him and his wee beefies indeed!'

'Ach, Bob is just an old-fashioned mannie,' said Tina indulgently. 'He has the old way o' talkin' and does no harm to anyone.'

'Ay, and wi' him being a lonely bachelor man he is a bittie out o' touch wi' the modern ways,' supplemented Kate. 'He has lived alone wi' himself for far too long but that will be changing now that Grace has had her way wi' him.'

'It's no' decent,' intoned Behag primly, entering the shop at that moment and immediately adding her contribution to the conversation. 'All these elderly folk wedding themselves to one another. That Grace should be ashamed o' herself, old Joe hardly cold in his grave and herself goggling away at Bob in a manner befitting a schoolgirl, and her a widow woman twice over.' Behag shook her palsied head and tucked a strand of wispy hair back into the confines of her headscarf. 'I canny understand it myself,' she went on with pursed lips, 'the attraction that ordinary wee body has over the menfolk o' the place. There was a time when she had three o' them after her at once, Joe, Bob, *and* Captain Mac...' At mention of the latter Behag sucked in her lips. 'Well, at least he is off her list, and that I canny rightly understand either. That Elspeth, at her age! Hooking an old sea dog like Isaac McIntosh! She'll be hard put to know what to do wi' him once she has the ring on her finger.'

Kate treated Behag to a deceptively charming smile. 'Ay, ay, Behag, it is indeed a thought. Elspeth and Mac on their wedding night, playing hide and seek under the covers and neither o' them too sure what it is they are looking for.'

'I wouldny put too much sillar on that,' Jim Jim piped up. 'Don't be forgetting, Elspeth was married to Hector Morrison, a hard-bitten seaman if ever there was one. He lived rough and he died the same and Elspeth has been a lonely woman all these years.' He grinned reflectively. 'You know, I mind her when she was just young. You wouldny think it to look at her now but she was a hot piece and no mistake. She raised the dust in many's a hayloft, if I'm mindin' right, and I myself escaped her by the skin o' my breeks on more than one occasion.' From the corner of his eye he spotted his wife Isabel hoving into view and hastily he composed his features into those of a man entirely innocent of the ways of the world.

'Are you ready to come home yet?' Isabel asked. 'I've been run off my feets all morning looking to see where you were.'

'Ay, ay, as ready as I'll ever be.' He rose creakily to

94

his feet and leaning heavily on his stick he hobbled away out of the shop.

'Are you no buying anything today, mistress?' Holy Smoke enquired rather peevishly of Isabel. 'I have some lovely pork sausages, freshly made and just burstin' wi' goodness.'

'Ay well, let them burst,' Isabel returned firmly. 'I'll buy them when I want them and no' before.'

Holy Smoke blew down his nostrils in disgust. 'You would think my sausages were poisoned, the way some people behave.'

Isabel disdained to answer and leaving the shop she crooked her arm to her husband and led him slowly along the road.

'Ach, poor Jim Jim,' sighed Kate solicitously, 'he is getting worse wi' the rheumies and could be doing wi' one o' they electric chairs to get around in. Our Nancy was after telling me she heard tell o' a body who got one and is never off the top o' the road wi' it.'

Tina banged a black pudding and a jar of liver pâté down on the counter. 'I'll be taking these, Mr McKnight . . .' She glanced at the clock on the wall and gave a mild cluck. 'Will you look at the time! I'm all behind wi' myself today. I should have been over at the Manse seeing to the minister but Grannie Ann and Granda John will be waiting for their dinner so I'll have to look to them first.' She glanced doubtfully at the black pudding. 'I wonder, will Granda John be able to digest a heavy thing like that? It gave him heartburn the last time and I said I would never get it again but och, I'm fair rushed and canny think what else to give him.'

'How about some nice pork links then?' Holy Smoke said in his best shop manner. 'As fresh as the morning dew and just the thing for old John to get his teeths into.'

Tina wrinkled her nose. 'He hasn't got any, that's why he is so prone to the heartburn, besides, I'm no' in the mood for pork links myself today.'

'You're no' in the mood! I thought you said you were buying the stuff for the old folks?'

'Och ay, I am right enough, but I'll be having a bite along wi' them and these links o' yours don't always agree wi' me. As I said, Granda John canny abide anything as tough as a sausage wearing a skin and Grannie Ann just sucks the meat out and leaves an awful mess on her plate.'

'This island!' Holy Smoke said despairingly. 'Half its teeths are missing or shoved to the back o' a drawer somewhere, and the other half is waiting for the dentist mannie to come and perform a miracle!'

Holy Smoke checked himself. It would never do to lose his temper with a customer, he needed all the business he could get on an island where trade depended on the locals for the greater part of the year.

Kate and Tina left the shop together, avidly discussing the latest mystery surrounding 'Fergus McKenzie's young woman'.

Behag followed fast on their heels. She had no intention of being left alone in the shop with the butcher man. She neither liked nor trusted him and it had always puzzled her how he tried so hard to ingratiate himself with her when she made no effort to hide her feelings from him.

'Miss Beag!' Holy Smoke's voice followed her out of the shop in no uncertain manner. 'You haven't bought anything yet! Also, I was wondering – would you like to come over to my house some night for a dram and a game o' cards?'

Behag stopped dead in her tracks, her heartbeat quickening, a flush spreading over her wizened countenance. A dram and a game of cards indeed! And him the so-called holy man who looked down his nose at the village men for their sinful liaisons with the bottle. The – the hypocrite! Just what did he take her for! She, Behag Beag, who never touched a drop and denounced card games as 'gambolling wi' the very de'il himself'. But worst of all! In the man's own home! Alone with him! Nobody else there, only him – and her ...

Behag shivered, she trembled. Pulling herself together she sprachled away down the road as fast as her spindly legs would carry her, straight to her very own medicine cabinet to withdraw an innocuous-looking brown cough bottle. Holding it to her lips she gulped deeply of its contents and then she sat back in her chair to stare at the wall and take a few deep breaths. Without a twinge of conscience she told herself that this was different, this was the uisge beatha, an entirely medicinal brew, the very water of life itself. The Lord Himself would surely not have denied her the healing draught in those fraught moments of her life.

She was vindicated, she was saved! Her palsied head bobbed on her thin shoulders, seeming to agree of its own accord with her puritanical thoughts. With

97

dignity Behag arose from her seat. Replacing the cough bottle very carefully back in the medicine cabinet she clicked the door shut and went to boil an egg for her lunch. She felt good and safe inside of herself, and she was glowing, there was no doubt about that; a gentle kind of glow filled with satisfaction.

Going to a drawer she withdrew her mail order catalogue and placed it on the table beside her plate. She would browse through the pages while she was having her lunch. Her medicine cupboard needed stocking up and the catalogue was a good way of getting life's little essentials without anybody knowing too much about her methods for getting them. Erchy the Post was the one drawback. When he brought her mail he always had a mite too much to say about the weight of her parcels. That glint in his eye, the knowing smirk on his face, no doubt wishing he had x-ray vision so that he could poke and pry into the private side of her life. It was a quirk of Erchy's nature which had always been a thorn in Behag's side. When he delivered her letters he was often able to tell her who they were from and where they had come from, simply because he made it his business to examine postmarks and study handwriting.

Behag buried her spoon into her boiled egg and snorted. A terrible thing just, to be inquisitive to the point of indecency! Everybody had a right to their privacy – everyone – even the very animals themselves liked to curl up in their own little corner in order to escape the world for a while.

Behag crunched into her toast and flipped through the pages of her catalogue with the utmost enjoyment, lingering over the displays of vests and knickers. She could be doing with some of those, the thermal ones with the nice long legs. No one, with the exception of the owner, knew what went on under a long skirt, not if a body had always kept herself decent and private – as she had – all her life! Of course, when she was younger, those scallywags of the island had been forever trying to make her do physical things, but she had been blessed with the strength to resist – except . . . maybe once or twice . . . nothing much of course . . .

Behag fell to daydreaming as she remembered little incidents, pleasurable sensations; perhaps if she hadn't been so adamant . . . She gave herself a mental shake. How could she? How could she even begin to think she might have wanted the likes of *that* – from a man! They were all the same when it came to the bit.

Look at Fergus McKenzie, for example, finding himself another woman as soon as his wife's back was turned. Of course, she wasn't really surprised, the McKenzies had always been a lusty lot, right down the line, as far back as she could remember . . .

She gazed again at the glossy display of undergarments. Those drawers looked really warm. It used to be only men who wore such things but times had changed and women had more freedom these days. Too much of it in some respects. She would never have worn 'the trouser', for instance, but she didn't mind the latest trend in sensible underwear, especially the long johns, they were so cosy and utterly comfortable . . . pity they didn't make them in flannel any more. As a girl she had worn flannel bloomers and once or twice – very daringly – she had treated herself to a red pair. They were still there, in her dresser, but getting a bit threadbare after all these years.

She turned a few more pages. Really! Some of that lingerie nowadays! It wouldn't decently cover a fly! It reminded her of that time when Elspeth Morrison had blatantly hung out frilly pants and bras for the whole island to see. It was as if she had gone off her head altogether, flaunting herself, acting like a teenager in the throes of growing up. Disgraceful behaviour in someone of her age! A voyeur with no sense of shame! Behag had read that word in a magazine and though she was only vaguely aware of its meaning she relished the sound of it and thought it applied perfectly to Elspeth.

Behag sat back in her chair, the catalogue momentarily forgotten. No one had ever found out Elspeth's reasons for hanging those provocative garments on her washline and Behag, more than anyone, was still incensed with curiosity about the episode.

Forgetting all about her recent views on the human right to privacy she gave herself up to the enjoyable pastime of wondering about the affairs of other folk, particularly those of Elspeth and Captain Mac. In her mind she needled into every little detail of their relationship and thoroughly enjoyed herself in the process. It was a terrible pity that the pair were planning to get married in Oban. Nobody would get the chance to see Elspeth in her wedding outfit and for

100

all anyone knew it might turn out to be just as daring as that underwear she had displayed on her washline.

Anything was possible with that woman, now that she had Captain Mac very firmly in her clutches!

Chapter Nine

The said Elspeth was, at that precise moment, sitting in Fergus McKenzie's kitchen, her back rigidly straight, her stoutly clad feet held one against the other in perfect formation, not flinching one inch when two of the resident cats took it into their heads to weave themselves round her lisle-clad legs and mew up into her face.

Her shopping bag was propped on her knee, her fingers curled stiffly over the handles with the knuckles showing white. The expression on her gaunt features was one of set determination; even the very hat on her head looked stern and unyielding with its grouse feather sticking straight up into the air in a distinctly regimental manner. She had sat thus for the last ten minutes, and though she appeared to be calm it was only an illusion. Every nerve was alert, every fibre ready for action, because, if truth be told, Elspeth was extremely wary of McKenzie o' the Glen, particularly so today, when she had taken it upon herself to arrive, unannounced, at his house.

On Rhanna, this was by no means an unusual occurrence. People popped in and out of each other's homes all the time. Hospitality was part and parcel of everyday life and it would have gone against the

Hebrideans' nature to have to knock at a door to gain entry or to make a formal arrangement to call in for a cup of tea and a chat. There were exceptions to this particular rule however. Where Laigmhor was concerned, Elspeth Morrison came into this category, and all because Fergus, in a turmoil of grief many years ago over the death of his first wife, had quarrelled with Lachlan. Ever since then, Elspeth had made no secret of her dislike of Fergus, while he had never made any bones about his lack of patience with her dour and critical nature.

She was certainly no stranger to the Laigmhor household, having entered its portals many times in the course of the years, especially when the motherly Mirabelle had been housekeeper and, more recently, when Shona had given birth to twin babies. But that had only been because a McLachlan had been involved, otherwise casual visiting was not on the agenda, except perhaps when she met Kirsteen on the road and was invited in for a cup of tea or if Phebie wanted her to take some message or other to Kirsteen.

So, with some trepidation, she waited for the master of the house to arrive. When eventually she heard him coming through the door her bearing became more taut than ever and she was the first to speak because there was no way she was going to allow him to have the first say. 'It is yourself,' she observed stiffly, unconsciously sticking her sharp nose in the air in a haughty gesture. 'I thought it must be you when I heard the door opening.'

A muscle worked in Fergus's jaw. She was the last person he expected to find in his kitchen. He had spent a good part of his morning in a fruitless search for Fern and he was in no mood to deal with Elspeth and her crotchety ways. At her words he glanced over his shoulder and said sarcastically, 'Ay, it must be me coming home to my own house, for I canny see anyone else at my back.'

Elspeth sniffed sourly but went on determinedly, 'I have spent the morning over at Slochmhor, seeing to Doctor Lachlan, and a good thing too for he's about as helpless as a newborn kitten unless he has a woman to look to him. Of course...' here she sniffed again, 'I wouldny leave a man like that on his own. He has worked hard all his days and Phebie would be better staying at home to fend for him instead o' gallivanting off to Glasgow without a care in the world.'

'Ay, ay,' Fergus broke in irritably, 'I know all about that, but it's dinnertime and I canny stand here listening to your blethers when I have so much else to keep me occupied.'

His tone put Elspeth on her mettle and it was with an effort that she swallowed her ire to say gruffly, 'Indeed, that is why I am here, Fergus. While I was busy wi' the doctor it came to my mind that Kirsteen too was away in Glasgow. I thought it would be only right for me to call in and see were you needing a hand to make your dinner, so I got the post bus to drop me at your road end. Mind you, that isny as simple as it sounds, that Erchy drives as if the de'il was chasing him and he went screeching past your gate so fast he just about killed us all.' She omitted to say that she had been the only passenger in the bus and she hadn't told Erchy to stop till they were almost at Laigmhor's gate, but she was an islander and she liked to exaggerate whenever she could.

Her words made little impression on Fergus. He wouldn't have cared if the bus had dropped her off on the moon, so unwelcome was she in his house. He knew why she was here. Not for his well-being, but to satisfy her own curiosity about the latest happenings at Laigmhor. She and that Behag between them were about the nosiest pair of old witches anyone could have the misfortune to meet and he had always tried to avoid them as much as he could.

Elspeth, ignoring the thunderous expression on his face, stood up and went over to the stove. 'Just you be telling me where everything is, Fergus, and I'll put on a peeny and get started. Of course,' she kept her face averted from him, 'I'll have to be knowing how many people I'll be cooking for, as I believe you have a young woman guest biding wi' you. I hear tell she came to your house in the dead o' night and had to be carried upstairs to bed. Folks are also saying that no one, not even Nurse Babbie who's so good wi' people, can get a word o' sense out o' her, but then there's some who will do anything to get the attention o' a man, especially one whose wife is safely out of the way for a while.'

It was pure and blatant snooping and Fergus was about to tell her where to go when something, a small devil inside himself, made him change his mind. Why not play the old yowe at her own game! It was high time somebody put her in her place and what better way to do that than throw it all back at her!

A strange little smile quirked his mouth, and when

he spoke his tone was even and relaxed. 'It's very good o' you, Elspeth, to take so much interest in my affairs. You'll find an apron hanging on that hook and food in the larder that Kirsteen prepared before she left. All you have to do is heat it. The lass you spoke about is upstairs resting in bed. She had a bad time o' it last night and I had to be in there with her to calm her down. I'll just go and see if she's ready to come downstairs, and also to make sure she puts some clothes on. I think she has the gypsy in her, the way she wanders about in bare feet, half naked.'

So saying he went out of the kitchen, leaving the door open. At the foot of the stairs he yelled upwards, 'Fern, my lass, dinner will be ready in a few minutes. Elspeth has come to cook it for us and won't mind if you aren't properly dressed. I'll come up and give you a hand to get out o' bed so bide where you are for a second!'

Elspeth turned an aghast face from the stove. Her mouth was hanging open, and her eyes were bulging in their sockets. So, it was true! All of it – and more! He and that strange young woman were alone with each other in the house! They must have spent the night together! And he didn't care! In fact – in fact – he was boasting about it! And Kirsteen not here to keep her eye on the pair of them. It was sinful! It was wicked! Downright wicked!

Of course, the McKenzies always had done things that no one else would have gotten away with! Take Alick, for instance, Fergus's brother, now deceased, and small wonder! In trouble from the moment he had drawn breath, getting into fights, involving himself in all sorts of mischief while he was still at school. It hadn't stopped there. Oh, no! At just fifteen years of age he had made a local girl pregnant and Malcolm, his father, had sent him away to school on the mainland to get him out of the way.

Then there was Shona, a wild little whittrock from the start, ingratiating herself into the McLachlan household, attaching herself to a decent laddie like Niall, wreaking havoc in his life by having his bairn out of wedlock. Mind you, there was an excuse for Shona, she had never known her mother, it was her father who had set all the examples, whether they be good or bad. A lass needed her mother; if it hadn't been for Mirabelle, devoting her life to the McKenzies, and in particular to Shona, God alone knew where any of them would have ended up.

There came a few thumps and bumps from upstairs. Elspeth's nostrils flared. *He* was in one of the rooms – with *her*! And by the sound of it they were having a high old time to themselves. The – the shame of it! Carrying on together, regardless of who was in the house. Well, she wasn't staying one moment longer in this den of vice! She had found out all she needed to know . . . and more . . . much much more, than she had bargained for. Untying her apron she threw it on the table and grabbing her bag she scuttled out of the house and away down the Glen Fallan road as if all the hags of hell were at her back.

As she neared the village the first people she saw were Kate and Tina, walking close together, heads wagging as fast as their tongues, so engrossed in their conversation they didn't see Elspeth bearing down on

107

them, waving her shopping bag in the air. It wasn't until she was almost upon them, gasping and wheezing from her brisk flight down the brae, that they became aware of her presence.

'What ails you, Elspeth?' greeted Kate. 'For a minute I thought it was Croynachan's bull breathing down my neck. You should be taking things a bit more slowly at your age.'

Elspeth ignored that. She was churning with the excitement of her discoveries and was fairly bursting to tell them to someone. 'I have just come from Laigmhor,' she panted, 'and I'll tell you this, it will be a long long time before I set foot in that house again. It's in their blood of course, has been from the start. The McKenzies were aye a family who did what they liked and now it's starting all over again, with Fergus the ringleader as usual!'

'Just what are you insinuating, Elspeth?' Kate had a dangerous glint in her eye. Despite their little differences she respected McKenzie o' the Glen and didn't like to hear anyone speaking ill of him, especially someone like Elspeth who was a troublemaker if ever there was one.

'I am not insinuating, I am telling you outright,' Elspeth returned with a lift of her chin.

'Outright! You have just spent the last few minutes going round and round the houses!'

'That was because I was so shocked I just couldn't bring myself to say what I saw and heard. Him and that new woman, alone wi' each other in the house, as cosy as you like, and from what I gathered they must have spent the night together. According to him she

108

floats around the house practically naked – the – the shameless hussy!' Elspeth digested her own words for a moment, while Kate and Tina eyed one another as they wondered what was coming next. 'He was upstairs wi' her when I left the house – ran from it more like. He told her he was coming up to help her to get out o' bed and not to bother getting dressed as I wouldn't mind. I heard them up there, cavorting about, banging and thumping and heaven knows what else.'

Skirls of laughter rent the air. Elspeth gaped in astonishment as Kate and Tina held on to one another and just about burst their sides with merriment.

'I can assure you this is no laughing matter,' Elspeth observed sourly. 'I am beginning to think this island is going to the dogs altogether! I was under the impression that you were two normal women wi' proper views about sin and corruption! And here you both are, just about dying wi' mirth, as if you were drunk and didny know any better.'

For answer, Kate and Tina hooted louder, and Elspeth was even more put about when Ranald, on his way home to dinner, paused to say with a twinkle, 'My, my, this is indeed a sight for sore eyes. Can I join in the joke or is it private?'

'Be on your way, Ranald McTavish!' Elspeth barked imperiously. 'You're much too nosy for your own good and would do well to mind your own business.'

Ranald, well used to Elspeth's sharp tongue, shrugged his shoulders and went on his way with a nonchalant whistle, even though his curiosity was well and truly aroused and he was agog to know what Kate and Tina were finding so amusing while Elspeth looked positively murderous.

It took several minutes for the two women to recover from their fit of laughter. Even then, they kept erupting into giggles, so that quite some time elapsed before Elspeth could get any sense out of them.

'Ach, my,' Tina wiped her streaming eyes, 'you can be really comical when you put your mind to it, Elspeth. I never knew anybody else who could keep such a straight face whilst telling a funny story.'

Elspeth was greatly upset by this. She certainly hadn't expected such an unusual reaction to her news and she could only stare wordlessly when Kate shook her head and said sadly, 'It must be wedding nerves, Elspeth, going to your head and making you say peculiar things.'

'Peculiar? Peculiar!' Elspeth found her tongue. 'What is so strange about an unfaithful husband, I'd like to know! Or am I just being old-fashioned? The odd one out in these days o' hippies and flower people sleeping rough wi' one another? And thon loud music that makes young folk dance all night like zombies wi' bulging eyes. Maybe if I became like that I would get on better for I'm beginning to see that a person wi' my principles is just an object for ridicule!'

Elspeth was somewhat out of touch about what went on in the mainland. Her racks were full of old magazines and newspapers and these she re-read from time to time so that she was still under the impression that she was thoroughly up to date about the 'state of the world'.

110

Kate, however, was much more informed. 'The flower people are no' so much in fashion as they were, Elspeth,' she said cheerfully, 'and somehow I canny see you as one o' them, flowers in your hair and strings o' beads trailing down your bosoms.'

'Ay,' Tina nodded her agreement. 'It would take an awful lot o' imagination to think o' you as one o' them.'

'Unless, of course, you were to dress up like that for your wedding,' Kate hazarded gleefully. 'A body can wear anything she likes on her wedding day and get away wi' it.'

Elspeth let out an almighty snort. 'Hmph! I can see I'm wasting my breath on you two. Here is Fergus McKenzie, carrying on wi' another woman and all you can do is laugh about it.'

'Ach, we're no' laughing at that,' said Tina as she hoisted up her shopping bag. 'It was just the idea o' Fergus having a wee bit fun to himself. He has no woman biding wi' him. The lass went off by herself during the night and the Lord only knows where she is now. I myself stayed the night at Laigmhor because Fergus was that worried about all the talk concerning him and the lassie.'

Elspeth stared. Her eyes goggled. A bright red stain crept over her face to the furrowed folds of her neck.

Kate shook her head and said heavily, ''Tis no wonder the man behaved as he did, Elspeth. There is enough rumour going about without you adding to it and I for one am glad he gave you a red face.'

Tina gave a sudden gasp. 'Och, my, I'm later than ever wi' the old folks' dinner, and gracious knows

111

what time I'll get to the Manse today to see to the doctor and the minister.'

She and Kate went off together, leaving Elspeth to stare after them. Her little vendetta against Fergus had backfired on her and she had never felt more humiliated as she stood there, wishing the ground would open and swallow her up.

When Shona came in to make her father's mid-day meal she found him sitting on a chair by the table, staring into space, not even turning when his daughter came into the room.

'What's troubling you, my lad?' Shona said in astonishment. 'You look as if you've just seen a ghost.'

'Not a ghost, that old yowe, Elspeth, here in the kitchen, as bold as brass when I came in at dinnertime. She pretended she had come on an errand o' mercy, but was only here to do her nosy, and like a fool I played along wi' her. Now she's away wi' a flea in her ear, probably gossiping her head off at this very minute about me and my philandering ways.'

'And were you – philandering?'

'Och! For heaven's sake, girl! You're as bad as she is! Fern isn't here, she went off last night and I don't know where she is!'

Shona flashed him a repentant smile. 'I'm sorry, I didn't mean it to sound like that, though in some ways I wasn't joking. Any man might be tempted to flirt wi' the likes of little Miss Innocent. She's all sweet and helpless on the outside but I have the feeling she's a lady who knows how to manipulate men in order to use them for her own ends.'

'You know, you're getting to sound like that witch Behag,' he said with what Shona called his 'black look', and with a laugh she kissed the top of his head and told him he would feel better after he had eaten.

'Just the same,' she turned from the stove, 'I think you should tell Kirsteen about her when next you phone. It would look bad if you didn't and if she hears it from other people it would really set the cat among the pigeons.'

Bob, coming in that moment in a gust of fresh air and a flurry of curses aimed at his dog, put paid to further family discussions. Fern's name was not mentioned once, as steak and kidney pie, followed by home-made apple tart, was dispensed and eaten with the greatest gusto and enjoyment.

That very evening however, Fergus paid a visit to Lachlan, who, deep in his first article about island doctoring, wasn't inclined for company.

'Go you ahead and phone, man,' he told Fergus, without looking up from his typewriter. 'I'm at a sticky bit here and can't leave it. I'm doing a piece about my years here as G.P. and I was just wondering what to call everybody. It's all very well to mention place names but I don't know if it would be wise to pinpoint people in the same way, particularly beings like Behag and Elspeth, they might end up suing me.'

Fergus gave a wry smile. 'I know what I would call those prying old bitches, Miss Nag and Miss Yowe, ancient crones wi' barbed tongues and long noses that have been poked in everywhere except the one place that might cure them o' meddling for all time.'

Lachlan threw back his head and roared delightedly. 'How about you doing this article for me?' he suggested cheekily. 'You've got the imagination for it and I could be doing wi' some help.'

'You're the man wi' the fancy words,' Fergus returned quickly. 'I'm only a farmer who's never had much to say and never will. Talking o' which...' He glanced at Lachlan appealingly, 'Could you dial this number for me? I'm as much good wi' telephones as I am wi' fine speeches and to tell the truth – I don't trust the damned things.'

'Och, alright then,' In his obliging way Lachlan abandoned his typewriter and went to dial Aunt Minnie's number. It was Phebie who answered it and husband and wife held a long, animated conversation before Lachlan handed the instrument to the impatiently waiting Fergus.

Kirsteen was delighted to hear the deep, lilting voice that she loved and he was equally pleased when her light melodious tones came over the line.

'I'm missing you, mo cridhe,' he told her quietly.

'Fergie,' she murmured softly, 'I miss you too, every minute, and I think about you, all the time. I hope you're lonely without me and that the house is so unbearably quiet you can't wait for me to get back.'

'Ay, that's true enough.' He took a deep breath, 'But the house isn't so quiet. In fact, since you went away I haven't had a moment to myself. It's been like Sauchiehall Street. The womenfolk of Rhanna seem to have joined forces and are never away from the place, cooking, cleaning... doing their nosy.'

'Oh, is that all,' she sounded relieved. 'Well, at least I know you're being looked after.'

'It isn't so much that, though of course Shona and Tina between them are spoiling me. It's just – well – you'll never guess what I found in the barn after you left.'

'Mmm, let me see, a litter o' kittens? Or of pups? A broody hen sitting on a golden egg?'

'No – not exactly, something a bit bigger than any o' those. A young woman in fact, sheltering in the hayloft.'

'A young woman? Who is she?'

'Well, that's just it, nobody knows. She was in a bit of a state when I found her, she must have knocked herself out on a beam and had a few cuts and bruises. I got Lachlan to help me carry her into the house.'

'But, last time you phoned you didn't mention her,' Kirsteen sounded puzzled.

'Och, you know me, mo cridhe, I never know what to say when I'm on the telephone and only remember what I should have said when it's too late to say it.' He was gabbling a bit and to cover his confusion he went on, 'Her arrival caused a bit of a sensation but she's gone now anyway, just upped and left last night without a word to anyone and nobody's seen her since.'

'Oh, the poor girl,' Kirsteen's voice was warm with sympathy, 'I hope she's alright, maybe she's suffering from loss o' memory. Anything could have happened to her. I'm surprised you didn't go out to look for her, Fergus.'

'I – did.' He felt a dreadful pang of guilt as he spoke, remembering how anxiously he had searched for Fern that morning. 'But I couldn't spare much time, Donald's still laid up wi' the flu and I couldn't leave all the work to Bob.'

'Well, you'll have to look for the girl again, as soon as possible, she might be anywhere and needing medical attention.'

'Alright, Kirsteen, I will.' His voice was husky; in those moments he appreciated his wife more than he had ever done. What other woman would have shown such sympathy for a girl she had never even met? There had been no hint of suspicion, no awkward questions, just complete trust and understanding.

'Goodnight, mo cridhe,' he said softly, 'don't worry about anything here, I'm fine and so is everybody and everything else.' Long after he had rung off he stood there, staring at the phone, thinking about Kirsteen and how much he loved her.

A hand on his shoulder made him jump. 'Good for you, Fergus,' Lachlan said approvingly. 'Talking of Fern, has there been any sign o' her yet?'

Fergus shook his head and Lachlan looked slightly worried. 'She really shouldn't be wandering about on her own like that. She took quite a knock on her head and would be better off resting in bed for a day or two.'

'What makes you think she's still on Rhanna? She could be anywhere by now. She seemed worried about staying at Laigmhor and begged me to let her go.'

'I know, I know.' Lachlan frowned. 'But she didn't seem to have any money on her and if she is still here she might have collapsed somewhere and be in need of help.'

'That's what Kirsteen said. She advised me to have a hunt for the girl.'

'Maybe we should call in the police,' Lachlan suggested. 'They might organise a search party and ease our minds a bit. The girl is certainly behaving in a very mysterious fashion and I myself am damned curious to know what's going on in her head.'

'No, no, leave the police out o' it just now.' Fergus rejected the idea quickly. 'She was adamant about not wanting them involved and she isn't likely to have changed her mind now. Let me do it my way and if I don't come up with anything you can send for Clodhopper – though for all the good he ever does he'd be better at home steeping his feet.'

Lachlan laughed. 'Ach well, time will tell all. Meanwhile, I'm relieved you told Kirsteen about Fern. It's one little weight off your chest and no doubt you'll feel the better for it.'

'Ay,' Fergus agreed, and then wondered why he still felt burdened down with guilt and anxiety.

Chapter Ten

Fergus stood on the headland of Burg, buffeted by a howling wind that tore at his clothes and threatened to sweep him off his feet with its relentless power. In front of him, the Sound of Rhanna was a tumble of blue-grey waves, crested by foaming white horses that rode and bucked and boomed against the stark black fingers of glistening reefs rising sheer out of the icy wet confusion of the ocean. Of all the bays on Rhanna, Burg was perhaps the most terrible, slashed as it was in winter by fierce Atlantic storms that caused havoc to the tiny pockets of fragile habitation along the shoreline.

Fergus had always hated the sea, its might and its power frightened him. The only boat he ever felt safe in was the steamer that plied between the islands, though even then he was never fully at ease and was always glad to step ashore. He had lost his arm in an accident in the dark relentless waters that swirled ceaselessly round the jagged finger of Port Rum Point. It had happened many years ago, but the deep sickening fear he had felt at that time gnawed at his belly and brought him out in a sweat whenever he thought about it. Even so, he never failed to be impressed by the ruthless strength of the ocean, just as long as his two feet were planted firmly on dry land.

His gaze travelled to the awesome spectacle of Burg, shearing starkly above the waves, a great gleaming fortress of treacherous cliffs, pocked with dank caverns, joining with the ragged bastion of Port Rum Point to protect the sheltered little harbour of Portcull.

Despite his feelings of relief at Fern's departure, Fergus had nonetheless experienced a strong compulsion to look for her, and for the last two days he had searched the island, scouring the moors from Nigg to Croy, the woods and copses surrounding the lochs and the hills. He had even tried the abbey ruins at Dunuaigh and the tiny islet on Loch Sliach, but had come up with nothing. Burg was his last resort and as he stood there, staring down at the crashing breakers, his stomach turned over and he found himself praying that her footsteps hadn't taken her to a Godforsaken place like this.

With Heinz romping along at his side he began to move down the cliff, following one of the numerous sheep tracks that led to Burg Bay. Here he wandered along, bent into the wind, knowing in his heart that no one in their right mind would seek refuge in such a wild and lonely spot.

He gave up looking when a brilliant watery sunset was spreading its light over the sky from the east, turning the Sound into a vast sheet of gleaming gold, and the bite in the wind was so icily intense he felt as if his face was being anaesthetised by it.

He was glad when he reached the familiar haven of the village. The little white-washed cottages looked homely and safe; Merry Mary was just locking up her

119

shop and she and Aggie McKinnon went off along the road, their voices high and fragmented as they shouted to one another above the wind. Ranald, whose craft shop was quiet in the off-season, was standing aimlessly in the shelter of his porch, but abandoned it with alacrity when Tam McKinnon and his cronies came noisily along, heading for the comforts of the Portcull Hotel, where it was their habit to consume a pre-dinner pint of Bull Bull McManus's draught beer, and maybe another for the road if funds and time permitted.

''Tis yourself, Fergus,' greeted Tam in some surprise, as McKenzie o' the Glen was inclined to keep himself to himself and only appeared in the village when he had to. 'A grand night for a walk, eh?'

'Ay, especially if it's only a short one to the hotel,' Fergus returned dryly.

'Ach well, 'tis the best place to be when it's cold like this,' Tam said jovially, blowing on his hands and rubbing them briskly together to emphasise his point about the weather.

'You look as if you could be doing wi' a dram yourself.' Todd the Shod eyed Fergus's wind-stung countenance. 'You could do worse than come wi' us for a quick one.'

'Ay,' agreed Ranald affably, all the while trying to calculate whose turn it was to stand a round. 'It would be an honour just, McKenzie o' the Glen, sharing a drink wi' his pals.'

'Thanks, but I'm busy,' Fergus said shortly.

'Oh ay,' Erchy tapped the side of his nose and winked. 'Hunting the highways and byways for that wee lassie who was biding wi' you, eh?'

Fergus's brow darkened. 'You could have had a go at looking for her yourself, instead o' wasting your time supping beer in the Portcull Hotel.'

The men shifted uncomfortably and Tam, acting as spokesman as was his wont, said rather lamely, 'Ay, well, Fergus, we had a mind to do that and had a wee bit o' a discussion about it. After a good bit o' argy bargy we came to the conclusion that she knew what she was about when she arrived on the island and would know where she was going when she went.'

'As simple as that, eh?' Fergus said heavily.

The men squirmed at his tone and when eventually they went on their way they did so in an awkward silence that wasn't broken till they had entered the well-loved portals of the hotel where a peat fire was leaping up the chimney in the Snug Bar.

Bull Bull McManus, named so because of his enormous head and rotund figure, padded up on slippered feet to take the order. He didn't mind being addressed by his nickname and would look bemused if anybody called him Duncan, which was the name with which he had been christened.

'Same as usual?' he nodded, flicking a damp cloth over the table and flipping open a discarded cigarette packet to peer inside it hopefully. 'Empty,' he pronounced dismally. 'It would be nice, just for once, if somebody left a fag or two, or better still, a bob or two, by way o' thanks for all the hospitality they get here.'

'Ay, I've often thought the same about our visitors,' Tam pondered thoughtfully. 'They come and they sup our tea and our whisky, they eat us out o' house and home and use our toilet paper, and never leave as much as a penny piece in return.'

'Ach, that's no' the same thing at all!' protested Bull Bull, fingering the point of his thick black beard and running his tongue over his full red lips, both of which gestures meant that he was getting annoyed.

'No, it isn't,' agreed Tam. 'You get paid for your food and drink – and you expect to get a tip for doing it.'

'Oh, so, you're grudging me an honest living,' Bull Bull began argumentatively. 'I work from morning to night for my bread and butter.' He eyed Tam speculatively, 'Pity I canny say the same for some people I know.'

'Ay, ay, right enough,' Todd, anxious to be served, spoke in a soothing voice. 'You do work hard, Bull Bull, and as well as all that, you keep the best cellar on the island.'

Since the Portcull Hotel was the only establishment of its kind on Rhanna, keeping the best cellar, as Todd put it, was not a particularly difficult achievement, but it was enough to mollify Bull Bull and he lumbered off to get the order.

A few minutes later, Bull Bull's wife, young, saucy, and as fat as a butterball, waddled over to the table with the drinks, bending low as she set them down so that her cleavage was exposed to full advantage. 'There you are, lads,' she said in her plump, hopefully seductive, voice. 'Nice and cold, the way you like it. If there's anything else I can do for you, just be letting me know.'

'Margie!' roared Bull Bull. 'Don't be taking all day

at that table! There's a mountain o' glasses to be washed.'

Margie giggled. 'Would you listen to him. Never lets me out o' his sight for a minute. He thinks all the men are after me for my body, as if I've ever encouraged anything o' that nature.' With a deep throaty chuckle she went off, teetering on high heels and wiggling her bottom for all she was worth.

'Would you look at the arse she has on her?' observed Tam, taking a hasty gulp of his beer.

'Ay, and those bosoms,' supplemented Todd, 'it's like looking down the sunny side o' the Clyde tunnel.'

'When were you in the Clyde tunnel?' Erchy asked obliquely.

'Quite a few times,' Todd asserted himself quickly. 'Glasgow is just teeming wi' relatives o' mine, and Mollie's too for that matter.'

'I didny know the tunnel had a sunny side,' Erchy continued to deviate in a most infuriating manner. 'Both ends always looked the same to me.'

Tam wasn't listening to any of this. 'By God! She certainly has got some arse on her,' he repeated meditatively. 'Like the rear end o' a suckling sow. I wonder if she would be like that naked – Margie, I mean, no' the pig, all pink and smooth and wobbling a bit.'

'Well, she wouldny have a wee curly tail for a start,' Erchy said decidedly, 'and you're never likely to find out about the other things, Tam, no' wi' Kate on one side, keeping her eagle eye on you, and Bull Bull breathing down your neck on the other.'

'Ach, well, never mind all that,' Tam's mind had

switched to other matters. 'I was just thinking about our conversation wi' Fergus regarding that lassie who is lost.'

'God, he's a dour bugger is McKenzie,' Todd grumbled as he settled himself more comfortably into the dented green leather of his favourite seat and proceeded to poke into the depths of an ancient briar with a pipe-cleaner that had seen better days.

'Ach, he was maybe right,' Tam said, sipping contentedly at his beer as he thoughtfully eyed the display of bottles in the gantry. 'We could have spared a bit o' time to look for that young woman. It would be terrible just if she was maybe lying somewhere, all twisted and bloody and McKenzie the only one caring if she lived or died.'

The others eyed one another uneasily. 'Ach, it'll no' be as bad as he's making out,' Erchy said hastily. 'The McKenzies were aye ones for a drama. She'll be in a city somewhere, living it up, glad to get away from the wind and the rain and the sheeps.'

'Ay, it might no' be as bad . . .' Ranald's tongue came out to mop up a moustache of frothy beer, '. . . on the other hand, it could be a lot worse. A similar thing happened in a book I read once. A lassie had a row wi' her parents and she went fleering out o' the house, saying she was going to lose herself in the hills. Everyone said she was just doing it to get attention and she would come home soon enough when her belly started to rumble. Well, she never came back, no' on that day, or the next.'

Ranald lowered his voice to a hoarse whisper. 'A search party was organised, but by that time the snow had covered the land, the winter winds were howling like ghosts in the corries, and the wild cats were so hungry they were baying like wolves in the wilderness. It was the worst winter that anyone could ever remember – and when it was over . . .'

'Ay, go on,' Todd urged, his eyes like saucers in his ruddy round face.

Ranald, who was thoroughly enjoying himself, dropped his voice even lower so that his cronies had to lean forward to hear what he was saying. 'When it was over, the lass was found, living in a lair like a wild animal. Her hair was matted and long, her nails like cat's claws, her teeths worn to the gum from living on the raw flesh o' mice and rabbits. She fought her rescuers tooth and nail for she didny want to leave the haunts she had grown used to. The only way they could get her off the hill was to wrap her in a straight-jacket bound round wi' the toughest rope they could find. She was never the same after that and would crouch in a corner, only eating uncooked meat and raw fish. Her parents were heartbroken for they said they had lost their daughter as surely as if she had died out there in the snow.'

'Och, the poor, poor lassie,' Todd's voice was husky with the suspense he was enduring. 'But what happened to her, Ranald? Surely she didny live the rest o' her life like that?'

'Oh ay, she did.' Ranald's voice was triumphant, he had a captive audience and he was making the most of it. 'When her mother, then her father, went to an early grave, she went back to live in her lair in the hills. As time went on she became more and more like

125

a wild beast, vicious and snarling if anybody dared to go near her.'

At that point Ranald appeared to sink into a trance-like state, staring into the fire, sipping absently at his beer.

'Is that the end o' the story?' Tam asked in disappointed tones.

Ranald started; he seemed to come back from a long way. His face was composed into serious lines, his eyes were sad. 'Indeed no, Tam, I was shocked, shocked to the core when I read the next bit o' the story. There is worse, much worse to come.'

'Ay, ay, get on wi' it, man!' encouraged Tam, almost beside himself with anticipation.

Ranald gazed round at all the expectant faces. 'This is hard for me, lads, very, very hard, for when I was reading the end o' the book I was greetin' like a baby and I don't want to be doing that in front o' my friends.'

'For God's sake!' exploded Erchy. 'We'll no' care if you drown yourself in tears! Just tell us what happened next!'

Ranald swallowed hard. 'Well, you asked for it and here goes. It doesny really bear thinking about but the truth is this, the lassie ended up living wi a family o' foxes! Untamed and as cunning as they were, she hunted alongside them and was sometimes seen, tearing at carcasses o' dead animals, her teeths dripping wi' blood, as savage as any beast o' the forest. When she died she was eaten by the very foxes she had befriended, and only her skeleton was found. But – and here is the strange and terrible crux o' the matter

126

– it wasny a normal, human skeleton that was found. When the experts examined it they discovered that her incisors had grown into fangs and her nails into claws – and also . . .' Here Ranald's face positively glowed, '. . . she had grown a tail – a big, bushy red tail – exactly like a fox's brush!'

'But how could she have a tail on her if she had turned into a skeleton?' Tam clamoured. 'It would have dropped off along wi' her skin when the foxes got her!'

'Ay, and how did anybody know the foxes had eaten her unless they were there to see it?' Erchy said scornfully. 'It could have been a wild cat or rats or – or even whole batches o' worms and grubs that had hatched out on her rotting corpse.' The picture that his own words presented appeared to upset Erchy greatly and he sat back, looking stunned and disgusted.

'Ach well,' Ranald shook his head. 'It just goes to show, every story has its weaknesses, and I have often thought I could do a better job o' writing books myself, if only I had the time to do it in.'

'You certainly have the imagination for it.' Todd sounded aggrieved. He had begun to feel somewhat queasy and couldn't face the last dregs of beer in his glass. 'I'll bet you ten pounds you made the last bit o' that story up. Next time I come to your house I want you to show me that book so I can see the truth o' it for myself.'

Ranald looked faintly worried by this. 'Och no, Todd, you'll no' be able to do that. I got it from the library and had to give it back after I had read it.'

'There is no proper library on Rhanna.' Todd said triumphantly. 'Only the one run by the Wimmen's Rural in that wee hut attached to the kirk. I've had a good look at it myself and it's mostly thon romantic novels and cookery books that's in it. There's nothing much for men at all except old Gaelic bibles and do-it-yourself magazines, so you must have the book in your house and I'll be round tomorrow to have a wee keek at it.'

'And then there was the question o' her teeths,' Tam was off on a slant of his own, still poking and prying into the all too obvious gaps in Ranald's story. 'You said they were worn to the gum from eating raw meat, so how could she have had those fangs you spoke about? Human people are no' like sharks. Sharks have rows o' new teeths growing all the time, shunting around in their jaws like they were on a conveyor belt. Folks like us canny grow new teeths to order, so how . . .?'

Much to Ranald's relief Bull Bull put paid to further argument by coming up to stare pointedly at their empty glasses, whereupon they rose as one and made their way home to their respective dinner tables.

Huddled into his jacket, his collar pulled around his ears against the biting wind, Fergus trudged up the Glen Fallan road, reflecting moodily on his actions over the last few days. He wondered what had possessed him to go looking for a young woman he knew so little about.

She meant nothing to him, nothing! All she had done was make a damned nuisance of herself by coming to his house, infiltrating his life, upsetting his routine, and having everyone running to her beck and call. And then she had just walked out! Without a word to anyone! Never a by-your-leave nor a word of thanks for all the trouble she had caused. If she was still on Rhanna she was making a damned good job of hiding herself! If she had left, then all his efforts had been in vain, and he had made a bloody fool of himself and wasted his time into the bargain! He had only allowed her to stay at his home out of common decency, and the only reason he had tried to find her was because he had felt himself to be responsible for her in some obscure way.

There was only one course open to him now: he would have to inform the police about her disappearance. More than likely they would send P.C. George McDuff, commonly called Clodhopper because of his clumsy great feet. What good he would do in a case like this was anybody's guess. Convinced that certain islanders were always up to mischief, he revelled in any excuse to come over to Rhanna so that he could have a go at trying to uncover unlawful misdemeanours.

One of his tricks was to hide behind the bushes near the hotel and pounce on the locals if he thought they'd had too much to drink. His other favourite game was trying to book people on drink driving charges, excelling himself on one occasion by stopping old Angus McBain on his bike and asking to see his driving licence!

Fergus had reached the track leading up to Laigmhor. It was growing dark; the hills rose up behind the white farm buildings, aloof and mysterious in the fading light. The highest and most rugged tip of Ben Madoch still wore its winter cap of snow, and the peaks of Ben Machrie were lit by the pink afterglow of sunset.

His gaze travelled back to the sturdy big farmhouse, sheltered from the prevailing wind by a grove of trees, surrounded by dykes and runs and an assortment of outbuildings. Normally he loved coming home to Laigmhor with its welcoming warmth and a hot meal waiting to be set on the table. But Kirsteen wasn't here! She was away in Glasgow. The house would be empty and unwelcoming . . .

Why, then, was there a light shining softly in one of the downstairs windows?

Perhaps Kirsteen had come home early . . .

Perhaps . . .

His heart began to pound in his breast and for reasons unknown to him he felt like a man hypnotised as he began to walk towards the beckoning light in the window.

Chapter Eleven

With his heart in his throat Fergus pushed open the door, almost afraid of who he might find waiting for him in his own kitchen.

At first he could see very little; only one lamp spread its glow over the room, combining with the firelight to create an aura of mystery that made his heart beat all the faster as he stood there, letting his eyes adjust. And then he saw her, huddled in a chair by the fire, silent, watchful, wary, that wonderful hair of hers framing her face, falling down her back in a waterfall of rich waves and curls.

'Fern – Fern Lee.' Her name escaped his lips, like the opening notes of a song, lyrical and sweet. He shook himself, as if awakening from a dream, and when next he spoke his tone had changed to harshness. 'Where the hell have you been?' he demanded. 'I've looked everywhere for you – I was just about to call the police . . .'

'Please,' she shook her head, her voice was frightened and pleading, 'don't be shouting at me. It's sorry I am for wandering off like that but my thoughts were in a whirl and I didn't seem to know what I was doing. I walked a lot at first and then I found myself in a derelict cottage and stayed there for a while. All of it happened in a daze but I kept thinking of you and it seemed only right – to come back here. It's wonderful to be in your house again, to feel the homeliness – the warmth. I'm so . . . cold.'

She couldn't go on, she was pale and exhausted-looking and she was shivering. Striding to the cupboard he took out a bottle of brandy and pouring out a generous measure he went back to the fire and shoved the glass into her hand.

'Drink it, every drop,' he ordered.

She glanced up at him, her eyes meeting his. He felt strange and breathless and going once more to the cupboard he poured himself a stiff dram and drank it down in one gulp.

He heard her coughing a little as she swallowed her brandy and without turning he said, 'That should make you feel better. Medicinal, that's what Mirabelle called it. She was housekeeper here for years and we all did what she told us.'

'I'm thinking I owe you an explanation for all this,' her voice came to his ears, low and subdued. 'I came to this island to get away from my husband who is a brutal and abusive man. He is never done drinking and fighting and hitting me if I dare to say one word against him. I just couldn't take any more of him so I smuggled myself aboard a fishing boat, never knowing or caring where it was going. I ended up here on Rhanna, staying hidden on the boat till I thought it was safe for me to be coming ashore. I only wanted a bit of shelter for the night and that was the reason I was after hiding myself in your barn. That was where you found me, having knocked myself out climbing up into the hayloft.'

132

Her voice faltered. 'I'm truly sorry for all the trouble I've caused, but I have to admit how glad I am to have found a man like yourself, so different from my own in every way that I can see. I knew you were special from the minute I clapped eyes on you – that's why I came back, why I'm here now. Let me be hearing from your own bonny lips that you're just a wee bit pleased to be seeing me again – after all, if you didn't care about me, you wouldn't have gone out looking for me, would you now?'

He turned slowly to look at her. 'You really canny expect me to answer that. I'm a married man – a happily married man – and I won't let anything or anyone jeopardise that. You do understand what I'm saying, don't you?'

She didn't answer. For reasons of her own she had to have Fergus on her side and she uncoiled herself gracefully from her chair. As she stood up her eyes were fixed on him, dark and compelling. Her body swayed as she came towards him, and the movements of her limbs were cat-like, flowing, sinewy, deliberate.

Before he could stop her she had wound her arms round his neck, ensnaring him in a circle of feminine softness, gazing up at him appealingly as she whispered, 'Please, Fergus, don't be angry with me any more, I couldn't bear it if I thought you hated me for all the bother I've been causing you.' Her eyes held his for a long moment, then she drew his head down till their faces were almost touching. 'Special man,' she murmured. Her lips touched his and then their mouths merged together, deeper and deeper, in a kiss that was warm, lingering, inviting, and utterly sensuous.

Temptation washed over him like a tide. He heard her voice in his ear, low and husky, begging him to let her stay with him. 'I feel safe here, Fergus. It wouldn't be for long, I am just needing a little bit of time to decide what to do with my life. I promise you won't regret it.'

Her breasts were soft and provocative against the hard wall of his chest, and he felt himself drowning in a dangerous sea of desire and longing. He fought against it, he couldn't do this, to himself, to Kirsteen, to his family. Even as he argued with himself he was aware of his mounting passions, his arousal, his overpowering need to make love to her even if it was the last thing on earth that he did . . .

And then he looked up to see his granddaughter, seven-year-old Lorna Morag McKenzie, standing watching him, her big gentian eyes filled with solemn wonderment.

'Lorna!' he cried, pushing Fern away to take a few deep shaky breaths. Striding over to the little girl he dropped on his knees beside her to ruffle her dark curls and gaze into her small sweet face. 'What are you doing here?' he questioned gently, all the while wondering just how much the child had witnessed. 'Surely – surely you didn't come on your own?'

Lorna was a young creature possessed of an intelligence that went far beyond her years. Her instinct for assessing the feelings of those around her had been born in her and she seemed to know just when to be silent and when to speak. Her eyes when she looked at him held a message and he knew without asking that she wouldn't make a fuss about what she had seen.

134

'Mother and Father and Douglas are just coming,' she informed him, her small fingers twisting nervously together as she spoke, the only sign of the agitation she was feeling at catching her adored grampa kissing a woman who bore no resemblance whatsoever to her equally adored gramma. 'We all came in Father's van to make your tea and I ran in first.'

The next minute the door opened and the room was filled with people all talking at once, while the youngest member of the family, five-year-old Douglas, screeched with delight at sight of Heinz, whom he regarded as his playmate.

'I thought it would be nice if I brought the tea and we all had it together here,' Ruth explained to her father-in-law, removing her coat as she spoke and shaking out her mane of golden hair. 'Douglas, don't pull the dog's tail,' she added in the same breath, rushing over to grab her son and smack him for his misdemeanour. It was then she saw Fern, who had returned to the fire to bathe herself in its warmth.

'Oh,' Ruth recoiled a little. 'I'm sorry, I didn't know there was anybody else here.'

At this point Fergus hastily intervened. 'This is Fern Lee, the lass who's been the talk o' the place since she arrived. She went away for a whilie but she's back again and needing her tea as much as anybody else here.'

With one accord everyone stared at the girl by the fire. Despite the discomforts she must have suffered over the last two days she still managed to look stunningly beautiful. Her skin was golden in the fire's light, while her beautifully formed body looked re-laxed and peaceful.

135

But it was only an illusion. Her great dark eyes were burning like lanterns in the sculpted perfection of her face, her head was proudly tilted, her blue-black hair cascaded round her shoulders, all combining to endow her with that gypsy-like quality that had so enchanted Fergus from the start. Heinz had fallen hopelessly in love with her and sat with his head on her lap, gazing soulfully up into her face with his big mournful eyes.

Everyone else, including the children, seemed mesmerised by the woman and Ruth experienced a pang of unease when she noticed that Lorn could hardly take his eyes off her.

'Right!' Ruth was the first to speak. 'It's high time we *all* had something to eat! Lorna, you set the table, Lorn, you can make yourself useful by unpacking the foodstuffs and putting them over there by the stove.'

Her voice was brisk and business-like, but Lorn knew his wife and when she was busy cooking the meal he went over to her and said quietly, 'What ails you, Ruthie? You're like a hen on a hot girdle and you've got that funny look in your eye.'

'Nothing ails me!' She flounced about, throwing bacon into one pan, breaking eggs into another. 'I'm just hungry, that's all, and needing my tea.'

'That isn't all.' Lorn's handsome features darkened, his brows came together. 'You're looking and sounding like a damt wee spitfire! Yet when we left home to come here you were like a bairn in your eagerness to surprise my father.'

'Ay,' her eyes flashed, 'if we'd come a bittie sooner we might have surprised him even more. He was all

136

hot and bothered looking when we came in and *she* was just acting too cool for words.'

'So, that's it, eh? You've got it in for her and you don't even know her.'

Ruth rounded on him. 'Oh, I know her alright! That sort o' woman is as easy to read as a book. And don't think I didn't notice the way you looked at her! As if you could have gobbled her up in one gulp and then gone back for more.'

'Ruthie,' he said warningly. 'If you go on behaving like this I'm going home.'

'That's right!' she flashed back. 'Run away, like you did the time you and Rachel had that affair. Don't think I've ever forgotten it! All men are the same when it comes to the bit!'

'I didn't run away, you did, and if you're going to start all that again then I really am going home and leaving you to explain to Father.'

She calmed down then and gazed at him with her huge expressive eyes. 'Oh, Lorn, I'm sorry, it's just – I can never forget the way we all suffered when you and Rachel did what you did. Deep inside I'm afraid it might happen again wi' somebody else. I couldn't bear to lose you – yet ... I know I couldn't forgive you ... a second time.'

'Ruthie,' he took her hands and held them tight, 'nothing o' that sort will ever happen again, I promise you. I was just looking, that's all, it's – it's the way men are made.'

She giggled. 'I've a good mind to blindfold you next time we come here, Lorn McKenzie, but if I did I wouldn't be able to make use o' you. Here, take these plates before everything gets cold. And don't drop them or you'll get a warmed lug and no tea!'

There was a rather awkward silence when at last everyone seated themselves at the table. The conversation was polite and stilted as salt and pepper, milk and sugar, were passed round with the utmost attention to the needs of table partners.

Even the children seemed struck dumb by the presence of the unexpected newcomer to Laigmhor's familiar scene. Douglas had to be reprimanded once or twice for openly following every move that Fern made, his eyes going from her plate to her mouth, her mouth to her plate, till in exasperation Lorn told him to stop gaping and get on with his own meal.

But gradually the atmosphere thawed and when it did, everyone began talking at once, as if vying with one another as to who could recount the most interesting tit-bit of news.

Fern, her eyes sparkling, listened for a while, and then she too began to add to the conversation, and when she did it was as if the atmosphere had been charged with something electric. Her elbows on the table, her clasped hands supporting her chin, she began to speak in her southern Irish lilt, simple little anecdotes, funny things that had happened to her, nothing startling or out of the ordinary, yet she made the commonplace sound exciting, the mundane exhilarating and hilarious.

By the end of the meal she had captivated everyone, including the children and the animals. Even Ruth couldn't help succumbing to her charms and felt quite gratified when she offered to help wash up the tea things.

138

'I am fair delighted to have found you all,' Fern confided to Ruth in her pleasing voice. 'If it hadn't been for Fergus I don't know what I would have done and everyone else has been so kind.'

She proceeded to tell Ruth her reasons for seeking refuge on the island. By the time she had finished speaking Ruth was overcome with sympathy and eager to help in any way she could.

'Ah, if only I could be staying at Laigmhor for a while,' Fern sighed. 'I feel so safe here, but it's difficult with Mrs McKenzie away and no one else in the house but myself and her man.'

'Oh, that's easily solved.' Ruth's face was flushed with earnestness. 'Lorna loves it here and would be only too willing to bide wi' her grampa for a whilie. Shona and myself take turns driving the bairns to school in the morning and it would be no trouble picking Lorna up from Laigmhor . . .'

Ruth halted. More visitors had arrived, this time Fiona and her husband Grant, Fergus's eldest son. With them they had brought little Ian, who wasted no time joining forces with Douglas who was intent on tying a woollen bonnet round Heinz's patient head.

Fiona's bright eyes took in the scene in one glance. 'I see you found your way back,' she addressed Fern appraisingly, all the while thinking how quickly the newcomer had made inroads into the family circle.

Grant said nothing but just stood looking at the girl, something in his dark eyes that wasn't easy to fathom. He was very like Fergus, both in build and looks, brawny and muscular, bristling with life and energy, his firm determined jaw bearing testimony to a nature

139

that could be every bit as stubborn as that of his father. Woe betide anyone who ever did wrong against a member of his family, especially if it involved his mother, of whom he was fiercely protective, having spent the first five years of his life in her keeping before she and Fergus got married. He didn't like the upheaval this girl was causing in the Laigmhor household and Fern, sensing something of his thoughts, was the first to look away from him with the feeling that his black steely eyes seemed to be boring into her very soul.

A silence had once more descended on the room and everyone experienced a sense of relief when it was broken by a noisy scuffling at the door which soon opened to reveal Tam and Todd, grinning their big grins, almost in unison whipping their caps respectfully from their heads and twisting them round in their large red hands.

'Ach, you're busy, Fergus,' Tam observed, his eyes roving round the gathering. 'It might be best if we came back another time.'

The cold night air was rushing in through the open door. 'No, no, come in,' bade Fergus hastily, 'you're letting all the heat out o' the house. Two more won't make much difference now,' he ended in some bemusement since the walls of the kitchen seemed to have shrunk in the last half hour.

Obediently Tam shut the door and came further inside. 'If you're sure it's no bother.' He was being at his polite best. 'We'll no' keep you long but after meeting you today we thought it only right to come here and offer our services.'

'Ay, ay,' Todd, not to be outdone, added his piece. 'While we were in the hotel we had a wee discussion about the things you were after telling us. There was the usual humming and hawing but in the end we came to the decision that we ought to offer to help find the lassie who is lost. It was after Ranald told us a terrible tale about a young woman who went missing in the hills and ended up being eaten by foxes . . .' He broke off; Tam was nudging him in the ribs and grunting in a most meaningless manner.

Todd blinked uncomprehendingly.

'There, man, there,' hissed Tam, gesticulating with his thumb in Fern's direction.

Todd stared at her as if she was a ghost but Tam, being Tam, soon recovered himself.

'I see you have found yourself,' he beamed at Fern. 'Well, well, is this no' a turn up for the books? Todd and me were just about to go out looking for you and here you are, bright as a moonbeam and as bonny as a morning rosebud.'

If Kate had heard this she would undoubtedly have crowned him with the nearest floor mop, since the only flower he had ever likened her to was 'a dead dandelion wearing curlers'. Kate, however, was not there and Tam felt free to let his tongue run riot, his reward for his chivalry being a thank you kiss on his cheek, planted there by Fern herself who seemed filled with appreciation for his apparent concern for her well-being.

'Well, well, this calls for a dram!' Tam, quite carried away with himself, spoke in a masterful voice.

'Ay, ay, right enough.' Todd, feeling cheated of

141

attention, was prepared to settle for a 'drop o' the cratur' as a reward for his good intentions. 'It's no' every night a lass is saved from the wilderness, is it now?'

Fergus capitulated. The drams were poured and passed round. Half an hour later a ceilidh was in full swing, with the menfolk vying with one another as to who could recite the best poem or recount the most interesting tale.

'We should have had Ranald here,' Todd cried. 'If anyone can make a body's flesh creep, McTavish is the man to do it.'

'Ach, we don't need him,' Tam said flamboyantly, one eye on Fern, whom he was trying hard to impress. 'All the best people are here at Laigmhor tonight. Get out your fiddle, Lorn, my lad, and we'll have a wee bit dance.'

Lorn always kept a spare fiddle at his old home and soon the reels and strathspeys were springing wildly from his flying fingers. Everyone danced, the menfolk making sure that Fern was never without a partner. Only Grant remained aloof, while Fergus was careful to keep his distance from her.

He watched her, though. When he was certain that everyone else was busy he noted the swaying of her lithe limbs, and the feline grace of her slender young body.

'She's recovered quickly enough.' Grant's voice at his elbow made Fergus jump. 'I thought she was supposed to have spent the last few days freezing to death and starving.'

Fergus's eyes glittered. 'Just what are you implying, son?'

142

'Och, come on, Father. Look at her, she's the picture o' health and vitality – and – and there's an excitement about her that I canny explain, as if she's got something to celebrate and is glad o' the chance to let it all out.'

Even as he spoke a wild cry rent the air. Lorn was playing a lively selection of Spanish melodies, and Fern had jumped up and was holding the floor. Swirling her skirt around her thighs, stamping her feet, she gave full rein to a wild Flamenco dance, showing her shapely legs, arrogantly moving her head from side to side, in the process effectively displaying her perfectly sculpted cheekbones and the entrancing little cleft in the middle of her chin.

'Phew, just look at those legs,' Tam hissed to Todd.

'Ay, she's a bonny lass and no mistake,' Todd nodded.

The rest of the men thought so too, if their rapt attention to Fern's every move was anything to go by. Then, just as suddenly as she had risen she sat down again, face averted, looking as if she was regretting having brought so much attention upon herself.

Grant and Fiona glanced at one another meaningfully. 'Are you thinking what I'm thinking?' Fiona asked her husband. 'That there's more to her than meets the eye?'

'Ay,' he returned darkly. 'But try telling that to Father –or anybody else for that matter. She's got them eating out o' her hand, but I'll be keeping a weather eye open for her, at least till Mother gets home.'

'She is lovely though, isn't she?'

'Devastating,' he admitted frankly. 'And she's using it like a weapon. She knows how to attract men alright but . . .' he grinned, '. . . not an old salt like myself who's spent his life dodging beautiful mermaids and witches and all the other fabulous creatures that the ocean ever had to offer.'

She giggled, but knew he meant what he said about keeping Fern under surveillance. When he set his mind to it he was like a dog with a bone and where his family was concerned he would never let go until all danger had passed.

Chapter Twelve

It was late when the visitors took their leave of Laigmhor. Ruth and Lorn were the last to go, lingering on for a cup of tea before they too departed into the night, leaving Lorna, who was delighted to be staying with her grampa.

'I'll look after him,' she promised her parents in her most grown up manner, and taking Fergus's hand she stood with him at the door till Ruth's little car was lost to view on the Glen Fallan road.

'Now it's just us!' Fern cried in delight. 'And we'll all have a wonderful time together.'

She seemed genuinely pleased to have the little girl in the house and set about bathing her and generally attending to her needs. 'There now, mavourneen,' she said as she finished brushing the child's curly mop. 'Into bed with you. I'll tuck you up all nice and cosy and then you must go to sleep like a good wee lass. You have school to go to in the morning and I'll have your breakfast all ready for you.'

But Lorna had other ideas. 'I have to look after Grampa,' she stated solemnly. 'Mother says he's lonely without Gramma and I'm going to read him a bedtime story and keep him company till he falls asleep.'

And she meant every word she said. The grown ups had very little say in the matter. Lorna was a true McKenzie and could be every bit as stubborn as any of them when she felt like it. With a determined set to her chin she left her own bed to go through to Fergus's room and climb into his bed.

'I'm waiting to read you a story,' she told him, and so saying she folded her hands over her chest and lay on the pillows with a look of utmost patience on her rosy, newly washed face.

'Alright,' laughed Fergus, who had a terrible soft spot for his eldest grandchild. 'I give in. What will it be tonight? Jack in the Beanstalk? Red Riding Hood?'

She gazed at him reprovingly. 'Grampa, those are for tiny children like Aunt Shona's twins. They're far too babyish for a big man like you. I thought you might like *Treasure Island*. It's in the bookcase in Aunt Shona's room.'

'*Treasure Island* it is,' he conceded, unable to smother his laughter. 'I'll go through and get it.'

He went across the landing but stopped short at the door of his daughter's old room. Fern occupied it now! And he didn't know if she had come upstairs or was still down below in the kitchen. Tentatively he tapped the door. There was no answer and snapping on the light he went in quickly to search through the bookcase.

'She's all there, that little one! She's got us both neatly sewn up and just where she wants us.' Fern had come in. She was right there, at his back, so close he could smell her perfume and feel the soft material of her nightdress whispering against his bare arm.

146

'I have just had a bath.' Her breath fanned his ear, her voice was low and seductive. 'Was it not my old grandmother who was always after telling me to waste not, want not, and leave nothing for the devil? I used Lorna's bathwater for it was still fine and warm, and here I am, all ready for the taking.' She laughed, and pressing herself up against him she allowed her lips to brush his cheek. 'Don't be forgetting now, the things my grannie used to say. It would be a terrible waste altogether if I had no one to share my bed with and myself chilled to the bone after all my terrible experiences.' Her hands came round to caress his chest. 'Don't be long with that story, Lorna's a tough wee thing but she's had a busy night to herself and should soon drop off to dreamland.'

'No!' He felt as if he was choking in a mixture of desire and rage. Fiercely he shook her off and spinning round he grabbed her wrist to hold it fast and look her straight in the eye. 'No more o' this! I won't have it in my house! I said you could stay till you got on your feet and that's all I meant. My granddaughter's in the next room, my wife will be home in a week or so, my family are never away from the place and I – I'm bloody well not getting myself into trouble, for you or anyone else!'

She held his gaze, her dark eyes flashed, and a husky mocking laugh rose up in her throat. 'Ah well, are you not the man of stone and steel? Here am I, a flesh and blood colleen, only wanting to show you how grateful I am for everything you've done for me, and here you are, boiling inside and trying to pretend you have a heart made of ice. But it will melt, Fergus, surely it will melt, the furnace in your belly will see to that, and when it does I'll be here waiting for you.'

Breathing heavily he pushed her aside and charged out of the room, forgetting all about *Treasure Island* in his haste to escape. Before facing Lorna again he paused to collect his senses. He was seething with emotions that he hadn't known for years! Awash with an anger that shook him! And something else that he could hardly bear to admit, even to himself.

It had been a struggle for him to reject her advances just now. He wanted to know what it would be like with her and the urge to rush back to her room was almost overpowering.

It was too much! All he wanted was peace in his own house, to feel he was his own man again!

All he wanted . . .

He didn't allow his thoughts to wander further. If he had succumbed to the persuasions of those young arms, that hungry mouth, he knew he would have lived to regret it for the rest of his life.

'You should see her, Kate,' Tam was enthusing to his wife as he partook of a late supper of melted cheese on toast sprinkled with pepper. 'It's no wonder McKenzie wanted to keep her all to himself, she's a beauty and no mistake.'

'Oh ay,' Kate sounded ominously calm. 'And I suppose you would know what to do wi' her if you had her all to *your*self?'

'What man wouldny?' Tam returned in muffled tones as he bit into his cheesy snack with relish.

Kate glowered at her husband's bald patch. 'You

dirty bodach!' she cried. 'What woman in their right mind would give the likes o' you a second glance! I only put up wi' you because at my age I canny get anything better.'

'Och, Kate,' he cajoled, 'that's no' a very nice thing to say to your very own man. You're a bonny woman and you know fine I wouldny change you for all the tea in China.'

'Do you really mean that, Tam?' Kate was somewhat mollified.

'Of course I do, mind you, what would I be doing wi' all that tea?' he continued jovially. 'I would rather have a hotel like Bull Bull's and put Fern behind the bar. I would do a roaring trade for she's a right wee shining star . . .'

His eyes gleamed. 'That dance, those legs.'

For answer, Kate bonked him on his bald patch with the empty teapot which, fortunately for him, was made of light metal. 'That's about the only stars you'll be seeing in this life, my lad!' she told him furiously. 'If it does nothing else it might knock some sense into that silly skull o' yours!'

'Och, Kate.' Ruefully Tam rubbed his head and gazed at her with reproach. 'There is no need for violence o' that sort. You like to know what's going on in the place and I was only telling you what I saw and heard on my visit to Laigmhor tonight.' Taking off his socks he wriggled his toes to the fire. 'Whether you like it or no, there's going to be a few jealous cailleachs on the island soon. That lass will cause havoc among the menfolk or my name's no' Tam McKinnon.'

Kate snatched his socks from the floor. 'There are holes in these as big as your head! Well, this time you can darn them yourself or – or get that Jezebel o' McKenzie's to do them for you! She might no' be so keen to flirt wi' bodachs like you if she got a taste o' your smelly drawers and sweaty socks and your boozy snoring in bed when you're sleeping off the dregs o' Bull Bull's beer.'

'Och, come on now, Kate,' wheedled Tam, 'that's no' very fair. You can raise the rafters yourself wi' your own snoring. Many's the night I've lain sleepless in the dark, thinkin' the world was crashing round my lugs wi' all the noise and thunder you make.'

'Tam McKinnon! I haveny finished wi' you yet and don't you try to change the subject! I haveny forgotton how you have to get up in the night to pee all your money down the drain, and here's me, needing a new winter coat and a decent pair o' breeks to cover my backside!'

Tam sighed; he said not another word but gazed into the fire, a little smile hovering at his mouth, and Kate, knowing that she had lost this round, threw his socks at him and flounced away to bed, silently cursing 'that woman o' McKenzie's' for all she was worth.

Next morning Shona arrived at Laigmhor to collect her niece for school. With her she brought her fair-haired little daughter, Ellie Dawn, who immediately vanished upstairs to seek out her cousin Lorna. Both little girls got on well together, and it wasn't long before their laughter and chatter came drifting down-stairs.

Left alone with her father Shona immediately demanded to know what was going on in the house. 'When Ruth told me about last night I could hardly credit that you were allowing that woman to stay here with only a bairn to act as chaperone! I hope you know what you're doing, Father!'

Fergus was immediately on the defensive. 'Of course I know what I'm doing – and see you keep a civil tongue in your head, my girl.'

'I'll say what I have to. I suppose you've told Kirsteen about this – this latest arrangement?'

'I haven't had time,' he said shortly.

'Then you'd better make time! Of course, if you weren't too cussed about getting the phone in there would be no problem about keeping in touch. I know fine Kirsteen would love one, even if it only meant she could blether to another woman occasionally. You should learn to consider her feelings as well as your own.'

'Learn! Learn!' Fergus nearly choked, a muscle in his jaw was working overtime. Father and daughter faced one another, their eyes blazing. Both were possessed of fearsome tempers and obstinate natures, with the result that neither would give in without a struggle.

'Ay, learn, Father, it isn't too late,' Shona returned coolly. 'I've never seen you like this with anyone before, far less a stranger who landed on you out o' the blue. She's spinning you fairy tales and you're allowing her to get the upper hand, but I don't think she's telling the truth.'

'How do you know?' he threw back. 'You've never spoken to her properly!'

'I don't have to, her story just doesn't ring true somehow. I think she made it all up. That business about losing her memory and taking shelter in a deserted house is nothing but a fanciful figment o' her imagination. If you ask me she's got something to hide and is just using you for her own ends.'

'Nobody is asking you, and if you ask *me* you're just jealous o' her and mad because she borrowed some o' your clothes!'

'Ay, and that's another thing!' Shona returned furiously. 'She did have a damned cheek helping herself to my things! I hope you make sure she washes them and puts them back in the condition she found them.'

'She had nothing else to wear.' His tones were clipped and cold. 'But don't worry, I'm sure there are other women on the island with more charitable inclinations than my very own daughter, people who won't grudge helping someone worse off than they are.'

She looked at him strangely. 'Haven't you ever wondered why she didn't take some of her own clothes with her when she left her husband? It's the sort o' thing that women do, no matter how much in a hurry they might be. And a handbag, women never forget their handbags, but she did and it just isn't natural.'

He glared at her. 'I can see it's no use talking to you when you're like this. You're determined no' to like or trust the girl, even though she's done nothing to you except sleep in your room and use bits o' clothing that you seldom wear yourself. I just hope, if ever you're in trouble, you'll come across someone who will help rather than hinder you and show you kindness when you most need it.'

One word borrowed another. By the time they had finished with each other they were livid with fury and hurt feelings. An atmosphere of unnatural silence prevailed, and they sat, one at either end of the cluttered breakfast table, neither of them moving or speaking or looking at one another.

It was as well that Lorna and Ellie Dawn came clattering noisily into the room, breaking the deathly quiet as Lorna announced proudly to Shona, 'I slept in Grampa's bed last night and told him a story.'

'Oh, did you now?' A twinkle appeared in Shona's eyes.

'He wanted Red Riding Hood, but I said *Treasure Island* would be better for a big man like him.'

'Ay, the big bad wolf got the heave last night,' Fergus said sheepishly.

'But he couldn't find *Treasure Island*,' Lorna continued innocently. 'It was in your room, Aunt Shona, and when he went in to get it the nice lady was in there too and made him forget all about it.'

'Oh, was she now?' Shona glanced quickly at her father. 'Maybe the big bad wolf *was* there after all, in the disguise o' a woman, waiting to gobble up the nearest man in sight.'

'No, Aunt Shona,' Lorna gave vent to an exaggerated sigh at the obtuseness she sometimes encountered in the adults around her. 'Nobody ate Grampa. He came back to bed and cooried down while I read him a bit out o' Gramma's magazine. It was a ghost story but he wasn't frightened and went to sleep because he wasn't lonely with me in there beside him.'

'I could keep him company too,' Ellie Dawn

chimed in, her amber-coloured eyes glinting at the thought. 'Lorna could read him ghost stories and I could sing to him. I learned lots of songs at school and I know all the words.'

Shona threw back her head and laughed delightedly at this and when she looked at her father it was to see that he was smiling too, albeit rather grudgingly.

'I hope the teapot's still warm.' Grant was trying to sound nonchalant as he popped his head round the door, 'I was along seeing Lorn and I thought I would look in . . .'

'To see if I was needing anything,' Fergus finished for his son. 'What the hell is all this?' he continued irritably. 'Nursemaids? Babymaids? Twenty-four hours o' the day and night?'

Grant shrugged his shoulders. 'Surely there's nothing unusual about a caring son keeping an eye on his father? I just wondered . . .'

He let the question hang in mid-air. Shona giggled and patted Lorna's head. 'Don't worry, Grant, Lorna's doing a fine job looking after her grampa. She's been reading to him and keeping him company ever since last night.'

'And I'm going to sing to him!' cried Ellie Dawn, not to be outdone.

But Lorna took Fergus's hand and held onto it possessively. 'No, it's just me Grampa wants when he's tired, isn't it, Grampa? You're just little, Ellie Dawn, and make too much noise.'

Ellie Dawn's lip trembled. 'I'm not too little, I'm six, and I can read stories too.'

154

'Anyway, there wouldn't be enough room in Grampa's bed,' Lorna ended the matter in her own determined way.

'The little spy in the camp.' Fergus chucked his eldest granddaughter under the chin and looked meaningfully at his daughter. 'It isn't fair to use an innocent bairn in such a way, and besides, she'll get bored here with only grown ups to keep her company.'

'I won't get bored,' Lorna stated firmly. 'I'll play games with you and talk to you and I'll help the nice lady to make your tea when I come home from school.'

The 'nice lady' appeared at that moment, looking more ravishing then ever after a refreshing night's sleep. Her golden-skinned face was glowing in its frame of glossy black hair, the white shirt and blue jeans she was wearing only serving to enhance her youth and her femininity.

Grant's eyes flickered as she entered the room and he was unable to help gazing at her admiringly, despite what he had said about her the night before. But he quickly recovered his equanimity and putting down his cup he folded his arms, crossed his legs, and settling back in his chair he said off-handedly, 'I'll just wait and get you along the road, Father.'

'I'm not going along the road,' Fergus replied testily. 'I'm going along to the fields, as well you know, and I haven't got on my boots yet.'

'I'll wait,' Grant replied laconically, and gazed at the wall.

'Perhaps you would like another cup of tea?' Fern was there at the table, looking at him enquiringly as she lifted his cup.

155

'Er – no – no, thanks.' Grant reddened and was heartily glad that Bob chose to arrive at that moment, leaving his boots and his shepherd's crook at the door and stamping his way into the room with the assurance of one who had been doing it all his life.

'Well, I'll be off.' Grant pushed back his chair.

'I thought you said you were waiting for me,' Fergus reminded him sarcastically.

'Ay, I was, but now that Bob's here you'll be blethering a bit and I never was one for all that farm talk.'

Shona, who hadn't uttered a word since Fern's appearance, whispered into her father's ear, 'Friends again?'

'Ay, friends,' he returned gruffly.

'I just don't want to see you getting hurt, Father,' she said quietly, and with Lorna holding onto one hand, Ellie Dawn to the other, she followed her brother outside with a toss of her red head.

Chapter Thirteen

The tongues had been busy, notably those of Tam and Todd, whose appearance in the post office that morning set off a clamour of questions from the other customers.

'One at a time.' Tam held up his hand importantly. 'If it's that lass o' McKenzie's you're on about then you would do well to mind what you're saying about her in my hearing. Todd and myself got the facts last night from her very own bonny lips, and 'tis a terrible tale just – ay indeed,' he finished with a sad shake of his head.

Both men had, in fact, only heard a few details from Ruth during the ceilidh, but Todd was basking in the limelight and did not therefore feel inclined to contradict his friend. Instead he added his own sanguine contribution to Tam's and, amid much interruption and prompting from that gentleman, the 'story of Fern Lee' gradually unfolded.

'She'll likely be an adulteress,' Behag decided unsympathetically. 'The man maybe had to hit her.'

'Well, whatever,' nodded Elspeth, memories of Hector's rough handling of her person springing into her head. 'Men can be brutes when the mood takes them. The girl could well be telling the truth.'

'Hmph! You've changed your mind,' accused Kate. 'You were all for condemning both her and Fergus that time you came fleeing from Laigmhor like a scalded cat.'

'That was then, this is now.' Elspeth didn't like Kate's tone one bit, and the look she threw at her would have withered an oak tree.

But Kate was made of stern stuff, and Elspeth had never intimidated her yet, as her next words proved. 'Ach Elspeth, you never could make up your mind unless everything was in black and white in front o' your eyes. But you're right enough about the lass, poor sowel, though I didny think so last night when Tam came in, stupid wi' admiration for her. It must have been terrible just, living wi' a cruel and drunken husband. Any man that lifts his hand to a defenceless woman deserves to be castrated.'

'Nobody could ever accuse you o' being defenceless, Kate,' Tam said dryly, last night's episode with the teapot vivid in his mind. 'In fact, it would make a change if I could have the last word wi' you sometimes.'

'You did last night,' Kate reminded him sourly, 'but all that is beside the point. This lass o' McKenzie's will have to be protected now that we know why she came here. Are you all agreed about that?'

There was a general murmur of assent.

'When I hear things like these, I'm glad I never got caught by a man,' stated Jessie McKinnon. 'I am all for keeping the girl out o' harm's way and if anyone comes asking about her I for one have never heard o' her.'

'Especially if Clodhopper comes sniffing around, or any stranger to the island asks questions,' augmented Kate. 'Just answer them in Gaelic and if they happen to know the language then mum's the word.'

Old Sorcha tuned up her hearing aid. 'Eh? What was that, Kate? Did you get it on your shoes as well? I myself stood on one this very morning. It's a disgrace! Folks seem to let their dogs run wild these days. The verges are just full o' them.'

'Full o' what?' Kate looked baffled. 'Dogs?'

'Eh?' Sorcha roared.

'Never mind, Sorcha, it's good luck,' grinned Tam as he grasped the old lady's meaning.

'It wasny good luck when I slipped on it and nearly broke my ankle. Like an elephant's it was too. The biggest dog turd I have ever seen.'

'Heaven help us!' cried Totie in exasperation. 'What kind o' place is this? Monumental things are happening in the rest o' the world and all you lot can talk about is dog mess! I have a business to run, and if you don't mind I'd like to get on wi' it.'

'Pay out time first!' Jim Jim reminded the postmistress. 'I've won that competition, Totie. I said the mystery girl was a prisoner on the run and I was right.'

'No you weren't,' objected Tam. 'She wasny escaping from jail, she was running away from her man.'

'Ay, because she was under his rule and was as good as his prisoner,' Jim Jim explained slyly. 'Anyway, I have no doubt that mine was the nearest to the truth.'

'He's right,' Totie spoke up in support of the old man as she took the slips of paper from the box and examined them. 'Jim Jim wins, all of five pounds, two

159

shillings and sixpence. That should help to boost your pension a bit, Jim Jim.'

She counted the money into the old man's waiting hand. Delighted, he retired to a corner to count it all over again while Ranald muttered darkly that it was a fix and it was the last time he would throw away good money.

At this juncture Shona entered the shop, having dropped the children off at school before going on to visit her sister-in-law, Fiona, to discuss the latest developments regarding Fern Lee.

'The sooner Kirsteen's home the better,' had been Fiona's opinion as she made each of them a large mug of coffee. 'The girl was positively flaunting herself last night, dancing and skirling around and lifting her skirt as high as it would go. The men just sat there and ogled her. Even ancient creatures like Tam and Todd were drooling at the mouth and looking as if they would like to eat her. Then she went all quiet and strange, as if she was regretting making an exhibition o' herself in front of everybody.'

'She *is* strange,' Shona had said decidedly. 'Not just in behaviour but in the things she says. Maybe I'm being unfair because, as Father wasn't slow to point out, I've hardly spoken to her. But I have this feeling about her, as if – as if – she has something to cover up and will do and say anything to protect herself. Even her name sounds odd, sort of theatrical and unreal.'

'It was her timing,' Fiona had mused, 'arriving as soon as Kirsteen was safely out o' the way.'

'Mmm, not exactly, she came the night before Kirsteen left to be precise. We have to be fair about it,

160

Fiona, even though I feel like clonking her over the head wi' the nearest flowerpot for all the bother she's causing.'

'Thank heaven she didn't land herself on my father . . .' Fiona's eyes had twinkled. 'And him with a book to write before Mother gets home.'

'I don't know what's gotten into mine,' Shona had confided, 'he seems smitten by the woman and stands up for her at every turn. We almost came to blows over her this morning and if it hadn't been for th bairns, him and me might still not be on speaking terms.'

'Och well, we'll just have to wait and see what happens. Meanwhile, we'll all make an effort to keep an eye on our Mrs Lee. Grant is making a good job o' doing just that at the moment, but he's only got a day or two left o' his holiday. When he goes back to work we'll have to take up the cudgels with a vengeance, till then, here's to our wee Lorna, long may she reign in her grampa's house, at least till her gramma gets home.'

After that Shona didn't feel like discussing the matter further, especially with those who were not members of her own family, and she was therefore annoyed to find the post office buzzing with talk about things that she considered were only of concern to those immediately involved in 'the Fern Lee episode'.

But this was Rhanna, everybody knew everybody else's business, she herself liked to know exactly what was happening on the island, and with a resigned sigh she marched over to the post office counter, aware that all eyes were upon her.

'It is yourself, Shona.' Kate had many tactics for extracting information, depending on who it was she happened to be targeting at the moment of interrogation. Mostly it was a direct approach, occasionally she 'went round the houses', and at other times she began by warming up gently before getting to the point.

This was one of those times. Shona was a McKenzie; all of the McKenzies and their satellites had to be handled with extreme caution, and Kate's expression, as she addressed this undoubtedly dominant female member of the clan, was one of benign deference.

'Ay,' Shona nodded her red head in agreement of her identity. 'It is indeed me, Kate, hurrying to get round the shops so that I can get home to relieve my husband of babysitting.'

Kate sighed. 'Life, these days, seems to be nothing but bustle and hurry. Of course,' she eyed 'Laigmhor's daughter' with sympathy, 'things will be busier than ever for you now, your man and your bairns to see to, no' to mention your father wi' all his bothers and worries.'

'You know, it's a strange expression that,' Shona parried thoughtfully. 'People say "not to mention" and in the next breath they do just exactly that.'

'Ay, I have often thought the very same thing myself,' Tam broke in, seriously undermining Kate's line of enquiry. 'Folks are aye saying things they don't mean and I have wondered to myself if it's got something to do wi' the English way o' putting words together. When, for instance, they say, "I don't think that's true," it should be, "I think that isn't true," because, put the other way, it sounds as if they're no'

162

thinking the very thing they're thinking.' In utter confusion Tam ground to a full stop and blinked at his wife, who was poking him in the ribs and hissing at him to be quiet.

'The man is just a walking wind-bag that thinks it's an encyclopedia,' she said apologetically to Shona. 'As I was saying, your poor father, he must be having a hard job coping while Kirsteen is away. As if that isn't enough he has to contend wi' these other burdens landing on his doorstep.'

'Ay, Kate, life can indeed be hard at times,' Shona nodded, determined she was not going to help Kate one bit.

Kate leaned forward confidingly, 'We were after hearing about the girl's troubles, running away from her man because he abused her. Is it no' terrible just, what we womenfolk have to put up with?'

'Terrible,' agreed Shona, 'and if I don't get a move on, my man will be abusing me wi' his tongue for taking half the morning to get a few supplies, and him wi' a surgery full of sick animals waiting for his attention.' With that she paid for her stamps and envelopes and left the shop.

'She wasn't giving much away,' Kate said peevishly.

'She's a McKenzie,' Elspeth said with a sniff. 'She'll swim against the tide just for the sake o' it.'

Kate, filled with chagrin at her failure to extract even the smallest tit-bit of news from Shona, turned her attentions on Elspeth. 'And I suppose you're swimming wi' the tide, Elspeth, when you elope to Oban to get married to Mac? A wedding should be a proud affair. It is the one chance a woman has to show herself off to the world. As it is, we'll never get to know if you went as a flower person or just plain old Elspeth, grouse feather and all.'

'Ach, you're too hard on her, Kate,' reproved Mollie as Slochmhor's housekeeper turned on her heel and walked hurriedly out of the post office. 'You've never got a kind word to say to her for all you are a sympathetic cratur to other folks hereabouts.'

'Ach well, she asks for it at every turn,' Kate defended herself. 'She's aye on the lookout for trouble and has to be kept in her place. Besides all that,' her eyes glinted, 'I'm mad at her for going to Oban to be wed! I'm dying to know what she will be wearing on the big day. It isn't fair o' her to deprive her friends of her own personal fashion show.'

'Her friends!' hooted Mollie. 'You can hardly call yourself one o' those, Kate. And since when did you come to be so interested in clothes anyway? You were never a body to bend to fashion – of any sort,' she ended, eyeing Kate's shapeless coat, her headscarf, the scuffed and clumsy black suede boots that Tam had likened to 'the fringed hooves of a carthorse'.

At this, Behag looked down her nose and pointedly turned up the collar of her mother's fur coat. 'Appearances do count, no matter where a woman happens to live. I myself have aye tried to look smart, even if it's only to the shops in Portcull, and, of course, to the kirk on the Sabbath. My mother, rest her soul, would be proud if she could see me now, making good use o' the coat she herself was so privileged to own.'

Kate's eyes travelled the length and breadth of

164

Behag's moth-eaten furs. 'Ay, as you say, Behag, just as long as you don't go wearing it to the midden for fear it might leap off your back and throw itself in.'

At that, the shop held its breath, Behag stalked out, and everyone erupted into gales of merriment.

'Och, you're a terrible woman, Kate,' Tam said as he wiped his eyes. 'If you weren't I couldny bear living wi' you for I wouldny know what to do wi' a wife who had nothing but good to say about everybody. It would be a tedious existence, just, and I myself would pine away altogether if I wasny on my mettle waiting to see where the next teapot was coming from!'

Elspeth was deep in thought as she sat by the fire, staring abstractedly into the flames. The things that Kate had said to her that day in the post office were rankling in her mind and no matter how hard she tried she just couldn't settle.

In the chair opposite, Captain Mac was asleep, his big slippered feet ensconced comfortably on the hearth, his great hairy hands folded loosely across the generous proportions of his stomach as he puffed and snored gently into his beard.

As a rule, Elspeth cherished this evening hour with Mac, sharing a companionship with him that she had never known with anyone else. Peace and contentment pervaded every corner of the house, making it seem like a little fortress that neither man nor beast could penetrate.

In a less tangible way, however, Kate had succeeded in doing just that, with her unthinking comments regarding Elspeth's wedding outfit, and Elspeth's mind was in a turmoil because of it.

'What ails you, lass?' Mac woke himself up with a mighty snort and looked at Elspeth sitting quiet and subdued in her chair.

'I was just thinking, Isaac, about the wedding. I have never been easy in my mind about a registry office ceremony. As you know, I have been a regular church goer all my life and this hole in the corner affair in Oban just doesny seem right to me.'

Mac wouldn't have cared if he had got married on a rock in the middle of the ocean! Better still, he wouldn't have minded carrying on 'living in sin', a state that had been attributed to himself and Elspeth by a few pious islanders, even though the physical side of 'the arrangement' in Elspeth's house had amounted to no more than a few affectionate hugs and squeezes. This had certainly unsettled Mac a good deal since he was, as Kate so aptly put it, 'a lusty big chiel' whose healthy appetite for women was well known throughout the Hebrides. But Elspeth's firm devotion to the Bible and its teachings had not allowed for much in the way of pre-marriage hanky panky and Mac had resigned himself to the fact that the ring would have to be on her finger before he could gain admittance to her bedroom.

But while he didn't give two hoots about where and how they were married he was sensitive to Elspeth's feelings on the matter and was therefore able to look upon her with kindness when she took him into her confidence that night.

'Get the rum, lass,' he said softly. 'You and me will

166

have a discussion about everything over a nice wee nightcap.'

Elspeth got up and fetched the rum bottle from the sideboard and while she set out the glasses Mac plunged the poker into the glowing depths of the fire.

'There now.' Settling back in his chair to wait for the poker to heat he gazed at her expectantly. 'Tell me what it is that's bothering you? We said a while back that we would try never to hide anything from one another and aye remember, a trouble shared is a trouble halved.'

'It's that shrew, Kate McKinnon,' Elspeth's eyes grew misty with self-pity at the memory of Kate's hurtful words and she proceeded to tell Mac about the scene in the post office.

'Is that so now,' Mac nodded when Elspeth had finished speaking. He allowed a few minutes to elapse, during which he plunged the glowing tip of the poker into each of the glasses and handed one to her. To Elspeth, this little ritual was one of the most pleasurable she had ever shared with anyone, safe from prying eyes, no one to criticise her actions, just herself and Mac at either side of the fire, the aroma of burnt rum hanging agreeably in the air as they drank and conversed in utter harmony.

'Here's to us, Isaac.' She clinked her glass against his.

'Ay, here's to us, lass.'

Mac put down his glass and picking up his pipe he pushed tobacco into the bowl with a stubby, tar-stained thumb. Elspeth didn't mind this part of the ritual and in fact revelled in it since the manly odour

167

of pipe smoke reminded her of the days when her father had been alive.

'Well,' Mac said at last, 'it sounds to me as if Kate is just mad because we aren't getting wed here, on Rhanna. I myself don't mind where we tie the knot but I somehow didn't bargain for a kirk wedding. At our time o' life it should be something a bittie special, so just you let me have a wee think about it and I'll see what I can come up with.'

A silence descended. The minutes passed, Mac's brow remaining furrowed in thought for quite some considerable time. When at last he came out of his reverie he did so with such force that Elspeth just about jumped out of her skin with fright.

'I've got it! I've got it!' he cried, slapping his knee and rocking back and forth in his chair, as excited as Elspeth had ever seen him. 'It's perfect! It's wonderful! Why did I no' think of it before?'

Elspeth waited for the perfect wonderful thing to be revealed.

'We'll get wed aboard *The Arian*! The very steamer that ties up here on Rhanna three nights out o' seven! Young Grant McKenzie is the skipper. I aye liked Grant and he's one o' you favourite McKenzies. He would be only too willing to help – and we could get our very own minister to marry us,' he added hastily, seeing the expression of doubt creeping over Elspeth's face.

Leaning forward he took her hand in his big strong one, his brown eyes glowing as he went on, 'Just think, lass, no one else on the whole of Rhanna has ever done anything like it! By jingo, you would be the toast o' the place and the envy o' all the women. You could set off a whole new trend, and everyone would get to see you in your bonny new wedding clothes.'

That last bit appealed to Elspeth, as Mac had known it would. 'Ay, Isaac,' she breathed, an excited glow spreading over her face. ''Tis a thought, a really grand thought.'

'We would have the wedding itself in the saloon o' *The Arian*,' Mac explained, 'and maybe a dram or two afterwards – just for those who want to attend the ceremony. After they have gone ashore the rest o' us can sail on to Oban for a wee reception in a nice hotel. I'll arrange it, Elspeth, I'll arrange everything, and maybe you could go to see the minister as soon as you can.'

'You have a silver tongue in your head, Isaac McIntosh,' Elspeth told him affectionately, utterly entranced by his proposals.

She had not, as yet, purchased any 'bonny new clothes' but that same night she got out her mail order catalogue to thumb happily through the pages, while Mac smoked his pipe and sipped his burnt rum, as contented as any man could be who has just put the world to rights for his woman.

Elspeth had a wonderful time with her catalogue. She spotted some lovely suits that would be just perfect for a special occasion but she couldn't make up her mind about the colour and asked herself, should it be pink or lilac or perhaps a combination of the two?

Her mind switched to the wedding guests. She would ask Phebie and Lachlan, of course, and their young ones, and the minister's wife, Doctor Megan, would have to be there too ... The only fly in the ointment was Mac's cousin Gus, with his disgraceful personal habits and his unsavoury appearance. Long ago, and to herself, Elspeth had christened him Dis Gus Ting and, as far as she was concerned, he had certainly earned every letter of the title.

But Gus wasn't the only one of Elspeth's worries; to a lesser extent there was Mac's sister Nellie to contend with. Nellie did not approve of her brother's relationship with Elspeth and had told him he was going 'soft in the head' to even consider marrying such a sour cailleach.

Resolutely Elspeth pushed Gus and Nellie to the back of her mind. She would deal with them as and when the need arose, meanwhile she was determined not to let them spoil her happiness.

At bedtime she took Mac's hand in hers. 'It won't be long now, Isaac,' she told him softly.

'No, lass.' His eyes twinkled. 'You've kept me waiting a long time and I canny promise to behave like a gentleman in the bedroom when the grand night comes.'

Her own eyes gleamed. 'If you did, I would throw you out, and that's a fact!'

She walked sedately to her own room but once inside the door she clasped her hands to her mouth and stared at herself in the mirror. Soon, soon, she would show Behag and Kate McKinnon that she, Elspeth Morrison, was a woman of considerable worth, and she could hardly wait to see their faces and hear their comments when they heard that she was to be married aboard *The Arian*. Let them find fault with that if they could! Jealous witches!

With that happy thought Elspeth went to bed to dream her happy dreams while next door Mac squirmed in his cold sheets and told himself that, for once, he would be glad to get married.

Or, should that be twice? He was startled at the thought, but it was right enough, first to Mary, now to Elspeth. Fancy the like! He, Isaac McIntosh, having the courage to twice take the plunge, though, mind, Elspeth did keep a good tight ship and deserved a second chance herself, especially when she had netted a good catch like himself – the lucky cailleach!

Chapter Fourteen

Rhanna was ablaze with spring colour; March had moved into April and tender green shoots were burgeoning everywhere. Fat sticky buds hung heavily on the trees, ready to burst open; the hill slopes were furred with young grasses, and the burns tumbled down through the corries, glinting and sparkling in the light of the sun.

Everything was new and fresh and as Fergus walked along the Glen Fallan road to Slochmhor he took a deep breath of the clean fragrant air and felt glad of his own company for a while. The last two weeks had been hectic; everyone, it seemed, had found a reason to visit Laigmhor. The door had never stopped opening, a regular stream of 'sightseers', as Bob dourly called them, coming to 'see was Fergus wanting anything', when all the while what they really wanted was to see Fern Lee and speak to her so that they could discover for themselves the gory details about her 'bad devil o' a man'.

The family, too, were never far from the place, with Fiona, Ruth, and Shona popping in at all hours of the day, and Grant, on the evenings that *The Arian* was berthed in Portcull, making sure that he spent a greater part of his off-duty hours keeping his father company.

To cap it all, Ellie Dawn had joined ranks with Lorna to 'look after Grampa' and Lorna, feeling ousted from her position as chief grandad-sitter, had, in an attempt to regain her leadership, been more assertive with Ellie Dawn than usual, the result being that both little girls were wont to snipe at one another and look to Fergus for his support in their small wars.

Fern Lee was not in the least perturbed by all this, rather she appeared to enjoy the whole thing, and when it was decided that Ellie Dawn should stay at Laigmhor to 'keep Lorna happy' she positively welcomed the addition of another child into the household and set out to look after them with such enthusiasm, it wasn't long before the children were incurably bewitched by her and more determined than ever to remain in the house till 'Gramma came home'.

Fern was recovering well from her recent traumatic experiences and was growing more attractive with each passing day. There was a life and a passion about her that was almost spiritual, an excitement in her that endowed her with a charisma that made her glow and sparkle as if she was illuminated by some inner light. She hadn't made any more flirtatious approaches to Fergus, but the promise of it was all there, in the flash of her dark eyes, the sensuous sway of her lithe body, the way she sat and moved, the intimate manner in which she brushed against him whenever she got the opportunity.

There was also a restlessness in her that Fergus found worrying. For days she would content herself and really seemed to enjoy being there at Laigmhor with him, then quite without warning she would disappear, often for hours at a time, and when he questioned her about it she became vague and uncommunicative and said she had been 'just walking'.

Yet she was never seen in the village or in any of the most frequented places on the island. Once or twice, and with much amusement, she would recount some meeting she had had with old Dodie or Canty Tam, the two people who were most likely to wander the solitary places of Rhanna.

Other than that she had nothing much to say about her mysterious sojourns away from the house and Fergus, himself desperate for some solitude in his life, could understand this. Also, he was becoming more and more convinced that she had the gypsy in her soul, not just because of her dark wild beauty, but from the way she moved and spoke and reacted to the world around her – in fact, all the aspects of her personality that he found so intriguing and difficult to resist.

Each day he felt himself to be less in control of his own mixed emotions, feelings that made him restless and anxious and definitely uneasy that his life had taken such a strange and unexpected turn. He told himself that he was glad Kirsteen was coming home within the next day or two, he was going to phone her now, to find out exactly when she would be arriving, and his steps quickened as he neared Slochmhor.

He found Lachlan writing furiously at his little desk in the parlour, hardly looking up when his visitor announced himself from the kitchen.

'Help yourself to the phone, man!' Lachlan called.

'It's in here but if you don't mind you can dial the number yourself. You ought to know it by now.'

Fergus found himself entering the sanctum on tip-toe. Lachlan had been writing almost non-stop for the past two weeks. One article was already away to a well known Scottish magazine, another was in the pipeline. He was a self-taught typist, banging away painstakingly with two fingers on his little portable. The results weren't always what he wanted them to be and crumpled balls of discarded paper had soon filled his waste-bin. After a few days, however, he had gotten into the swing of things; even so, it all took a great deal of time and effort, and he had practically shut himself away from the outside world in order to concentrate.

But that didn't stop the outside world coming to him. Elspeth, confined to her own house with a bad dose of flu, hadn't been able to make her usual contribution to his welfare, but Fiona was always stopping by to make sure he was feeding himself properly; Ruth brought him tasty morsels from her own table and gave him helpful advice about his writing; Shona supplied him with hot meals along with reports on island activities, while Tina did wifely things for him, like taking home his washing, laying out his clean underwear, and generally doing for him in her placid, unobtrusive fashion.

So all things considered he was being well taken care of and was progressing well with his journals, determined as he was to let Phebie see that he hadn't been idle during her absence.

* * *

175

Ruth arrived while Fergus was on the phone. He could hear her and Lachlan in the kitchen, chattering away about books and writing. He found their voices distracting and at first didn't fully take in the fact that Kirsteen was telling him she wouldn't be arriving home as planned.

'Aunt Minnie isn't coming along as fast as we thought. The doctor says it's her age and wondered if we would mind staying on a bit longer. Fergie, are you listening to me? I said . . .'

'Ay, I know what you said . . .'

His mind began racing as he thought about the complications that her delayed homecoming might evoke. How could he continue living under the same roof as Fern and manage to remain detached from her? It was a dangerous situation, one that was growing more difficult with the passing days. His mind rejected involvement with the girl even while his body cried out for her with all the raw emotions of a man who was fast approaching a crisis point.

He couldn't go on resisting her – he just couldn't! It was too much to ask of any hot-blooded man. He couldn't stand any more of this aching, terrible yearning that gnawed at him day and night. Even with the children in the house, there was plenty of opportunity for him to go to Fern if he allowed himself to give in to his desires. And Kirsteen was unwittingly making it easy for him – the fates seemed to be aiding and abetting this devil that had taken possession of him!

His heart began to beat strangely. Something terrible had happened to him. If he was honest with himself, he had to admit that he was glad – glad – that Kirsteen wasn't coming home just yet. In the next instant a black tide of deepest guilt swept over him and he asked himself how could he? How could he ever think such a thing? His Kirsteen! The woman he had once loved with a passion beyond endurance! The woman who had borne his children, who had shared his life so sweetly for so many years. The woman who not only owned his heart but his very soul and one he would do anything for.

Yet, despite the knowledge of these things, despite his love for his wife, his voice, when he spoke, uttered words of deception that seemed not to come from him. 'Kirsteen, I don't know what to say about this,' he began hesitantly, 'I'm missing you, mo cridhe. I was all prepared for you coming home. I want you here beside me . . .'

'Oh, Fergie,' her voice was immediately filled with loving concern. 'I'm sorry, I should have considered you first. I won't stay here after all, I'll come home, Phebie can manage without me, my place is with you on Rhanna . . .'

'No, Kirsteen, I'm the selfish one, the old lady needs you more than I do. I'm managing fine here, the womenfolk are making sure o' that, and the wee ones watch over me day and night. Lorna reads to me . . .' he chuckled, 'tales that she thinks I'll understand and that are befitting to a man of my tender years, and Ellie Dawn sings to me in her tiny little elf of a voice. They're like a couple o' bookends in bed, one on either side o' me in case I fall out, at least that's what Lorna told me. They fight like a pair o' shrews and try to get me to take sides but they're great bairns and Fern likes having them around.'

'Oh, yes, Fern, I'm glad she came back, poor lass. How is she? I was so sorry when you told me she had run away from her husband because of his cruelty to her.'

Her voice was warm with compassion and Fergus answered her quickly, 'She's fine now, and she keeps herself busy around the place. She's a good cook too and aye has my meals on the table, even Bob approves of her cooking.'

'I see, I'm beginning to feel I'm not needed there anymore. What about Shona? Doesn't she feel ousted from her position as head daughter o' the house? Surely her nose must be out o' joint just a teeny weeny bit?'

He didn't reply immediately to that. Shona had not accepted Fern's presence in the house, rather her resentment had strengthened and she hadn't taken kindly to another woman in Laigmhor's kitchen in her step-mother's absence. But he wasn't going to tell Kirsteen that. She might start asking too many questions and his life at the moment was complicated enough as it was.

'She has her own lot to see to, but she mucks in with Fern when the need arises and she and Ruth, Fiona and Grant, make a point o' coming along to keep an eye on me and make sure I never feel lonely.'

'Sounds like a full house. Will there be any room for me when I finally get back?'

'Mo cridhe, you're the one who keeps us all together and well you know it. But you can't let either

Aunt Minnie or Phebie down so just you bide where you are for as long as you're needed. I'll be fine, and I'll keep in touch, I promise.'

They said their goodbyes and Fergus turned gladly away from the phone to go to the kitchen, where he discovered that Erchy the Post had arrived to swell the ranks, thus giving Fergus no chance to tell Lachlan that the return of their respective wives would be delayed for a while longer.

'I don't know why I'm so thirsty this morning,' Erchy said ruefully, dumping a sheaf of letters on the table as he settled himself on a chair. 'I am just after delivering the mail to Croft na Beinn. While I was there I had a wee blether wi' Nancy so maybe that's why my tongue is sticking to the roof o' my mouth. She can talk the hind legs off a donkey, can Nancy Taylor.'

'And I suppose you just sat there like a mouse and listened,' suggested Lachlan with a twinkle.

'Ach well, I did put in the odd word or two but in the end it's the womenfolk who have the biggest say.'

Wetting his lips, he picked up a cup to peer into its empty depths and Ruth laughed. 'Hint, hint! Why can you no' just come right out wi' it and ask for a cup o' tea, even though I'm sure you got one at Nancy's. It's a wonder to me you ever manage to deliver any mail with all that liquid you consume on your rounds.'

'Ay, it can be a problem,' Erchy agreed, 'but nothing that a wee tin under the driver's seat canny cure.'

'Spare me the details,' Ruth said and went to put on the kettle.

'I've brought you a letter, Lachlan,' Erchy announced rather cryptically, peeping at Lachlan from under the brim of his hat.

'Well, you don't say, now? And here was me thinking you were delivering daffodils. If I'm seeing right, you've brought me not one, but several items of mail.'

The conversation was suspended for a moment as Ruth came back with the tea which she dispensed into cups and passed round.

'Ay, but this one's special.' Erchy picked up the threads of the conversation as he sipped contentedly at his tea. 'I had a quick glance at it as I was coming along and I just happened to notice it had a wee address printed on the back o' the envelope.'

'You never fail to amaze me,' interceded Lachlan sarcastically.

Erchy crunched noisily into a gingernut biscuit. 'Ay, and I was after seeing it was from that very magazine that is so popular wi' everyone. The one that has these nice pictures o' Scottish scenes on the front cover.' He delivered this last piece of information with great aplomb, calm sounding and seemingly more interested in the plateful of tit-bits that Ruth had placed on the table in front of him.

But for all that, his words had the desired effect. Lachlan and Ruth just stared at him, Fergus paused with his cup half-way to his mouth, even Heinz, who was under the table waiting for crumbs, popped his head up to look at everyone with comical expectancy.

'Well, let me see it, man,' Lachlan found his voice. 'It is my letter we're talking about, after all.'

With maddening calm Erchy picked up the bundle of mail from the table and slowly removed the elastic band surrounding it. 'Let me see now, some o' these are for the new bungalows, these two are for you, Fergus, this one's for Murdy, just one o' they circulars that clog up the rubbish bins. I didny have time to sort them all out at the post office and just stuck them all together in my rush . . .'

'For heaven's sake!' Lachlan exploded. 'I'll clonk you over the head wi' that plate o' biscuits if you don't get a move on, Erchy McKay!'

'Oh, well, now, there is no need for threats o' that nature, Lachlan.' Erchy looked hurt, nonetheless he knew when he had gone far enough and at last delivered Lachlan's letter into his waiting hand.

There was silence at the table as he tore it open, a hushed, waiting silence that lasted for fully ten seconds till Lachlan broke it with a wild whoop of joy.

Waving the letter in the air he yelled, 'Subject to editorial adjustment my article's been accepted and will appear in the July issue o' the magazine. It will have a little column all to itself and, if it takes off, they want it to be an ongoing thing! To cap it all, they've enclosed a nice little cheque in advance of publication!'

'Lachlan! That's wonderful news!' Ruth rushed round the table to give him a resounding hug, while Heinz barked with excitement and Fergus uttered his congratulations.

Erchy, waiting till all the fuss had died down, grinned at Lachlan and dared to say, 'I don't suppose you'll be telling us how much they paid you, will you now?'

'You suppose correctly, Erchy,' Lachlan returned promptly.

Erchy remained unperturbed. 'A pity, a great pity. A writer's income has aye been a wee curiosity o' mine. Take Ruth here, for example, none o' us are knowing if she's a millionaire keeping a low profile or if she's just keeping a low profile hoping to become a millionaire.'

He looked hopefully at Ruth but she just laughed and set about clearing the table while Lachlan, still floating on air, disappeared into the parlour to regale Phebie with the news over the phone.

'Lachy! That's wonderful!' she cried. 'Och, I'm so proud o' you! I would love to be there to give you a hug but it will have to wait now till Aunt Minnie's feeling better.'

'Eh! I thought you were coming home tomorrow or the next day?'

'Didn't Fergus tell you? He's not long off the phone to Kirsteen.'

'Erchy came in, Ruth was here too – in all the excitement he probably didn't get the chance.'

'Och well, it won't be for all that much longer, and it's maybe just as well, it will give you time to get cracking on your next article. It's marvellous news, Lachy, darling, wait till I tell Kirsteen and Aunt Minnie. I'm going to have a marvellous time basking in all the reflected glory so don't you dare sit back on your laurels. I have a reputation to keep up and you'd better not let me down.'

When Lachlan got back to the kitchen it was to find Ruth gone and Erchy just leaving, grumbling in his good-natured way because he still had a whole load of mail to deliver before going on to his part-time job as driver of the island bus, a ramshackle Bedford O.B. he had purchased some years ago to supplement his income from the post office.

'My regular passengers will kill me if I keep them waiting,' he predicted cheerily, and went off whistling, his steps more hurried than usual, eager as he was to regale everyone with Lachlan's good news.

Fergus remained to chat briefly to Lachlan before he too departed into the sunny glen, his mind brimming with a million thoughts and mixed emotions. As he neared Laigmhor his footsteps faltered a little and he wondered if it would be wise to go home rather than return to work in the fields. The children were at school, only Fern would be in, and she would be alone, dangerously and excitingly – alone . . .

His black eyes glinted, he pulled back his shoulders. It was his house – and it would soon be dinnertime. It would be silly to turn back now, he wasn't used to calculating his every move and he was damned if he was going to allow his life to be ruled in this way! Despite his decision, his progress along the farm track was as slow as he could make it. Visions of Kirsteen kept tormenting him, her smile, the way she held her head, the love in her blue eyes when she looked at him, how she had cherished and cared for him all these years.

By the time he reached the back door of the house he was feeling miserable and mixed up, yet he couldn't resist the forces that were leading him on – into certain self-destruction.

But the house was empty. Fern had gone off on one

of her lone wanders. He told himself it was a reprieve from something that he wanted no part in, even while a torrent of disappointment raged through him and he didn't know whether to laugh or cry as he stood there alone in the deserted kitchen, hearing only the ticking of the clocks and the sad lost bleating of an orphaned lamb in a basket beside the fire. Fern had found the frail little creature lying beside its dead mother and had carried it home to tuck it into the wickerwork basket that had been bed for generations of canine pets in the Laigmhor household.

Heinz himself had occupied it as a pup and he had been intrigued when the new arrival had been deposited in it and wrapped in a blanket. Now he went over to the motherless baby to sniff at it and give it a good wash with his big floppy tongue.

The lamb was happy to see this great mutt of a face so close to his own little white one and emitting a milky burp he rolled over and tapped the dog's nose with one small hard front foot. Heinz blinked and let out a squeak of surprise, his tail beginning to swing in an apologetic fashion as the lamb reached up and tried to suckle his nose.

This time Heinz was not amused. Backing off he knocked over a footstool and slipped on the rug and Fergus forgot all about his feelings of vexation, so entertained was he by the antics of the animals in a house that was definitely far from empty.

Chapter Fifteen

Several days later, a red-nosed Elspeth presented herself at the Manse, still sniffling a bit after her bout of flu but in reasonably good fettle for all that.

'Come in, come in,' invited the Reverend Mark James in his warm hospitable manner, ushering her into his study as he spoke. 'You must forgive the mess,' he went on, ruefully glancing at the pile of paperwork on his desk and the mountain of books stacked up beside a scuffed green leather armchair by the fire. 'I was doing some research work and I'm afraid I'm not one o' those tidy people who clears everything away after them.'

To herself, Elspeth wondered why on earth he employed the services of Tina if she didn't even have the decency to lift a finger to dust the place. Elspeth was not familiar with the cleaning arrangements of the Manse. Only in extreme circumstances did Tina enter the workrooms of both the minister and the doctor, usually when the dust could no longer be ignored; other than that she applied her gentle administrations to the bedrooms and those parts of the house which were 'open to public inspection'.

Both Megan and Mark were entirely satisfied with Tina and her methods and wouldn't have had it any other way. Elspeth, on the other hand, prided herself on her housekeeping, and when she beheld the jumble in the minister's den she told herself it was a disgrace, taking good money for keeping the place like a boorach and Tina herself creating such a fuss about 'working to the Manse'.

The two dogs, Muff and Flops, who never allowed their master to go anywhere without them, were decorating a couple of lumpy armchairs near the fire, opening one eye each at the intrusion of the visitor, the remainder of their anatomy cascading over the cushions in a hotch-potch of ears, paws, and tails. Inspection time over, they displayed no further interest in the newcomer and promptly went back to sleep. But their repose was short-lived, and their indignation great, when they found themselves being decanted from their favourite chairs and deposited out in the lobby.

With an apologetic grin, Mark James dusted the hairs from the cushions with a few flicks of his hand, and politely bade Elspeth to 'take a pew'.

Elspeth did not appreciate this flippancy, especially from the minister himself, and when she condescended to lower herself into the chair indicated it was to sit stiffly on the edge of it, her back as ramrod straight as her shoulders.

Her eyes roved round the room, coming to rest on the mantelpiece where sat pictures of the minister's first wife, Margaret, and his small daughter, Sharon. Both of them had been killed in a car accident some years ago and Elspeth, for all her sour ways, had become quite sympathetic over his loss and was able to see now why he had married again. The child in the photo was laughing, her eyes sparkling with the joy of living. Elspeth had always wanted children herself and she thought how awful it must have been to have had such a beautiful child taken away – in the midst of life . . .

Loneliness was a terrible thing, as she herself very well knew, and she found her eyes growing a little misty as she realised how alone Mark James must have felt when first he had come to Rhanna.

'Relax, Elspeth,' smiled the minister, mistaking her silence for disapproval of his untidy ways. 'I'm not going to eat you . . . I leave that sort o' thing to the dogs,' he added, his smokey grey eyes twinkling with devilment.

Elspeth lowered her shoulders a fraction and permitted herself a watery smile. 'I doubt that, Mr James, they look as if it takes them all their energy to eat their own dinner.'

'Oh, they soon waken up when it comes to meal-times,' he assured her with a laugh. 'Talking o' which, it must be nearly time for elevenses. I'll get Tina to bring it to us in here.'

He disappeared for a minute, but was soon back, rubbing his hands in his enthusiastic fashion as he said, 'We're in luck this morning, Tina's just made a batch o' muffins, piping hot straight out of the oven.'

As if on cue Tina came in with the tea, laying it on top of an occasional table after first scooping maga-zines and papers off its surface with the edge of the tray. 'Now then, Elspeth, how many spoons o' sugar do you take?' Tina enquired with great decorum.

187

Elspeth didn't immediately answer, so incensed was she with annoyance at the sight of the newspapers lying where they had fallen on the worn Axminster rug.

'I don't take sugar, thanking you,' she returned with equal politeness, all the time wishing she could teach Tina a thing or two about good housekeeping. 'And just a thumbnail amount of milk, if you would be so good.'

A smile flickered across Tina's face. Having poured the tea she stood back and eyed Elspeth's blotched countenance. 'Ach my, poor soul, you look terrible just,' she observed sympathetically as she folded her hands over her ample stomach, an indication that she was getting set for a good gossip. 'It isn't the minister you should be seeing, it is the doctor.'

'Yes indeed,' Elspeth looked mollified by Tina's concern. 'But knowing how busy she is I thought it better no' to bother her. I just followed the advice Doctor Lachlan used to give me when I had the cold, and that was to stay in bed, keep warm, and drink plenty o' liquids. His methods were simple but they aye worked and there's many a body alive today to tell that tale.'

Mark James could cheerfully have strangled her at that point and he thanked providence that Megan wasn't here or she might have done the job for him!

'Och, ay, Lachlan, the good soul that he is,' Tina responded thoughtfully. 'And we all loved him when he was the doctor. But Doctor Megan is here now and she is equally as good as Lachlan used to be. Speaking for myself, when it comes to all the wee problems o' womanhood, I find it a rare treat to have a lady doctor tending me. There is no need to feel embarrassed when you have to talk about all the wee personal bits she herself has been used to all her life, and you can say things about them that you might no' say to a man. Is that no' right, Elspeth?'

Mark James could have hugged Tina there and then and was most gratified to see a faint flush creeping over Elspeth's face.

'Never mind,' Tina went on, as if she hadn't noticed anything amiss. 'You'll soon be feeling as right as rain, even though it was a really bad flu. It must be going the rounds, wi' first one, then another, dropping on their feets like flies. Our own Donald was laid up wi' it and is only now getting out and about.'

At some juncture in the conversation Elspeth had been regretting her uncharitable thoughts about Tina, but at mention of Donald she froze. For all she knew Tina could have carried the virus from him; she was as strong as a horse herself but could easily be a carrier.

Elspeth clamped her lips tightly together. There was a lot she could have said to Tina, but not here, in the minister's study, and certainly not in front of him. In many ways she respected him, even though she hadn't always agreed with some of his modern methods of religious teaching. In an effort to control her chagrin she took out her hanky and enclosed her nose in its folds, a loud honking sound rent the air, and both the minister and Tina looked surprised that any human appendage could produce such noisy emissions.

'There, that's better.' Elspeth treated her nose to a

189

last satisfying pummel and placing her hanky carefully back in the pocket of her brown tweed coat she went on in nasal tones, 'It has indeed gone the rounds, Tina. I myself am a healthy body as a rule, but there are those selfish craturs who rise out their beds, still crawling wi' germs, and those who carry other folks' illnesses around wi' them, contaminating innocent people. I blame my cold on them and have often thought there should be a law against it.'

'Try a muffin, Elspeth,' Mark James offered quickly, afraid that she might start listing all the 'selfish craturs' she believed had infected her.

Tina's muffins were good, even Elspeth had to admit that; they were steamily warm and delicious, and as she bit into one she got her hanky ready to mop up the melted butter on her chin.

Pleased at the praise from this most critical of sources Tina departed to resume her duties, leaving Elspeth to get down to the reasons for her visit.

Mark James listened patiently to the long monologue that followed and which ended with, 'I will feel better wi' my own minister to perform the ceremony, and wi' Isaac being a man o' the sea all his life, it seems fitting that he should tie the knot on board a boat he once skippered.'

Mark James looked at her. On occasion he had been on the receiving end of her spicy tongue and many's the time he could have brained her with his own bare hands. Despite that he had often felt sorry for a woman who was obviously as lonely as she had been before the advent of Captain Mac into her life.

'I will of course be glad to officiate at your wedding,

190

Elspeth,' Mark James said with all sincerity, 'and I think it's a wonderful idea to have it aboard *The Arian*. You'll be the envy o' every eligible woman in the district and you shouldn't be surprised if they all want to follow your example.'

'Och well, it was Isaac's idea.' Elspeth was honest enough to give Mac his place. 'He has imagination and wanted the day to be that wee bittie special for both o' us.'

A date was arranged for the middle of June because, 'Phebie would surely be home by then.' When Elspeth finally took her departure from the Manse she was walking on air and, on meeting Doctor Megan on the steps, she hailed her with great levity and told her she was 'doing a great job as the island medic' and to 'keep up the good work'.

'To what do we owe the honour and what was all that about?' Megan laughingly asked her husband as soon as she got in.

'A wedding.'

'Oh, yes, *the* wedding. I thought she was to be married in Oban.'

'She's changed her mind, as women do, dear little wife o' mine. Seemingly she feels uncomfortable about a registry office so she and Mac between them cooked up the idea of having the marriage aboard *The Arian* with yours truly at the helm.'

'Well! Wonders will never cease!' gasped Megan. '*The Arian*, no less. At least it will be different from the usual and should cause quite a sensation. No doubt Kate McKinnon will be delighted to get seeing the wedding outfit and Behag will likely turn up with

191

her spyglasses smuggled aboard under her fur coat! As for myself, I'd better start thinking about what to wear. I might just be a poor second to Lachlan but I am also the minister's wife and as such I have to set a good example.'

He laughed and kissed her and arm in arm they went into the kitchen where Tina was agog to know why Slochmhor's housekeeper had taken so long with the minister and just what had they been up to, other than eating hot muffins and picking dog hairs off their clothes.

Elspeth's next port of call was Mairi's Hairdressing Salon, which place of business was interred within the crofthouse occupied by Mairi and Willie McKinnon, the last named being a direct offspring of Kate and Tam McKinnon.

Elspeth had some misgivings about her visit to the kind-hearted but artless Mairi, remembering the time when a goodly number of Rhanna women had turned up in kirk sporting bright blue rinses that had verged on the vulgar. Nevertheless, there was no other choice, it was Mairi or nothing, since she was the only hairdresser on the island, and surely she must have learned her lessons by now and improved with time.

Resolutely Elspeth entered the tiny room in the house that had been converted into a beauty parlour some years ago. It was a simple arrangement, no more than a washbasin, a few kitchen chairs, two ancient hairdryers, one mirror needing to be re-silvered, a small table piled high with magazines dating back four years, and a trolley containing an array of bottles, manicure equipment, and heaps of hairy-looking rollers spilling out of their trays. Scott Balfour, the laird of Burnbreddie, had officially opened the place in 1964, with a little plaque fixed above the powder-blue washbasin to prove it.

Mairi had recently expanded her venture to include the sale of cosmetics and hair beautifying aids. On a clothes rail, crushed into a corner, hung an assortment of hand knitted woollens, together with different coloured T-shirts bearing a map of the island and the logo, *Rhanna, Tir nan Og,* which meant *Land of the Ever Young.*

'We sold a lot o' these last summer,' Mairi entered the room and gave this information to Elspeth who was over at the rack fingering the garments. 'Especially the T-shirts, wi' them being cheaper than the woollies.'

'I have no doubt,' Elspeth snorted. 'Some folk will wear anything if they think they're getting a bargain. I myself would never put the likes on my back wi' all that writing on them.'

'The young folks like them,' Mairi said in her gentle way. 'And it's nice for them to go back to the mainland wearing their wee map so that people will know where in the world we are placed.'

Elspeth wasted no more time on small talk and got down to business with a vengeance, impressing on Mairi her need to have a very special hair-do for her wedding day and wondering if she ought to have some sort of rinse to complete the job.

'Should it be blue or lilac?' she muttered worriedly. 'Or would it be best to just leave it alone and be content wi' the colour God gave me?'

193

In the end Mairi made up her mind for her. 'I have the very thing! It's called Silver Cloud and it is the latest colour from the manufacturers. I got in a batch o' half a dozen bottles the other day and I just know my customers will be queuing up for it when they see the results.'

'Silver Cloud?' doubtfully Elspeth repeated the words.

'Ay, and just think, Elspeth, no one else on the whole o' the island has used it yet. You would be the first to pioneer it on your wedding day and no' a soul to touch you for glamour.'

'Silver Cloud.' This time Elspeth savoured the name. It sounded wonderful, and she was intently studying the colour chart that Mairi had produced for her inspection when Fern Lee walked into the room.

Turning her radiant smile on the island hairdresser she said she wanted to buy a hairbrush. In spite of all the talk Mairi had heard about 'the goings on at Laigmhor', she immediately melted in the warmth of that smile and went to fetch a selection of brushes while Elspeth, ensconced in a chair with her colour chart, made no response whatsoever.

When Mairi came back she and Fern went into a huddle as they mulled over the various merits of the brushes, Fern eventually deciding that one with stiff bristles would be the most suitable for her particular requirements.

'I don't suppose it will need much attention, other than washing and brushing it,' Mairi commented admiringly as she touched one of the blue-black, naturally curly ringlets cascading round the girl's shoulders.

'Sure, and you're right enough there, I just wash it and allow it to dry any old how. It has a mind of its own and won't do anything I want so I've learned to let it have its own way.'

'And the colour is just lovely too,' Mairi said this with a glance at Elspeth's back, before rushing on to inform Fern about the forthcoming marriage and Elspeth's momentous decision to have the Silver Cloud hair rinse.

Elspeth bristled. She fumed. That Mairi! She never could keep her mouth shut! It was not business etiquette to reveal personal matters to outsiders, particularly one who had the label of 'McKenzie's woman' on her!

'You've got really good hair,' Fern was at Elspeth's back, running a finger over her short, crisp, iron grey locks. 'It's got a nice natural wave to it and will look a treat with that rinse Mairi was after describing. If it would be pleasing you, I could do your make-up on the morning of your wedding.'

'Make-up!' Elspeth half screamed the words. 'I have never used any o' that rubbish on my face in the whole o' my life. It would make me look like a hussy!'

'Not at all, mavourneen, it would be that subtle you would never notice it was there at all – a touch of pink lipstick, a hint of lilac eyeshadow to set off those nice greeny-grey eyes and fine brows of yours. A lot of women don't know they've got what they've got, and no matter how old or how young she is, a woman should always try to look her best for her man.'

Fern had a very persuasive way of talking and Elspeth found herself softening. 'Well, maybe just a wee smear here and there. But if that besom Behag ever finds out about this I will personally take and skelp your backside, and that is a promise!'

Mairi, quite carried away with excitement, clasped her hands together and enthused, 'Och, my, I can see it all now, Elspeth, your bonny head floating down the aisle in a cloud o' silver and your face all sparkly and flushed wi' happiness.'

'I will not be going down the aisle, floating or otherwise,' Elspeth said dryly, even as a small tingle of anticipation seized her and she wondered if she should mention that she was taking the plunge, as it were, aboard *The Arian*.

The temptation was too much for her; the whole place would know soon enough anyway. The minister was bound to tell Tina, who would undoubtedly spread it round the island like wildfire. Mairi and Fern were in raptures at the news and for the next half hour all three women had a marvellous time, discussing clothes, make-up, and weddings, till Fern glanced at the clock and regretfully announced she must be going.

'I've really enjoyed talking to you both,' she told the older women. 'There's nothing like a good chin wag to cheer up the day and myself is honoured to be part of all your lovely wedding plans, Elspeth. I'm really looking forward to doing your make-up and I promise with all my heart not to be letting anyone else in on all the wee secrets we've been sharing.'

'Charmed, I'm sure,' returned Elspeth in rather a flustered fashion, mad at herself because it was all she could think of to say.

Fern beamed at them both and made to depart, but on the way out her attention was arrested by a display of children's hair ornaments. 'Would you look at these now, they are just what I've been looking for. Fergus was kind enough to give me a shilling or two for doing some odd jobs for him and I think I'll buy a set each of these clasps for Lorna and Ellie Dawn. I have come to love those wee ones, they're so pretty and clever for their age, and really funny in the things they say.' She paid for her purchases and departed, leaving Mairi and Elspeth to look at one another.

'Hmph! Paid her indeed!' was Elspeth's comment as soon as she heard the outer door closing. 'I wonder what else she did for him other than a few bit chores. And it's Fergus mark you, no' Mr McKenzie or anything as respectful as that – nor Mrs Morrison either, come to think o' it. She's a flatterer if ever there was one and just says what she thinks folks might like to hear. But she's no' a judge o' human nature or she wouldny come her smarm wi' me and I for one am no' taken in by her.'

'Well, I think she is beautiful just!' cried Mairi in a gluttony of admiration. 'Her nature is as sunny as a summer's day and because she has no envy in her she is able to praise the nice things she sees in other people.'

'I have to admit, she is quite a presentable young woman,' Elspeth conceded unwillingly, peering at herself in the mirror as she spoke and patting her hair.

'Ach, Elspeth, why can you no' just come right out and say you like her? It's the first time I've ever spoken to her and I hope it will no' be the last. She has

197

the men eating out her hand and the women like her too – even though some o' them hated her at first.'

'Ay, that is quite an achievement,' Elspeth said slowly. 'She has certainly got a lot o' charm – cheek too when she puts her mind to it. But she isn't the wicked woman I took her for in the beginning, I have to say that, and she does have an eye for a body's good points.'

Elspeth gazed at herself in the mirror. Fern was right, her eyes were a nice colour, and she did have well shaped eyebrows – funny she had never noticed these things in herself before now. It was as if she was viewing herself from a different angle altogether – seeing herself through the eyes of a bonny young girl whose face somehow haunted her and whose enchantment had bowled her over – and for Elspeth that was such a new and strange sensation she wasn't completely sure if she liked it or not. It was far safer to remain aloof from people; in that way there was less risk of being disappointed by them in the long run.

Chapter Sixteen

Fern was feeling exhilarated when she left Mairi's house to make her way through the outskirts of the village. She had just made friends with Elspeth Morrison of all people, a tartar according to Kate, one who was renowned for making people cringe with her snide remarks and her condemnation of the supposedly corrupt and sinful ways of others.

It was she who had come to Laigmhor with the sole purpose of poking her nose in where it wasn't wanted. But Fergus had soon sorted her out. Fern had heard all about that from Tina, who was a good and reliable source of information. In her candid way, Tina let slip lots of little interesting snippets, and Fern found herself mopping it all up so that she was soon quite up to date with the activities of the island. She had been most appreciative of Fergus's handling of nosy old Elspeth and had thought it would be fun to try and cultivate such a being, even if only to try and discover if she was as hard as she was made out to be.

Meeting her in Mairi's had been purely chance, but it had been now or never to take the bull by the horns, and she had won! She had succeeded in piercing through the hard shell that Elspeth presented to the world and Fern smiled triumphantly to herself as she walked through Glen Fallan with a spring in her step . . .

'*Tha Breeah*!'

Fern swung round to see Dodie bearing down upon her in a very determined manner, his long loping gait carrying him swiftly towards her. Fern had encountered the old eccentric quite a few times in the course of her own travels around the district and as she waited for him to catch up with her she prayed that he had bathed since their last meeting. The various smells that had emanated from him had been overpowering to say the least and she had quickly learned to keep her distance from him during their conversations. She had also discovered his speech impediments and the fact that he spoke in a mixture of Gaelic and English which made him even more difficult to understand. But, being Irish, she knew something of the Gaelic language, and despite his drawbacks she had come to like him and to feel a sympathy for a being who had endured, and in many ways overcome, the rigours that life had obviously doled out to him.

With all that in mind she was able to greet him with genuine warmth and to patiently wait for what he had to say to her, as, for quite a few minutes, all he did was to stand and stare at her with an undefined expression in his dreamy grey-green eyes.

The plain truth of the matter was that Dodie had fallen under the spell of this vibrant newcomer to the Rhanna scene. To him she was like one of the beautiful mermaids in Canty Tam's marine tales and he could just picture her, sitting on a rock on the seashore, combing out her long dark tresses while she chanted out a haunting sea shanty.

There was a rumour going about the island that some of the caves on the eastern shores were receiving visitations from a beautiful elusive being, with a voice like an angel and a form more enticing than any of the fabled creatures ever to have roamed the high seas. Some of the local fisherlads had reported several sightings of this magical figure but, as yet, not one of them had dared to go into the caves to ascertain the true nature of it.

The more cynically minded of the population put it all down to figments of the imagination, others said it was just modern day sea lore, dreamed up by lads who had become bored with the old tales of hags and water witches and wanted to try something new. Only a minority thought there might be something in the rumour but wouldn't admit to it for fear of ridicule. Others, like Hector the Boat, fully believed every word that was said, while Dodie was so enthralled by it all he began to imagine that it was none other than Fern that the fishermen had seen, flitting about in the great caverns, singing pensive airs and lullabies to the seals as they gathered in the bay to listen to her.

He was inclined therefore to hold her in utter deference and today was no exception. All he wanted was to stand there drinking in his fill of her for as long as she would let him, and if he could have put her in a picture frame and hung her on his wall just to gape at her, he would have done so willingly.

Fern Lee, however, was very much a flesh and blood creature, and she made this plain to Dodie when she said with a laugh, 'Come on, now, Dodie, say what you have to be saying to me for I'm as hungry as a horse and late for my dinner as it is.'

Dodie roused himself from his trance, one big rough hand sliding into a pocket buried somewhere in the folds of his greasy raincoat. 'I have a present for you,' he whispered in an agony of shyness. 'It isny much, just a wee thing I had a mind to do when I learned o' the bonny name you have on you.'

Dodie always apologised for the simple gifts he gave to the people he liked best, things gleaned from the natural bounties of sea and land and painstakingly fashioned into objects of rare and sensitive beauty.

When Fern saw the large oblong stone that he handed her, decorated with a hand-painted fern frond of palest green, the initial 'D' shakily scrawled underneath, tears filled her eyes and reaching up she kissed him gently on one nut-brown cheek.

'You're a very special man, Dodie,' she murmured, quite overcome with the emotion of the moment. 'But there you are now, I knew you were different the first time ever I spoke to you. Don't be taking offence at that for I mean it in the nicest way possible. I'll keep this stone always, and every time I look at it I'll remember you.'

Dodie's face burst into a riot of blushing colour. Placing a callused finger on that most favoured spot on his cheek he backed away, staring, staring at her in mesmerised wonderment, before he took to his heels, his boots half tripping him up as he galloped away in the direction of the village, looking back over and over to wave to her, dazed with delight, trying to assemble in his mind what next he could give her that

202

would make her smile at him the way she had and call him a special man.

Fern went on her way, Dodie's stone nestling in her hand, feeling strangely honoured to have been singled out by him in such a touching manner. She knew he had spent his entire life on Rhanna, that he was Hebridean to the core, and it would therefore be in his nature to size people up before placing his trust in them. That he had done so with somebody who was new and strange to him made her feel good inside of herself and her heart was light as she went on up the glen, glancing about her with pleasure at the trees and the wildflowers and the river thundering along.

She loved this glen, she loved this island, she hadn't been here for very long, but already its beauty and tranquillity had carved a niche in her heart. It was so far removed from everything that was discordant and ugly and she had vowed to herself that she would stay for as long as she could. She felt safe here. Laigmhor was like a haven, and Fergus McKenzie was like a rock, just thinking about him made her feel good and she prayed that he wouldn't get tired of her and send her away. She very much needed such a man in her life at the moment, and at sight of Laigmhor's chimneys prodding into the watery April sky, she found herself hurrying.

On reaching the track leading up to the farm her pace quickened even more, and she started to run as she approached the sturdy white farmhouse building that she had begun to think of as home.

It was well after mid-day and Fergus was alone in the house, Bob having gone on ahead to the lambing fields.

'It's sorry I am for being so late,' Fern apologised as soon as she got inside. 'I am after meeting old Dodie on the road and he spent several minutes just looking at me before giving me this lovely painted stone.' Uncurling her fingers she showed Fergus her prize before going on, 'You will never guess what else happened to me on this day of rich adventure! I came across Elspeth Morrison in Mairi's place and before I knew it, my tongue ran away with me and I told her I would help her to get ready on the morning of her wedding. At first she was all starchy and stiff and wailing like a cat with its tail in a trap but she soon melted when I spun her a bit of the blarney and told her she had nice hair.'

Fergus stared, then he laughed. 'That old yowe! Melted! What did you do? Pour boiling oil on her?'

'Ach, no, nothing so drastic. Am I not after telling you? I gave her a taste of the Irish and in two shakes of a lamb's tail we were blethering away like old pals in a pub. Mairi was fair tickled by it all and began making plans in that nice daft way she has about her.'

'I was right about you,' Fergus said appreciatively, 'you are a witch, one who can wind anybody round her little finger . . .'

'Anybody? Have I done it to you? Have I bewitched you, Fergus?'

'Bewildered me, more like,' he answered gruffly. 'I don't know whether I'm coming or going these days and I was thinking – maybe the time has come for you to find somewhere else to stay. It would be the best thing for everybody in the long run. I – I'm buggered if I know how to handle this anymore.'

'Fergus.' His name came out in a whisper. Dread, stark and naked, looked out of her eyes. 'Come on now, you can't just send me away like that, there is nowhere else in the world for me to go, it isn't safe for me out there. I have nothing, nobody else . . .'

With one quick movement she was beside him, pulling his dark head down towards her, kissing him over and over, her hands sliding under his shirt, gliding over his skin.

'No!' Roughly he tore himself away from her. 'I won't let you do this! I can't cope with this sort o' thing! You're young, only a lass – I'm . . .'

She gazed at him standing there, black eyes wild and burning, his body firm and weatherbeaten, his face ruggedly handsome, and she smiled, a small, lingering, secretive smile. 'Surely you know you're at your peak, Fergus, the sort of man who would appeal to any woman of any age. You're as strong as an oak tree . . .' She ran her hands over his shoulders, her fingers playing with the crisp black tendrils at the nape of his neck, 'Ah, is it not a real man you are? I can feel your heart beating against my breasts, wanting me as much as I am wanting you . . .'

He could stand it no longer. The last remnants of his resistance fled, he wasn't aware of where he was, nor did he care. His mouth came down on hers, drowning out her words, engulfing each of them in a tidal wave of excitement as they went wild together, kissing, touching, lost in a world of fierce and untamed longing . . .

The creaking of the opening door came to Fergus through a welter of dazed emotions. Looking up he saw

Bob framed in the doorway, mouth agape, face a study of blank disbelief.

Bob had come back because he had forgotten his pipe, and he immediately forgot it all over again as his astounded eyes absorbed the scene before him. Rough and tough as he was from a lifetime of shepherding and farming, Bob was first and foremost a gentleman, one whose loyalty to the McKenzies had never faltered through all the years he had known and worked with them. He recognised their strengths and their weaknesses and knew things about them that no one else outside of the family would ever know. Their secrets were safe with him; he had tried never to interfere with their lives, though there had been occasions when it had taken him all his time to hold his tongue.

This was one of those occasions, and it was maybe just as well that the said organ had stuck to the roof of a mouth that had gone suddenly dry with dismay and shock. That, however, was only a temporary condition. He would have his say later. By God and he would! This was more than just a household concern, unless it was stopped it could affect every member of the family, including him! And he was damned if he was going to stand by and allow that scheming little minx of a girl to ruin the good McKenzie name!

The knuckles of Bob's hands grew white on the stem of his shepherd's crook. He clamped his lips together. It wouldn't do to start ranting, not in front of a stranger. His dignity had always been important to him and he had no intention of losing it now, in spite of what he had just witnessed. With that in mind he muttered, 'Begging your pardon,' and hastily withdrew, venting his anger on Gaffer who, expertly tucking in his rear to avoid the tackity boot aimed at him, made off down the track with all haste.

'Christ! That had to happen!' Fergus said worriedly. 'And Bob of all people! I'd better go after him.'

'I'm sorry, Fergus,' Fern said in a quick, strange, breathless voice. 'I only want to please you and give you the things that I know you want from me. All I ask in return is a roof over my head and food enough to fill my belly. I'll work for all of that if only you'll give me a chance to gather my wits together. Terrible things have happened to me – if only I could tell you . . .'

Breaking off she held onto his arm and gazed up at him beseechingly. 'I'll do anything you ask of me, if you see fit to grant me this. It's worse for me at night, when I'm alone and my head won't stop going round in circles. I'm frightened of the dark and the silence and all I want is a bit of human company. If you care for me at all you'll come to my room tonight when the little ones are asleep. I'll be ready for you and I'll bless you for your kindness.'

Fergus didn't answer. Going to the door he shoved his feet into his boots and hurried to catch up with Bob just as he was opening the gate into the fields. Without a word he fell into step beside the old shepherd. There was silence for a few moments then, unable to keep quiet a moment longer, Bob turned to glare at his companion. 'You're playing wi' fire, Fergus,' he snarled, 'I know fine you're going to tell me it's none o' my business, but if I were you I'd leave that girl alone.'

'You aren't me,' Fergus grunted, 'and you're right, it is none o' your business.'

'Bugger it, man!' With clenched fists Bob swung round to face Fergus, stopping so suddenly in his tracks he tripped over Gaffer who had been skulking along at his heels in a very subdued manner. Bob released a string of oaths, and the dog retreated to the safety of the trees, there to flop on his belly onto the grass and wait till it was safe for him to come out.

By this time Bob was boiling with rage and he didn't mince words when he roared at Fergus, 'It is my bloody business! I consider myself to be part o' your family, and I'm damned if I'm going to sit back and watch you ruin your life for a slip o' a girl who means nothing to you! I've known you since you were born! I thought I knew all there was to know about you but I was wrong, today you are a stranger to me and I don't like the man I see! If I wasny so old and you wereny so tough I'd have a go at knocking some sense into that bloody stubborn head o' yours!'

The minute Bob had started shouting Heinz had started growling, warning sounds that rumbled deep in his throat with ferocious intensity. He was quivering from head to foot; his whole being had undergone a metamorphosis in the last few minutes. No longer was he the friendly domestic creature that everyone knew and loved. His lips were drawn back over his fangs, an action that moulded his nose into fearsome furrows that gave him an alarmingly savage appearance.

He looked ready to spring on Bob at any given moment and sharply Fergus ordered him to, 'Stay back and be still!'

Bob paid no heed to the dog. He was breathing heavily, his nose was running, and impatiently he drew a hand across it. Shaking his head he went on in quieter tones, 'That lassie will only wreak havoc in your life if you don't get rid o' her. There's something gey strange about her. I've seen her, wandering about on the shore over by Camus nan Uamh, searching amongst the rocks . . .' Bob looked uneasy, he shuddered slightly, 'And that's a dangerous place for anybody to be, never mind a young lassie who says she doesny know the island. I'm no' a one for idle gossip, as well you know, but I canny help thinking there's more to her than meets the eye and I wouldny trust her as far as I could throw her.

'She's up to no good and yet, there she is in your home, as bold as brass, behaving as if she owns the place and owns you wi' it. Instead o' kissing and cuddling her you should be trying to find out more about her. She's trouble, lad, trouble, and if you carry on as you're doing you'll live to rue the day!'

He glared at Heinz, who was sitting back on his haunches, licking his lips. 'And it's about time you trained that dog o' yours to be a dog and no' a wild beast! One o' these days it will hurt somebody and if it ever goes for me I'll kill the bugger wi' my own bare hands!'

With that Bob spat viciously onto the grass, called on his own patiently waiting dog to 'come ahint', and strode away, bristling from head to foot with emotion, blue eyes glinting fire, shoulders back, gnarled fingers holding on tightly to his shepherd's crook as if he badly needed its support in those fraught moments.

Fergus, who had been stunned into silence for the last few minutes, held onto Heinz's collar and watched till Bob was out of sight behind a hillock. Never, in all the years of knowing the old shepherd, had Fergus heard him expressing himself with such loquacity, and in his heart he knew that Bob was right to have spoken out as he had; but the heart and mind of Fergus McKenzie of Laigmhor were two very different entities.

'Pig-headed as a mule's arse!'

Mirabelle used to say that about him, and if she had come back that day and seen the set expression on his dour, dark handsome face, she would have uttered those self-same words all over again, and maybe a bit more besides. Because, where Fern Lee was concerned, Fergus had no intention of lying down meekly to the laws laid down by anybody, far less Bob Paterson, whose views of the world around him were old fashioned and outdated in the extreme.

All Bob had done was to weaken Fergus's earlier resolve to tell the girl she had to go. Let her stay! For as long as she liked! It was his home and he was the boss! Bob and all the rest of them could rant and rave forever if they wanted but in the end what he said went and that was an end to the matter!

So Fergus convinced himself as he commenced his belated afternoon's work, but somehow it didn't make him feel any better. No matter how hard he tried he couldn't get Fern out of his mind, and he went over every detail of that breathless interlude he had recently shared with her.

He remembered how excited he'd felt at her nearness, the softness of her mouth on his, the pulsating sensations he'd experienced at the feel of her hands caressing him. He ached for her and wanted only to know again the sweetness of her young body next to his own, her perfume in his nostrils, the sensual feel of her hair gliding through his fingers.

She had brought him to a pitch of unbearable longing and for the rest of that afternoon he could hardly concentrate on what he was doing. He wished only for teatime to come, that he might see her again and read in her eyes the messages that he wanted to know.

Chapter Seventeen

That night Lorna and Ellie Dawn were in a lively mood and had no intention of going early to bed. They were delighted with the clasps that Fern had given them to adorn their hair. After they had soaked in lathers of scented bubbles in front of the fire, nothing would do till their locks had been shampooed and dried and the clasps tried out in different hair-styles.

'I want mine in plaits, Aunt Fern,' Lorna decided, preening herself in front of the bedroom mirror.

'And I want a ponytail,' Ellie Dawn nodded, her lip jutting a little as she tried to elbow Lorna away from the mirror.

'Ach no, your hair's too fine for a ponytail,' Fern said patiently, running her fingers through the child's silken blonde tresses, 'and yours is a bit too curly for plaits, Lorna. How would it be if I just gave each of you a good brushing and we'll try out the clasps in the morning?'

Ellie Dawn clapped her hand over her mouth. 'You don't brush people, Aunt Fern,' she admonished with a giggle, 'only dogs and cats and monkeys and horses and nephelants and . . .'

'Elephants,' corrected Lorna triumphantly. 'It's

elephants, Ellie Dawn, I'll show you tomorrow on the blackboard and maybe if we're very quiet we'll see a real live one grazing in the woods by Loch Tenee.'

'Nephelants don't live there!' cried Ellie Dawn in shock, her eyes widening, her lip trembling. In a faint voice she added, 'They really and truly don't, do they?'

'Come on you two,' laughed Fern, 'you'll be seeing pink elephants in your dreams if you go on like this.'

Lorna shook her head. 'You don't get pink elephants, Aunt Fern, only grey ones and green ones and sometimes white and maybe a blue one like Neil Black paints in his colouring book in school.'

'Bed!' Fern herded the pair of them across the room and they were soon tucked cosily in between the sheets.

'Is Grampa coming up?' Lorna asked. 'I want to read him a story.'

'And I've learned a new song specially for him,' Ellie Dawn added importantly.

'He is a busy man and he had to go out again but I'll send him up the minute he comes in,' Fern promised, dropping a kiss on each of the rosy cheeks before crossing the landing to her own room.

Much later, when the children had exhausted themselves entertaining their beloved grampa and the room had grown still and quiet, Fergus, in an equal state of exhaustion, threw himself into a wickerwork chair near the window and closed his eyes.

The even breathing of the children filtered peacefully through the silence, the 'grand old lady' in the hall chimed out the hour of eleven o'clock, and the wind sighed soulfully through the windbreak of trees round the house. He opened his eyes and turned his head to stare at the silhouette of the dark night hills outside the window. Rugged, powerful, eternal, they stood sentinal over the land, hills that he had gazed upon since boyhood and which had always given him a restful sense of security.

But he could find no solace in them tonight. His senses were in a turmoil, his mind wouldn't be still; all sorts of thoughts were crowding into it, the uppermost being the scene with Bob in the fields, to be quickly followed by the cause of it all, the unsettling interlude with Fern in the kitchen.

Try as he might he couldn't rid himself of visions of her and he moved restlessly, wishing his stomach would unwind, wishing all sorts of things but most of all wishing to God he'd never clapped eyes on the girl! All she had ever done was disrupt his peace of mind and destroy the very things he had worked all his life to build up.

Because none of it seemed to have much meaning anymore, nothing mattered as much as it had. All he could think of was her, lying there in the next room, waiting for him to come to her . . .

He was damned if he would give in! How could he even contemplate such an act with his grandchildren here in the house, lost in their innocent repose, trusting that he would be there should they waken and need the comfort of his presence.

Fern could wait forever for all he cared! She meant nothing to him! Nothing!

The touch of her mouth on his swam into his mind.

It was as if she was there in the room with him, the sweetness of her perfume drowning his senses, her lips tempting him beyond endurance, her eyes beckoning him, her lithesome body swaying seductively as she moved slowly towards him. Sweat broke on his brow. Getting up he paced the floor in his stockinged feet. Up down, up down, he padded, like a caged animal yearning for its freedom, wanting only to escape the bondage that held it captive, to break away from a life that was repetitive, dull, and meaningless . . .

Abruptly he stopped pacing, knowing that he would have to do something, anything, to rid himself of this turmoil of mind and body. He would go down to the kitchen and make himself a cup of tea.

Mirabelle had been a great believer in tea as a remedy for a great many maladies. 'It's good for sleeplessness as well.' He could hear her voice now. 'Just get up and make yourself a good hot cuppy, it's the finest night nurse of all and afterwards you'll sleep like a babe in arms.'

Soundlessly he went downstairs to throw open the kitchen door. It was warm and drowsing; the clock on the mantelpiece ticked, the cats lazed and stretched and purred on top of the oven, the lamb was in its basket. Heinz was in his usual place on the hearthrug, his muzzle resting on his paws, one eye opening under the wrinkled canopy of his brow, his tail beginning to flick lazily as he prepared to welcome his master into the domain that normally belonged to himself and the cats at this hour of the night.

But tonight wasn't normal; human beings had infil-trated the sanctuary, seriously disrupting the well-

215

deserved slumbers of a good honest dog who was tired out after his labours of the day. But these were people that he loved to have in his world, no matter the hour, and he was puzzled that neither of them was paying much heed to him, particularly his adored master who seemed suddenly to have turned to stone as he stood framed in the doorway, not saying a word.

As for Fergus, he could hardly believe the sight that met his eyes as he was about to enter the room, and for one stunned moment he wondered wildly if he was witnessing a re-enactment of that other memorable night when he had come home from Lachlan's to find Fern emerging from the bathtub.

For here she was again, newly bathed, towelling herself briskly in front of the fire, her hair a mass of damp black ringlets that fell about her face and shoulders to almost touch her slender waist. She was leaning forward. Her breasts, her buttocks, those lovely long legs of hers, all were silhouetted against the soft, enchanting glow of firelight. She was like a golden statuette in all her perfection for she too had frozen into immobility soon after the opening of the door.

All she could do was stare at him, he at her. Time hung suspended, and everything in the room seemed to fade into another sphere. It was as if they were the only two people on earth, gazing transfixed at one another.

She was the first to break the spell. 'Fergus.' His name came out, husky and low. 'I was just coming up...'

He didn't let her finish. Unable to contain his feelings a moment longer, he covered the distance that separated them, in a few quick strides. And then she

216

was in his embrace, he was smothering her in kisses, her mouth, her neck, his breath rapid and harsh in his throat.

Her own breath caught. Tearing open his shirt she moulded herself into him so that the perfect young breasts he had dreamed of were pressed excitingly against the hardness of his chest. She moved even closer; those supple, shapely legs of hers were wrapping themselves around him, holding him captive, forcing him ever closer to those warm, damp, secret parts of her body, driving him crazy as she allowed him to do as he would with her . . .

Now there was no turning back, not till he had found his release with her, not till he had assuaged this aching, burning heat that surged through every fibre of his being. Heart pounding in his breast he gasped and moaned and whispered her name – and then he turned his head and caught sight of a picture of himself and Kirsteen on the mantelpiece, heads close together, laughing out at the world, safe and happy in their love for one another.

Something snapped in his mind. Sanity returned. It was as if he had been doused with ice cold water. Dazedly he struggled to regain control of his emotions, feeling as he did so that he was spinning back from some alien place, travelling towards a light shining at the end of a tunnel.

Kirsteen! His Kirsteen! The light of his world. The love of his life. With her he had shared every meaningful moment of his existence, to her he owed his allegiance and everything else that was precious and good between them.

The enormity of what he had been about to do was like a physical blow to his brain. He had very nearly betrayed his darling wife's trust in him. All for a few moments of pleasure with this young woman, whose tempting beauty had mesmerised him as easily as if he was a simpleton with no mind of his own.

With a snarl of shame and rage he hurled Fern away from him to say in a tightly controlled voice, 'Enough! I want no more of you! It's finished! Tomorrow you'll get out o' my house. And by God! I mean every word I say! Get out and never come back again! Ever!'

She was staring at him, her huge, dark eyes filled with disbelief, her breasts rising and falling in rhythmic time to her breathing. 'But, Fergus,' she faltered, 'I thought . . .'

'I know what you thought, but it's over. I was a fool to let you bide here in the first place. You're a dangerous young woman, Fern Lee. I have a feeling that you've cheated and lied to me ever since you got here but I tried to be fair to you because, fool that I am, I was drawn to you against my better judgement. All that is over with, tomorrow you go. You'll find somebody else to take you on, all you have to do is bat your eyes and wiggle your hips, you're an expert at both.'

Throwing her clothes at her he ordered her harshly to get dressed and then he blundered away, a man torn apart by guilt, regret and self-loathing. He had said some terrible things to Fern, had more or less accused her of being a hussy, but he was only too well aware of the darkness lurking within his own soul and he didn't like the feeling one bit.

'Fergus,' Her voice followed him from the room. 'Surely you must know I can't leave here, I – I won't leave. I have nowhere else to go, nobody else to turn to. Will you not take pity on me and let me be staying till all my bothers are sorted out?'

At the foot of the stairs he paused. There was pleading in her words, pathos in her voice – all mixed up with another factor. He recognised it for what it was. She was afraid – of something – or somebody. The man she had escaped? Or some other matter entirely? Something so terrible she would do anything, anything at all to avoid facing the reality of it, even if it meant ruining the lives of other people in the process . . .

Fergus hesitated; he shivered slightly. Where would it all lead? How would it end? Because he knew for certain that tonight was somehow only the beginning of his troubles where Fern Lee was concerned. He was caught up in a situation that wasn't of his making, yet like it or no he was one of the main players in the drama.

Somehow, sometime, somewhere, everything would come to a head and God alone knew what would happen then. People were bound to be hurt and it was up to him to try and protect his own family as much as he could. He had made a start by ordering the girl out of his home and his life. It was final; there was no turning back now. Having made that decision, he went on up to bed, feeling weary and oppressed, a chill in his marrow that did not owe itself to the cold.

The next morning events took an unexpected turn when Kirsteen arrived home, bubbly and excited, calling, 'Surprise, surprise!' as she rushed into the kitchen to throw herself at Fergus, who was sitting at the table finishing his breakfast.

At sight of her he experienced an overwhelming sense of relief. 'Mo cridhe,' he whispered, staring at her as if she wasn't quite real. 'You look wonderful, but I don't understand, you never said . . .'

'I know, I know,' she laughed, 'I thought it would be fun to just sneak home and catch you getting up to mischief!'

He looked at her quickly, wondering if she had already been exposed to gossip concerning himself and Fern. There was plenty of that going around, some of it was bound to reach Kirsteen's ears . . . He didn't allow his thoughts to wander further, he would deal with such eventualities if and when they arose, Right now, all he wanted was to enjoy these precious moments of just savouring her presence, taking his fill of her nearness, seeing the joy on her face as she gazed into his. Her arrival couldn't have happened at a better moment and he felt as if a weight had been lifted from his heart; the whole world seemed lighter and brighter.

'Mo cridhe,' he said again, pulling her towards him to kiss her tenderly, 'it's grand to have you back, it's been – so strange here without you.'

She snuggled against him, her blue eyes shining. 'Perhaps I should go away more often, it would be worth it to get a welcome home like this every time. As a matter o' fact, Aunt Minnie's decided to release the moths from her purse and wants to take me and Phebie on a cruise this autumn. Phebie, the besom, did hint at something o' the sort while we were there and out o' the blue the old lady announced that she needed a holiday and thought a cruise to sunny climes would be just the thing. She enjoyed our stay with her and put up quite a tearful scene when we announced to her that we were leaving.'

'A cruise?' he frowned. 'Away from your own country? Away from the island? To strange places you know nothing about?'

She giggled. 'Fergie, Fergie, home-loving man that you are! You just can't understand anyone wanting to leave Rhanna to visit foreign lands, can you? I myself felt a bit like that when I left to go to Aunt Minnie's and that was only to Glasgow! I see it now from a different angle, it was good to get a change of scene and it's made me appreciate my home all the more.' She kissed him on the tip of his nose. 'Stop fretting, it's months away yet. Right now . . .' she gazed around the familiar room, '. . . it's wonderful to be back, I've missed it all so much.'

Fern chose to enter the kitchen just then. At sight of Kirsteen she paused for a few seconds, then she came forward, hand outstretched, a smile lighting her face. 'Sure now, and you must be Mrs McKenzie, I couldn't be mistaking you for anyone else for I've heard that much about you and of course seen pictures of you in the house.'

For a few moments Kirsteen could only gaze word-lessly at the vision of youth and beauty that Fern presented, before hugging the girl to her and saying warmly, 'And you must be Fern Lee, I've been hearing about you too, though I must say,' here she glanced at her husband, 'no one told me you would be quite so young and bonny.'

Fern's dimples showed, 'Ah, men, they're a strange breed of folk to be sure. They're always so busy with their own concerns it's a wonder they notice anything that goes on outside their own wee worlds. Would you be agreeing with me about that, Mrs McKenzie?'

'Mrs McKenzie!' Kirsteen laughed. 'I'd almost forgotten I had such a title. Everyone calls me Kirsteen and I hope you will too, or I'll feel a stranger in my own house.'

Fergus watched the two women. Their faces were animated as they chatted; they might have known one another for years instead of just the few minutes that had passed since Fern's appearance. The girl was being at her most charming and it soon became apparent that Kirsteen had rapidly fallen under her spell.

To swell the ranks even further Tina popped in on one of her goodwill missions, bearing a freshly baked currant loaf and an apple tart, knowing how much Fergus liked them. She was thrilled to see Kirsteen again and greeted her affectionately before plunking herself down at the table, declaring that she was 'fair wabbit after the walk and gey thirsty into the bargain'.

Fern, knowing the routine by this time, fetched the kettle to make another pot of tea. All three women settled themselves around the table to laugh and blether, to drink tea, and devour a greater portion of the apple tart and half the currant loaf.

Fergus's brows knitted darkly. No one was paying much attention to him, not even Kirsteen, and feeling

222

unwanted he went off without a word, uneasy in his mind, unsure of how to handle matters as they stood.

His authority was slipping further and further away from him. He was no longer his own or anyone else's master. Fern had no intention of obeying his wishes of the previous night. That much was obvious from the way she had immediately taken advantage of Kirsteen's timely return, using it to strengthen her position in the Laigmhor household.

Fergus gave himself a little shake. It was a beautiful day, the sights and sounds of early summer were everywhere; a Hebridean song thrush was singing its heart out in a wooded glade; furry golden bumble bees were prodding busily into the spring flowers growing along the wayside; a lizard darted under a stone; a tiny frog blinked sleepily amongst the uncurling ferns; in the sky above, a skylark was trilling out a song of pure ecstasy while near at hand a little streamlet burbled musically over the stones, much appreciated by a blackbird who was making a great fuss with his morning bath, splish-splashing water everywhere, shaking the sparkling droplets from his wings and digging his bright orange beak in and around his feathers to make sure every part of him received attention. Somehow the beauty of the morning brought everything into a clearer perspective for Fergus. He told himself that time would resolve everything, that nothing was as bad as it seemed; and Kirsteen was home – that alone was enough reason for rejoicing. He hoped and prayed that she would never discover the guilty secrets that hung so heavily on his conscience. The knowledge that Kirsteen herself had indirectly saved him from that final act of betrayal made him feel weak with relief.

Calling on Heinz, who was sniffing curiously at the frog, he went to join Bob and Donald who were driving the cows onto the pastures on the lower slopes of Ben Machrie. Newly released from their winter byres, the animals were in a frisky mood, kicking up their hooves as they ran, jostling and butting one another, releasing torrents of dung and steaming rivers of urine in their excitement at being free. Gaffer, taking advantage of the situation, nipped at a few passing heels, Bob swore and wielded his crook at his dog, Donald grinned, so too did Heinz, and Fergus laughed because suddenly he felt good and right with a world that was as familiar to him as the very air he breathed.

When the children came home from school they screamed with delight at sight of their gramma and hurled themselves into her arms.

'I've been looking after Grampa,' Lorna announced proudly.

'Me too!' Ellie Dawn piped up.

'You've both done a great job,' Kirsteen told them as she cuddled them. 'In fact, I think you've been overfeeding him, he looks so well and happy.'

'I can't tell you how pleased I am to see you, Kirsteen.' Shona, who had collected the girls from school, spoke with feeling and took her step-mother's hands in both of hers. 'The place has been going to the dogs without you.'

'Eh?' Kirsteen glanced around her in surprise, 'It all looks fine to me.'

'Och, no, I don't mean that...' Shona glanced first at her father then at Fern, who was standing watching her with a strange expression on her face. 'It's just that – well – it will be lovely to have everything back to normal again, just you and Father here at Laigmhor, the way it always was before.'

It was Kirsteen's turn to look quizzically at her step-daughter but she didn't pursue the subject and said with a laugh, 'I can't promise it *will* always be like that. You shouldn't have chased me away to Glasgow like you did because now that I've had a taste o' the big bad world I'm going to be spreading my little wings even further afield.'

She went on to explain about the proposed cruise, the news of which brought an unexpected reaction from Shona who commented, 'Ach well, it won't matter so much if it's later on in the year, as long as you bide where you are till things have sorted themselves out at Laigmhor.'

Kirsteen was more puzzled than ever by all these cryptic remarks, but Shona gave her no opportunity to pursue the matter. 'I'd better take the bairns home,' she decided briskly, 'you and Father will be wanting the house to yourselves and Ruth is missing Lorna as much as I'm missing Ellie Dawn.'

'Och no!' protested Kirsteen. 'Let them stay till after tea at least. I've got presents for them and want to be here when they open them.'

Ellie Dawn clapped her hands. 'Like Christmas, Gramma?'

'Ay, like Christmas,' agreed Kirsteen with a smile.

* * *

Fergus had had no chance to talk to Fern about her leaving, and over tea she played another of her trump cards. Leaning towards Kirsteen, she said beseechingly, 'I hope you'll be letting me stay here a wee while longer, Kirsteen. I promise I'll be no bother and I'll do everything I can to earn my keep.'

'Of course,' Kirsteen looked taken aback, 'I'm surprised the question even came up. Where else would you go? And what made you think you had to move out because I've moved back in? It's going to be nice having another woman to talk to and I'm looking forward to it.'

She gazed out to the hills beyond the window. 'It's so wonderful to be back on Rhanna, I've missed it more than I could believe possible. But Glasgow's a busy place, there was always so much bustle and things happening. It's going to take me a whilie to get used to the quiet again so I'll be glad o' some company when Fergus is out and about.'

Fern looked at Fergus, a triumphant smile lifting the corners of her mouth. The gleam in her black eyes was something more than just gladness to be staying on. She was silently daring him to contradict the things his wife had just said and he knew that she wasn't going to let go of him so easily. Nothing was resolved, he was back to square one, and the look he threw back at her was a mixture of frustrated anger and growing defeat.

Tea over, the little girls sat happily on the rug, playing with the toys Kirsteen had brought them, but when Shona and Niall arrived to take them home to their respective houses they set up wails of protest.

'We have to stay here, Grampa and Gramma both need us,' Lorna decided in her quaint, old-fashioned way.

'Yes.' Ellie Dawn supported this with a vigorous nod of her fair head. 'Gramma's tired and needs me to sing to her and Grampa likes the stories Lorna tells him.'

'Hey!' Niall swung his little daughter high. 'Don't you want to come home to your daddy? I've missed you pinching me awake in the morning and the twins need you to tell them about the three bears.'

Ellie Dawn weakened at once and placing a hand in each of her parents' she began pulling them towards the door.

Not so Lorna, eyes swimming, lip trembling; she gazed at Fern and whispered, 'I want to stay here, with you, Aunt Fern.'

'Mavourneen.' Fern folded the child into her arms and kissed her rosy cheek. 'Your mammy and daddy have been awful lonely without you and want you back with them. Besides all that, I'm going to be here to look after Grampa and Gramma and there wouldn't be room for us all. You can come and visit whenever you like and we'll make pancakes and sticky buns for you to take home for your own daddy's tea . . .'

'Can I speak to you for a minute?' Shona, her face like thunder, put a firm hand under Fern's elbow to propel her through to the parlour, where she spun her round and glared into her face. 'Just what do you think you're playing at?' Shona blazed, her blue eyes sparking fire.

Fern's own eyes glinted. 'Sure now, I'm not playing at anything, you're the one who seems to be doing enough of that for both of us.'

'Oh, am I? Well, let me tell you this, Mrs Lee, you *are* playing a game, a deadly one at that! I don't know what you're up to and I don't want to know because I think it's something rotten! I've stood by and watched you teasing and tormenting my father and he wouldn't listen when I warned him you were up to no good! All that's finished now, Kirsteen is home and you can go somewhere else. You aren't staying here to manipulate my family any longer. Whatever you have in mind is finished and I want you to stop wearing my clothes and to get out o' my room, just as quick as you like.'

'Ah now, so that's it!' Fern flashed back. 'The truth of the matter is coming out at last. You're jealous because your father let me sleep in your room and allowed me to wear some of your rags. Well . . .' She tossed her hair back from her livid face. 'I have no need of them now, Kirsteen has said I can use her things and I'll be getting some of my very own just as soon as I can. I met Elspeth this afternoon and she has invited me to her house to have a wee look through her mail order catalogue. I'm getting on like a house on fire with that one and I am invited to her wedding which is more than you'll ever get, you being a McKenzie and all. The folks on this island are getting to really know and like me and any one of them would take me in but . . .' She laughed. 'I'm staying put – right here. Was it not Kirsteen herself who said I could stay? For as long as I liked, and herself only too glad of the company. In the spare guest room too, which is bigger than yours, so you can have that back, just to let you see what a generous lass I can be when I put my mind to it.'

Shona almost exploded. It took every ounce of her willpower not to strike out at the beautiful face before her. 'You will get what's coming to you, Mrs Lee,' she ground out. 'It might be sooner, it might be later, but it will come.'

'Ah, mavourneen, you really do want to punish me, do you not now? But I'll tell you one thing that might relieve your mind. I will be going from this island, sooner or later, I will be going, but not before I'm ready, mavourneen, not before that.'

Shona could barely contain herself. Hands curling into fists at her sides, she turned and left the room without another word, leaving Fern to gaze after her, the victorious expression on her face quickly fading to one of terrible uncertainty.

Part Two

SUMMER/AUTUMN
1968

Chapter Eighteen

It was the day of Elspeth's wedding and no one could have wished for better weather. Tiny puffball clouds sailed serenely across the pale blue dome of the sky; millions of sun diamonds sparkled on an ocean that was a dazzling expanse of deepest ultramarine; a medley of little islands shimmered in the distance in softest shades of purple and blue and green; tall ships with white sails fluttered lazily over the waves; frothy wavelets lapped the white sands in the bays; seabirds drifted like snowflakes above the cliffs and everywhere the birds were singing ecstatic praises to a world that was new and fresh and young in its cloak of many colours.

Elspeth had been up since the crack of dawn, anxiously rushing around and trying to do a hundred things at the one time till Mac laid a steadying hand on her arm and made her swallow 'a wee taste o' the cratur' for her nerves. Elspeth did as she was bid, in her excitement downing more of the whisky than she had intended. For fully ten minutes she managed to sit in a chair and remain immobile and reasonably calm, but then Nellie, Mac's sister, who had arrived the night before from the island of Hanaay, appeared in the kitchen in dressing-gown and curlers to seriously disrupt Elspeth's composure by demanding to know the whereabouts of the iron so that she could smooth away the travel creases from her best frock.

Nellie had never approved of her brother's liaison with 'the moth-eaten cailleach' as she called Elspeth behind her back. When she realised for certain that Mac was hell bent on marrying the said cailleach, she had been outraged and even more outspoken than usual.

'You have gone soft in the head altogether, Isaac McIntosh!' she had told him on his New Year's visit to the old family croft on Hanaay. 'Our dear good mother and father would turn in their graves if they knew that you were wedding yourself to that sour prune o' a woman. You had a good marriage to Mary, God rest her too, and her memory should have sufficed you till the end o' your days. Now, here you are, full steam ahead on the road to hell. You know what they say, marry in haste, repent at leisure, ay, and you'll repent right well, my lad, if I'm a judge o' human nature.'

'Ach, come on now, Nell,' Mac had protested, 'I'm no' marrying in haste, as you make out. I gave myself a long time to think about it before deciding to take the plunge, and if you wereny so stubborn you would soon see for yourself that Elspeth isny the ogre you make her out to be. She's a good woman, Nell, she looks after me right well and we're that contented wi' one another I canny think what I would do if she wasny there.'

'Hmph!' Nellie's jaw jutted worse than usual. 'Only time will tell us that, Isaac McIntosh. Meantime, I'm that mad wi' you I just don't have the heart to give you my blessing and might decide no' to come to your wedding when the terrible day comes.'

Now the terrible day had come and Nellie was there alright, standing in the middle of Elspeth's kitchen, as large as life and twice as formidable in her fearsome-looking spiked curlers and bilious green dressing-gown, splayed matchstick legs stuck into large brown-check bootees which had seen better days.

Elspeth fetched the iron, she fetched the ironing board, she made the breakfast, and performed a hundred and one small tasks that would have been unnecessary had it only been herself and Mac to cater for. Over and above all that she couldn't get Mac's cousin Gus out of her mind, and imagined a hundred and one possible catastrophes that he might perform to ruin her big day.

Halfway through the morning she was in a dreadful state of nervous anxiety. Her fingers were all thumbs, she couldn't concentrate on anything, Nellie moaned and complained and generally made life difficult, and to cap it all Mac wasn't there with his stout shoulder to cry on since he had taken himself off to Tam's to get himself ready, it being bad luck for the bride and groom to see one another in their wedding finery prior to the ceremony, as Elspeth herself had told Mac when she had been whole and hearty and all in one piece before the advent of her future sister-in-law into her home.

To make matters worse, she hadn't been able to spare one single minute to do anything about her appearance; her hair was a mess, her nails were worse, she had bags under her eyes and a spot on her chin, her feet were aching from rushing about all morning in her slippers, and over and above all else she was experiencing such a sense of overwhelming hope-lessness she doubted if she had the will to attend her own wedding, never mind get ready for it.

After all her wonderful plans too, her happiness, her visions of Kate's astonished face, Behag's envy, as they gaped at her in all her glory. It was done, it was finished. Nellie had won. No one would miss her if she just went back to bed for the rest of the day to sleep away her misery and disappointment.

Then Fern appeared; like a ray of sunshine peeping over a grey cloud she put her head round the door and beamed her radiant smile on Elspeth, who was sitting forlorn and drooping on a straight-backed kitchen chair.

From that moment on Elspeth's day took off. Fern carried her away on a magic carpet of energetic enthusiasm, straight to Mairi's to sit her down beside the powder-blue washbasin where she was plied with strong hot tea to calm her nerves before the serious business of beautifying got underway.

Mairi, at her motherly best, clucked and fussed and made soothing noises as she listened to Elspeth's woes of the morning. Then she got down to work, enveloping Elspeth's head in generous mounds of perfumed shampoo bubbles, rinsing it, enclosing it in a large fluffy towel, before busying herself mixing the Silver Cloud hair rinse in a chipped delft bowl. The rinse was then applied to Elspeth's head, and while she was waiting for it to do its stuff, it was Fern's turn to take over. Directing Elspeth to sit back and relax she got to work on her nails, manicuring them, buffing them, finally coating them in a tasteful shade of delicate pink nail varnish.

'Now for your feet, mavourneen,' Fern said with a little smile, knowing there would be a reaction of some sort to her words.

She was right.

'My feets!' gasped Elspeth in utter shock. 'You canny do my feets! Only hussies paint the nails o' their feets and I'm no' going to stoop that low. It's no' as if I'll be taking off my shoes when I wed myself to Isaac. I would be the laughing stock o' the whole place and what's the use o' painted toenails when no' a soul in the whole world is likely to set eyes on them except myself!'

Fern and Mairi looked at one another. 'Are you perfectly sure o' that, Elspeth?' the latter said in her gentle way. 'Tonight you'll be two instead o' one.'

'To be sure you won't be going to bed with your socks on,' Fern added mischievously. 'So just you be taking off your stockings and let me do my bit. I won't be painting your nails unless you want me to, I've brought along some lovely herbal oil to massage your legs and feet and I promise you won't regret any of it. You'll be walking on air by the time I'm finished with you and will just float right into the arms of your new husband. Come on now, you know you can trust me, mavourneen.'

Elspeth was silent for a moment as she digested all this. She had indeed come to trust Fern implicitly and wouldn't hear a wrong word said against her, while

Fern, in her turn, had developed a real liking for Elspeth, the result being that she had gained that woman's confidence and extracted far more response from her than many who had known her all her days.

'Ach, to hell!' Elspeth's face was suddenly animated. 'Why no' go the whole hog? I'm never likely to get married again so just you do as you will wi' me, lass, and don't spare any o' it.'

With that she rolled down her stockings and kicked off her shoes in a burst of total abandon. One stout brogue landed amongst the hairy hair rollers in Mairi's trolley, the other whizzed across the room to attach itself by its heel to a hook on the wall where hung the protective shoulder capes. 'I could never have done that if I had tried!' gasped Elspeth, and all three women collapsed in a state of merriment that lasted all through the rest of the proceedings.

The pedicure and the massage made Elspeth feel wonderful, and when she beheld the finished results of her Silver Cloud hair-do she stared at herself in the mirror and thought she looked like a film star she had once seen in a Hollywood movie. Mairi had done a really good job; the soft, wavy style softened the angular lines of Elspeth's face, and the colour was perfect, even if one streak above her right eyebrow was more silvery than the rest. It didn't matter, she would be wearing a hat anyway – and what a hat! She could hardly wait to show it off! Elspeth hugged herself with glee and was unable to take her eyes off herself.

'Ach my.' Mairi, delighted with her efforts, combed and patted Elspeth's gleaming locks and enveloped them in enthusiastic jets of hairspray that made everyone cough. 'I canny rightly believe 'tis yourself, Elspeth, you look just a treat and I'm that proud o' myself I could burst.'

The next stage of the beautifying process was soon under way as Fern got to work on the rest of Elspeth's person, thoroughly cleansing her face, plucking her eyebrows, smoothing on subtle hints of rouge, powder, lipstick, eyeshadow, and a smidgen of mascara.

The transformation was complete; anyone who knew the staid, colourless creature that had been the Elspeth of old, wouldn't have believed it was the same woman if they had chanced to look in at that moment. She could hardly believe it herself. A metamorphosis had taken place. She was shining, that was the word best to describe her vastly changed appearance, yet Fern had done such a good job of making her up there was nothing that could be pointed out as being overly artificial.

Elspeth was overwhelmed and with tears in her eyes she hugged first Mairi, then Fern. 'Ach, my,' she said huskily, 'I don't know what I would have done without you both, and that's a fact. This morning I felt like Cinderella among the cinders, now I feel as good as the Queen herself and maybe a mite better, for I doubt if she could be as happy as I am wi' all my good friends around me.'

'My, my,' Mairi wiped her eyes with a corner of her apron, but the emotional moments soon passed when Fern produced a small bottle of champagne and ordered that a toast be drunk to the 'bonny bride-to-be' and could it be quick as time was marching on.

The bottle was soon depleted, the next customer was at the door, and Mairi, anxious that Elspeth's Silver Cloud should not be exposed until the big moment, swathed it in the concealing layers of a chiffon scarf which she tied in a firm knot under Elspeth's chin.

At the last moment she realised that that lady was still in her stocking soles and, giggling, she retrieved the errant brogues from their unusual resting places, and after shoving them firmly onto their owner's feet, she handed the whole bundle over to Fern.

Elspeth, her head reeling and hardly realising what was happening, was hurried away from the hairdressing premises and back to a house in which reposed a smug Nellie, all dressed up in a frock of green and white daisies adorned by a buttonhole of pink carnations, her salt-and-pepper hair rolled into a tight sausage round her head, her generous feet encased in a pair of navy, double 'E' fitting, shoes.

When she saw her future sister-in-law being smuggled into the bedroom, her head smothered in a diaphanous array of floral chiffon, the rest of her in everyday garb, her smug look blossomed into a triumphant grin and she settled back to await the first viewing of the apparition which would eventually emerge from the bedroom – not that it would be much, Elspeth's idea of fashion was as out-dated as was castor oil for constipation, and twice as nauseating!

Elspeth had chosen a lilac suit of fine linen material and a showy wide-brimmed hat trimmed with purple orchids. It looked wonderful perched on her Silver Cloud hair-do. The straight skirt of the suit was daringly short, the jacket figure hugging, but on her ultra-thin form the whole ensemble was elegant and utterly fashionable and there were gasps of surprise from the womenfolk as Lachlan's car stopped at the harbour and the bride-to-be stepped out in all her glory.

'Well, would you look at that now!' gasped Kate. 'I would never have believed our Elspeth could be so bonny. Her hair is a treat and the colour is nicer than anything I have ever seen. I wonder if Mairi could do that for me. The fly besom never mentioned she had anything like that in stock when I was in yesterday having my hair done.'

'Indeed, she is beautiful just,' agreed Jessie McKinnon, her bright beady eyes devouring Elspeth's apparel in one fell swoop. 'If I didny know better I might have thought she was a gentry lady in all that finery.'

'Ay, she has excelled herself,' nodded Aunt Grace Donaldson, now Mrs Bob Paterson, having quietly married that gentleman the week before. 'Of course, she always did have good features, all they needed was a wee bittie encouragement to bring them out.'

Behag, herself outstanding in a heather-hued tweed suit and a Robin Hood hat sporting a green and purple duck feather, had different opinions. 'Hmph!' she snorted. 'She has certainly done that wi' her legs! Imagine, at her age! Her skirt halfway up her backside! And the only lady she will ever be is the landlady who managed to hook her lodger! As for looking bonny, her face is plastered wi' make-up, anybody wi' half an eye could see that! I myself would look a different body altogether wi' all that powder and paint on my face.'

Kate looked her up and down consideringly. 'Ach no, Behag, make-up alone wouldny do that, it would have to be combined wi' a miracle. And why can you no' just admire Elspeth like the rest o' us? I know I've been critical o' her in the past but I aye give credit where it's due and today is no exception. The cailleach deserves a bit o' praise on her wedding day, even though she's a sour old prune on every other occasion.'

'No doubt that young woman o' McKenzie's had a hand in it.' Behag, determined to have the last word, glowered at Fern as she too alighted from Lachlan's car. 'She's been hanging on to Elspeth like a tick to a sheep for weeks now, and to my way o' thinking it's just no' healthy for a strange lass like that to make friends wi' a strange body like Elspeth. No good will come o' it, they'll end up doing one another a mischief, that girl is out for what she can get, she'll rob and cheat whoever she can and when she's had enough she'll just up and leave the island, as quickly and as slyly as she came.'

Elspeth was beyond caring about the opinions of beings like Behag. She had taken another 'wee drop o' the cratur' before leaving the house and her silvery head was floating on a cloud of pure delight mixed with unequal proportions of whisky and champagne.

Nothing mattered, not even Nellie with her critical eyes and Gus with his soup stains. She was in a small, private world of her own where all the good things in life seemed to be happening to her all at the one time. It didn't even matter that her new white court shoes were pinching a bit, everybody was watching her, everybody was admiring her, she was the envy of every other woman there and she knew it.

Fern was at her side, as she had been most of the morning, whispering words of encouragement and humour into her ear, telling her how good she looked, how well she was doing. The girl was a prop in more ways than one and placed a supporting hand under her arm when she stumbled on a cobblestone on her way to *The Arian*.

Everything at the harbour was light and bright and airy that glorious day in early summer. The ship itself looked proud and shining, decked out as it was with flags and bunting and little banners proclaiming messages of greeting and goodwill. Much of this was due to Grant, who had had a big hand in arranging everything. He was there at the foot of the gangway, smart and handsome in his captain's uniform, saluting Elspeth as she went by. The rest of the McKenzies were there too, even Fergus, because Mac had insisted on it.

'Let bygones be bygones,' he had said cheerily, 'for one day anyway,' he had added, with a mischievous twinkle in his eye.

Mac was waiting for Elspeth in the flower-bedecked main saloon, resplendent in his McIntosh kilt and black Prince Charlie jacket, his fine hairy legs encased in cream wool hose, his feet in black kilt shoes with laced-up fronts. White hair and beard brushed and shining, ruddy face glowing, manly chest bulging, he was the epitome of Scottish manhood and Elspeth, her head whirling with whisky and happiness, was so glad to see him that the tears sprung to her eyes and she could have hugged him there and then.

Mark James, in his robes, was tall and dark and wonderfully calm as he waited for the coughings and the rustlings to die down in the packed room. Mac glanced at Elspeth, she at him, he winked, she smothered a giggle, silence descended, and the ceremony began.

Mark James said his piece, Mac said his, it came to Elspeth's turn . . .

'Do you, Elspeth, take this man . . .?'

'Indeed I do,' she responded with alacrity, 'and the sooner the better.'

'Just listen to that,' Nellie hissed into one of Behag's long lugs, 'she canny wait to get her clooks into my poor brother.'

'Shameless,' Behag declared succinctly. 'Ever since Mac went to lodge wi' her she's behaved like a Jezebel and doesny care who knows it.'

'. . . to be your lawful wedded husband,' the minister continued in his deep, unruffled voice.

'Have I no' already said so?' Elspeth returned flippantly.

Despite these little interchanges the rest of the ceremony went smoothly and before long Mac and Elspeth were pronounced man and wife. They kissed and cuddled one another before the gathering descended on them to shake their hands and kiss them all over again. Mac's back was thumped, the womenfolk smiled tightly at the new Mrs McIntosh and said her hair was lovely.

Phebie, the picture of rosy womanhood in a pink floral dress with a matching hat, took her old housekeeper into her arms and congratulated her profusely, delighted on two counts, one for Elspeth, the other for herself and the freedom she might have in her own kitchen now that Elspeth would be kept doubly busy in hers.

Elspeth wept, gazing fondly at Lachlan and at Niall and his children; she glowered at Fergus, she grimaced at Shona, and then her eyes came to rest on Cousin Gus. Gus was just recovering from a dose of gastric flu, 'And no wonder, wi' all the germs he breeds in his house,' opined Nellie. He was pale and rather thin but, if one didn't look too closely, surprisingly smart looking in a somewhat moth-eaten kilt and lovat green jacket which bore a few faint stains of indistinct origin.

'I gave myself a good steep in the sink, Elspeth,' he hazarded, thinking maybe he had better explain that fact to her in case she should order him home.

In the sink! Elspeth's eyes bulged. It didn't bear thinking about. And he was proud of it! As if the sink was a fit place in which to scrub any portion of the adult human anatomy! And how had he fitted into it anyway! Only children and dogs ever got bathed in a sink. She had done so herself when she had been young ... at her mother's instigation, of course ...

Her face reddened, and she turned away. As far as she could see, Mac was the only decent surviving member of his family, and it was as well that she had rescued him before he had become too set in his ways.

'Elspeth! Oh, I do love your outfit!' Prunella Sweet, the wife of a retired lawyer from Portvoynachan, had joined the party and was trumpeting her approval all over Elspeth. 'You did say anyone could come and as I was passing . . .'

Prunella Sweet was dressed for a wedding; one did not casually walk about Rhanna in a veiled hat and smart navy suit. Elspeth made no comment however, instead she smiled sweetly at the ex-lawyer's wife, bade her welcome, and forgot all about Cousin Gus as Todd and Graeme struck up on the pipes.

The party had begun with a vengeance, the bar had never been busier, and Elspeth graciously accepted a brimming glass of champagne from Mac's very own husbandly hand.

Chapter Nineteen

Dodie appeared halfway through the reception, looking very respectable in a soft hat and clean raincoat and smelling profusely of apple blossom. This was all thanks to Mairi, who had made him soak in bath fragrance before scrubbing him with a long handled brush which had made him yell in protest. After that she had trimmed his baby fine hair and supervised his choice of clothing before shutting up shop for the rest of the day in order to attend the wedding herself.

Dodie, always uncomfortable in any crowd, was inclined to slink about on the perimeter in the hope that he wouldn't be noticed, but on this occasion he made straight for Mac and handed him an untidily wrapped parcel which soon proved to be a delicate little pastel painting of a rather squinty ship with red sails gliding along on a blue and peaceful sea.

'By God, Dodie, it's the nicest present I ever had!' cried Mac enthusiastically. 'Whenever I look at it I will think I'm drunk even when I'm sober and all without spending one penny on "the cratur".'

Dodie blinked, unsure of whether he was receiving a compliment or an insult. He looked ready to cry, his big, callused hands went up to his eyes, and Mac hastily threw his arm round the old man's bent shoulders.

'Ach, Dodie, you're a sensitive soul to be sure. I love this picture, it will remind me o' happy days sailing the high seas and I'm going to hang it opposite my bed so that I can look at it every morning when I wake up. Cheer up now, this is a wedding, no' a funeral, so just you come over to the bar wi' me and let me be getting you a dram.'

Dodie wasn't used to strong drink, he didn't like the taste nor the smell of it, but he enjoyed the feeling it gave him of being on top of a buoyant happy world and Mac was right, this was a wedding, not a funeral, even though a lesser man than Mac, taking on El-speth, might have chosen to think otherwise.

Dodie consumed not one, but several drams. By that time he was feeling wonderful and capable of anything, even brave enough to seek out Fern who was having a breather on the deck.

'*Tha breeah*!' gabbled Dodie, utterly fascinated by this young creature in her white floaty dress and tiny garlands of wildflowers braided into her blue-black tresses.

'*Tha breeah*, Dodie,' she greeted him kindly. 'It is indeed a marvellous day and I hope you're enjoying it as much as I am.'

'I have another wee present for you,' he told her, before his courage deserted him. Rummaging in the recesses of his coat he proudly brought forth an oblong piece of wood, painstakingly cleaned and var-nished and bearing the inscription *Sea Witch*.

Dodie was always combing the beach and finding small treasures which he could take home. When he had lived in his tiny cottage in the hills it had been almost entirely furnished with fishboxes and bits of driftwood tacked together, but when he had moved into Croft Beag on the edge of the village, Mairi had soon changed all that.

'You'll be getting a lot more visitors now, Dodie,' she had told him, 'and you canny have folk sitting about on smelly fishboxes and planks wi' nails jagging their backsides.'

Thereafter Mairi had raked the 'For Sale' columns of the *Rhanna Roundabout*, the local rag printed and published monthly by two brothers from a back room in their cluttered crofthouse in Portvoynachan. The *Rhanna Roundabout* was a recent innovation and 'The Brothers Haig' as they were collectively known, were astounded by its runaway success. Gossip, news items, births, deaths, anything and everything, went into the paper, even, astoundingly, a lonely hearts section, and everybody eagerly turned to it for its comforting sustenance the minute it hit the post office counters.

Mairi had soon furnished Dodie's house to a comfortable if haphazard standard and before long Dodie had no more need to rummage the shores for his bits and pieces of home-made furniture.

Beachcombing was in his blood, however, and when Fern beheld the piece of wood in his hand and asked where he had got it he beamed and replied promptly, 'In the water, lots o' things floating on the edge o' the water. It was attached to a plank o' wood but I took it home and sawed it off and rubbed it wi' a wee bit sandpaper before I polished it. Now it's yours, all for you, nice it will look hanging up on your wall.'

So saying he thrust the thing at her and stood back, hands folded over his stomach, waiting for her approval.

Fern's reaction to all of this was startling. Her eyes had grown enormous in a face that had turned white; then she began backing away from him in horror. 'What – what else did you find, Dodie?' she stammered through pale lips. 'You know you said you would tell me if you came across anything . . . unusual.'

Dodie didn't answer; a veiled expression had crept into his dreamy eyes, he averted his head and wouldn't look at her.

'Take it back, Dodie, I don't want it,' she told him breathlessly. 'Take it home and burn it.' Gripping the cuff of his coat she gazed up at him beseechingly. 'Please, Dodie, if you care at all for me you will do as I ask of you. It's bad luck, just look at the name it has on it, you know how afraid you are of sea hags and witches and this piece of wood came from the sea – sent by one of those horrible creatures you and Canty Tam told me about.'

Dodie's grasp of both reading and writing was of a restricted nature and he had merely a vague idea of what was written on the piece of wood. He only knew how nice it looked, how hard he had worked to make it that way, and this rejection of it was more than he could bear. He stumbled away, his hands going frequently to his face and nose to scrub away froths of mucus mixed with the tears that were blinding him.

But when he got home he didn't burn the precious nameplate. He had put too much of his loving labour into it to even think of destroying it and carefully he placed it in his bedside drawer, next to a waterproof wallet containing a bundle of papers which he had fished out of the water that memorable day with Hector at the Bay of the Caves. The wallet, together with a bulky little drawstring bag, had attached itself to one of Hector's little marker buoys and Hector had been so preoccupied staring into the caves he hadn't noticed Dodie stowing his find into one of his ample pockets.

Dodie paused for a minute, remembering that day, then he extracted something from the packet to gaze at it with reverence. 'Lovely photy,' he murmured, and raising one large finger he touched the spot on his cheek that Fern had honoured with her lips when he had stopped her in Glen Fallan to give her the stone he had painted.

He gazed again at the picture. The face that looked out at him was that of Fern Lee, serious and unsmiling – not at all like the real, live, young woman that he knew – the one that he had privately christened Kalak Dubh, which was the Gaelic for Dark Maiden.

There were other items in the wallet, mostly documents with a lot of writing on them, none of them holding any interest for Dodie since he couldn't understand much of what they said. There was also another picture, that of a ruggedly good-looking young man with crisp dark hair, snapping black eyes and a wide, cruel, unsmiling mouth.

Dodie hardly gave him a second glance. It was Kalak Dubh he loved to look at, only Kalak Dubh who held his interest, and as he stood there gazing at her photograph a sob caught in his throat as he wondered what he had done to make her behave so strangely in rejecting the gift he had prepared for her with such tender devotion. Yet he was still enchanted by her and he felt he had every right to keep some of her things. When first she had come to Rhanna she had spoken to him a lot and had asked him to keep an eye open for any unusual items he might find on the shore. But to his way of thinking there was nothing extraordinary about a few papers and a couple of photos. Besides it was too late now, he had held on to them for too long; Clodhopper was soon due to pay one of his visits, and Dodie daren't risk him finding out about the wallet. It would only get him into trouble, Kalak Dubh would be involved as well, and Dodie couldn't bear the thought of that.

He stood there for a long time, the picture of Fern Lee held gently in his big callused fist, his mind roving hither and thither, his breath catching in his throat as he suddenly remembered something.

She hadn't wanted the piece of wood, but she would want one of the other things he had found when he had been with Hector at Camus nan Uamh. Something nice and shiny, oh, ay, Kalak Dubh would like that alright, she was such a sparkly lady herself.

It would all depend on Hector the Boat. He had showed no inclination to go back again to Camus nan Uamh and that was where Dodie had to go if he was to get the things he wanted for Kalak Dubh. Somehow he had to try and persuade Hector to take him back to that lonely wild place with the cliffs and the caves all around, even though Hector had said something about being afraid of a hobgoblin that lived there.

Dodie didn't know what a hobgoblin was, it sounded a bit scary, but he would do anything, anything at all, if it meant pleasing the dark-haired maiden who looked at him from the picture he held.

'Nice and shiny.' Dodie whispered the words to the empty room and felt much, much better.

Elspeth was having an ecstatic time; never before on Rhanna had anyone held their wedding reception aboard a ship and the novelty of it was fully appreciated by one and all, the credit for it given wholeheartedly to both herself and Mac. Not only that, everybody had congratulated her on her appearance, even the menfolk had been most complimentary, with an inebriated Jim Jim going as far as to wink at her and remind her slyly of far off days when youthful romps in the haysheds had been part and parcel of growing up.

'Ay, those were the days, Jim Jim,' Elspeth nodded reminiscently, 'too bad we all had to grow older and wiser and lose all those nice wee innocent ways we had as bairns finding out about life.'

'Ay, ay, but no' always as innocent as you make out, Elspeth,' Jim Jim pursued wickedly. 'I mind that time you and me . . .'

His voice droned on but Elspeth was no longer listening. Her attention had been diverted to the buffet table where sat Cousin Gus with several of his dreadful cronies. Most of them were deaf and they were talking in loud voices, criticising everything and everybody, oblivious to all but themselves, blowing obnoxious billows of pipe smoke all over the food, doing rude things with their noses and other parts of their anatomy, in Gus's case picking crumbs from his beard and absently fidgeting with himself in a most alarming fashion under cover of his rather bald sporran.

Elspeth went hot and cold but she told herself to keep calm; as long as Gus confined himself to the table all might be well, the other guests were too busy enjoying themselves to bother with a bunch of old men gossiping away amongst themselves.

Then Gus did a terrible thing. Right there in front of everybody he poured his tea into his saucer and slurped it up with rude enjoyment, and that was only the beginning. In the course of the next half hour he removed his teeth from his mouth, wrapped them up carefully in a floral napkin, and stuck them into the top pocket of his jacket, after which he got to his feet to perform a creaky Highland Fling, his kilt flying about his knobbly knees, breaking wind as he fleered around, clearing the floor as effectively as if it had been announced that he was suffering from a dose of the plague.

'I've never been so black affronted!' Elspeth hissed at Mac, whose ears had turned red with embarrassment at the sight of his own flesh and blood performing so rudely in public. It was bad enough in the privacy of his own home, but that he should do so on this day of all days, when there were Elspeth's feelings to consider, was practically beyond bearing.

Mac, however, was a man who had seen and endured many unusual things in the course of his maritime career. He had his own way of dealing with such matters and had no desire to create a scene in front of the gathering, especially with the minister and the doctor present and that strange garrulous female, Mrs Prunella Sweet, who was renowned for her loose tongue.

With all that in mind he laid a placating hand on his new wife's arm and said quietly, 'Ach, come on now, lass, don't fash yourself, everyone knows what Gus is like and later on you'll look back on all this and wet your breeks laughing.'

Elspeth wasn't so sure, 'It's bad enough doing these sort o' things here but he's supposed to be coming wi' us to Oban for the family reception and the hotel people will think we are just a rough bunch o' heathens from the islands.'

Mac looked at Cousin Gus. The old man had re-inserted his dentures in order to sample some cold meats from the buffet table. He was humming and hawing and making derogatory comments about a piece of roast venison he was having difficulty chewing. He seemed hell bent on making trouble of one sort or another and Mac, with a gleam in his eye, went to seek out Tam to have a quiet word in his ear.

Tam grinned, he nodded, and in his turn sought the services of Todd whose craggy face broke into a wide grin as he listened to what was being said to him. Without ado, both men intercepted Cousin Gus and, escorting him over to the bar, they challenged him to drink dram for dram with them.

Fingal, Erchy, Ranald, and quite a few others, weren't slow to join in the fun and all of them were legless by the time the boat was ready to leave the harbour.

Only Tam and Todd remained comparatively sober; they had made a promise to Mac and somehow they were able to keep it. Arranging themselves on either side of Gus, whose legs had crumpled under him, they took him home and put him to bed where he remained for the next few hours to snore off his excesses, while Mac and Elspeth sailed happily over the sea to Oban, to enjoy the remainder of their wedding with chosen kith and kin who had travelled from all the airts to participate in the second reception of that memorable day.

The very next morning Jim Jim presented himself in Doctor Megan's surgery where he prevaricated for fully ten minutes before he muttered bashfully, 'It is my water, doctor, it has a terrible head on it so it has, and I wouldny have come only Isabel made me, and you know what Isabel's like when she sets her mind to something.'

Megan sat back in her chair and studied the old man. She had treated him for years for his weak bladder, though it was only under great duress that he ever came to see her personally, preferring to send his wife to collect any medication that had been prescribed for him. He must therefore have a good reason for being there that morning and Megan wasn't slow to notice how anxious was his demeanour as he twisted his cap round and round in his rheumy hands.

'A head, Jim Jim?' Megan began encouragingly. 'On your water?'

The old man squirmed. 'Ay. Like the froth you get on a good pint o' Bull Bull's best beer.'

Megan tried hard to keep a straight face, no easy matter when faced with some of the more whimsical modes of speech used by various islanders.

'When did you first notice this, Jim Jim?' she managed to ask seriously.

'This morning, when I had to rise to use my chanty – I mean my chamber pot, doctor. I got a terrible fright just. I was drinking a wee bittie more than usual yesterday, it being Mac's wedding, and though I usually have to get up in the night it's never as much as that.'

He stopped fidgeting, his eyes growing wide at the memory of his brimming chamber pot. 'It just kept on and on, and the froth kept building up, mixed wi' funny looking white patches floating on the top. Before I knew what was happening the whole jing bang o' it overflowed onto the floor and of course Isabel got up to see what all the fuss was about. When she saw the head on that water o' mine she near died and nagged away at me till I said I would come here to see you.'

Megan was nonplussed for a moment till she remembered the last part of the reception when it seemed nearly half of the island hadn't been able to stand up straight.

'Did anyone see you home yesterday, Jim Jim?'

'Ay, now that you ask, doctor, Tam and Todd took Gus McIntosh home to his house, then they came back for me, seeing as how I was just no' at myself and had a wee bittie trouble putting one leg in front o' the other.'

'Aha, Tam and Todd . . .' Megan looked thoughtful. From her window she had just espied those very same gentlemen and turning to her patient she said urgently, 'Hurry, Jim, Jim, up on the couch with you, lie still, close your eyes, try to look half dead and don't ask questions. Just trust me and do as I ask.'

A startled Jim Jim found himself being heaved onto the couch and ordered to remain silent, and then Megan, much to the astonishment of her waiting patients, dashed past them in the hall to wrench open the back door and yell on Tam and Todd to come in for a minute.

They approached slowly and warily, tripping over a dozen feet before entering the surgery to behold Jim Jim lying pale and supine on the couch. They gulped, they glanced at one another sheepishly; as one they whipped off their caps and spun them round and round in their fingers in a most agitated manner. Like a couple of schoolboys on the mat they stood in front of the big desk, heads bowed, feet shuffling, the epitome of meek and mild manhood.

'It's Jim Jim,' Megan wasted no time. 'He indulged himself at the wedding yesterday and now believes there is something drastically wrong with his kidneys. He was up all night worrying about it and came to me in a dreadful state. At his age a fright can be danger-ous, as I'm sure you both know.' She glanced from one crimson face to the other, 'Could either of you throw some light on the matter? Perhaps you know of someone else with the same symptoms as Jim Jim? Unusual manifestations such as frothy urine? Much as you might get on a pint of Bull Bull's best beer, for instance?'

'Ach, doctor!' Todd, looking ready to burst, could hold himself back no longer. 'It was us! It was only a

258

joke! We put bakin' sody in Jim Jim's chanty when we helped him home yesterday. I thought at the time that a whole tin was too much and if Mollie ever finds out I stole it she'll kill me and throw me out the house!'

'BAKIN' SODY!' screeched Jim Jim, getting down from the couch with rage-propelled agility. *'Bakin' sody*! A whole tin! Mollie's no' the only one who will get you and kill you! And I thought you were my friends! All my life I thought you were my friends, and this is how you treat me . . .' He came to a full and sudden stop. 'Bakin' sody,' he repeated meditatively, and then he began laughing, his hands clutching his stomach, his head thrown back, exposing his tonsils, his old whiskered face a picture of comical delight.

Tam and Todd stared at him anxiously, then when they had ascertained that he wasn't in the throes of some sort of seizure, they joined in his merriment, screeching and guffawing, in between repeating snatches of Megan's afore-mentioned interrogation, while she, thinking it was the funniest episode to have happened in her surgery since taking over the practice, added her peals of laughter to theirs till the whole place rang with mirthful sounds.

One or two of the patients in the hall glanced at one another meaningfully and shook their heads.

'It's no' as if we're waiting here for the good of our health,' Peggy McAlastair, sister of Hector the Boat, spoke mournfully.

'Ay, you're right there, Peggy,' nodded Winnie Nells, an ancient old crone of a creature who also happened to be Canty Tam's gloom-ridden mother.

'I've been sitting here for the last half hour and my feets are freezing in the draught from that door. I feel worse than I did before I came and certainly no better for hearing our own doctor shrieking her head off in that den o' hooligans in there.'

Isabel, awaiting the emergence of her so-called hooligan husband, fairly bristled with indignation at this description of him, and turning to the cheerless pair she informed them that laughter was, after all, the best medicine, and if they were lucky enough to gain admittance to the den of ruffians, the doctor might prescribe some for them too!

Chapter Twenty

The weather remained good that summer on Rhanna. June slipped by in a balmy haze of warm days and honey-pink sunsets, when the horizon never grew fully dark and little islands seemed to float in an eternal glow of golden light that painted fiery banners on the sea and daubed wondrous hues of flaming red into the deep purples of the furthest reaches of the star spangled sky. Great moons waxed and waned and it seemed as if darkness would never again fall on the land; the air was perpetually drenched with the warm sweet scents of summer; wildflowers starred the moors; the green of the machair became hidden in a deluge of yellow buttercups; fields of white daisies shimmered like blankets of snow; the broom was golden on the hill, vying with the white flowers of rowans and elders. And in the woods the bluebells carpeted the leafy earth, the heady sweet fragrance of them wafting out of the trees to meet the evocative smell of the summer hayfields falling to the reapers.

Up on the normally deserted moors the islanders were out in full force, cutting the peats for winter fires, frequently stopping to mop their faces and swipe biting insects from their bare, sunburned limbs. They told one another that the heat was 'terrible just' and it was a good thing that it wasn't always like this or they would never get any work done, but just the same they revelled in the feel of the sun on their backs and the menfolk had ample excuse to quench their thirst in the Portcull Hotel when the day's labour was done.

There was always something to look forward to, some small event to be savoured, be it a birth, or a christening, or simply the latest edition of the *Rhanna Roundabout* to devour in one gulp if there was nothing much happening elsewhere.

The advent of the magazine containing Lachlan's article was a different matter entirely. It had been long awaited, not only by the McLachlans themselves, but by every interested member of the island's population, agog to know what he had written about them.

Here was something different, a departure from the norm that some people found rather worrying, since it would, no doubt, involve most of them personally. They had all been Lachlan's patients at some time or another in their lives and it was with some trepidation that they anticipated this particular issue of what was normally an extremely popular publication.

What, they asked one another, had he written about? *Who* had he written about? Which of them would be first to come into the limelight? It had been hinted that there might be more of the same, month by month, which meant that one by one, they would come under public scrutiny, whether they liked it or no.

Those that definitely didn't were not slow to air their opinions on the morning the magazine appeared on the

post office counter, an event that attracted an aston-
ishingly sparse number of people to the premises, for
the simple reason that the more shy members of the
community had taken the precaution of ordering their
copies some weeks in advance. One or two were bold
enough to appear in person, pretending to want something else; others, like Behag, for instance, made no
bones about her reasons for being there.

'He'll be exposing our private parts for all the world
to see,' she sniffed with tight-lipped disapproval. 'In
my view, anything that goes on between a doctor and
a patient should be sacrosanct forever more. Folks
these days get away wi' far too much and I for one
have no intention o' putting up wi' it.'

'Och no, it isn't like that at all,' mumbled Ranald,
nose deep in the controversial pages. Then he looked
up and his eyes gleamed. 'Ay, well, you're maybe
right at that, Behag, just listen to this:

'One of my most memorable patients was Miss Behag
Beag, the then postmistress of the village, who came to
me seeking a cure for constipation. Well, I tried everything to get her moving, pills, powders, potions of every
description. In the end I had to resort to the tubes and
never have I had to treat a more difficult patient. There
she lay, squealing like a pig from both ends, making
enough noise to attract the entire village to the surgery
door, all of them believing that a murder was in progress . . .'

'Here, let me see that!' A purple-faced Behag
snatched the paper from Ranald's hand and began

furiously to read, her lips moving as she devoured the words, head wobbling alarmingly on her thin shoulders.

'That's quite enough o' that, Ranald McTavish,' Totie intervened. 'Lachlan has used different names throughout the article, as fine you know, and he's written it in such a way that it's difficult even to tell which island he's talking about. It's a fair treat to read and I only hope it won't be the last o' it's kind we'll be seeing.'

A shamefaced Ranald made to slink from the shop till Totie stayed him with a sharp order. 'Not so fast, you mean bodach. Don't think I didn't see you devouring that magazine from cover to cover! It has your dirty fingerprints on it so just you be putting your money on the counter like everyone else, my lad.'

'But I only read the bit wi' the article in it,' Ranald protested vehemently, shocked at the idea of having to pay for that privilege. 'It's no' the sort o' paper I read in the normal way o' things, and besides. I'd be doing somebody else out of one if I had to buy it.'

For answer Totie held out her hand and said grimly, 'Money, Ranald McTavish, and you're lucky you're getting off so lightly. You dirtied the one underneath wi' those tarry fingers o' yours and should really be paying for two.'

At that opportune moment, Phebie and Ruth came bursting into the shop together, giving Ranald the chance to beat a hasty retreat outside without parting with one penny.

'Quick!' panted Phebie. 'Before they all go. I want six copies to send to my relatives. Lachy only got one complimentary edition and I'll never hear the end o' it if Aunt Minnie doesn't get hers as promised.'

'And I want four,' added Ruth, 'I wrote and told Rachel about it and she's desperate to get her hands on it. Jon's mother is dying to read it too, she misses the island and loves to read anything to do wi' it. She can hardly wait each month for her copy of the *Rhanna Roundabout* and if it's a day late she isn't slow to let me know.'

'Ah, yes, big Mamma Jodl,' Totie nodded as she busily jotted Ranald's name into the I.O.U. section of her memo pad. 'Do you think she'll ever come back to Rhanna?'

'Oh ay, most definitely, it seems she's never enjoyed herself as much as she did last year when Rachel had her baby.'

Totie's eyes twinkled. 'I don't think I'd be far wrong in thinking she has her sights set on Rab McKinnon. They all had a marvellous time playing cards in Aggie's house and if I'm minding right, Rab used to call for Mamma in his tractor and nearly scared the shat out o' her driving her along the Burg road.'

'She's a character alright,' laughed Phebie. 'A formidable one at that. She came to our door once asking to see the doctor and when I told her he was retired she just about bit my head off and stomped away in high dudgeon, muttering something about us all being heathens who had never heard of civilised things like medicine.'

Totie wasn't listening, she was craning her head in order to get a better view through her cluttered window. 'Is that Clodhopper I see? No doubt snooping around looking for trouble. I think it might be a good idea to warn some o' the menfolk that he's here as I know fine that one or two o' the rascals have been sticking beer labels on their vehicle windows in place o' their expired licences.'

Ruth turned red. Her very own husband, Lorn, was one of the rascals, since, in his opinion, it just wasn't worth forking out money for road tax when the island highways and byways left so much to be desired.

Rhanna, in common with other Hebridean islands, was exempt from the M.O.T. test that was compulsory on the mainland, just as long as the vehicles remained on the island. Many of the inhabitants believed that they should be exempt from road tax also, and delayed buying a licence, with the result that a visit from Clodhopper always caused a stir as everyone scrambled to lock up their various modes of transport in sheds and barns.

Ruth hurried away on her warning mission. So did several other people, because Clodhopper had indeed come to the island to sniff out the licence dodgers.

His appearance in the village caused a very strange reaction in Fern, who was chatting to Todd the Shod as he polished his Rolls-Royce outside the smiddy door.

Todd had won the car in a competition many years ago, but despite its age it was in wonderful condition, the pride and joy of its owner, even though it hadn't been run for some time owing to the fact that it needed some drastic work done on the engine.

Todd therefore had no need of a licence of any sort

266

at that moment in time and the sight of Clodhopper's bulky figure approaching his gate instilled no pangs of conscience in him whatsoever.

Not so Fern; grabbing Todd's arm she said urgently, 'Would you be an awful good friend and tell him I'm your niece? Quick now, he's coming this way, and he's got a very suspicious look on that funny big face of his, as if he's looking for trouble and thinks maybe he'll be finding it sooner than he thinks.'

'Ach, he always looks like that,' said Todd in some bewilderment. Nevertheless, when Clodhopper ambled to a halt at his gate, he beamed in his friendly way and said affably, 'Well now, if it isn't Constable McDuff. You've picked a fine day indeed to be visiting the island.'

'Ay, but I'm no' here for the pleasure o' it,' Clodhopper said sourly, gazing contemplatively at Fern as he spoke.

'This is my niece,' Todd made the introduction hastily.

'Very nice too,' the policeman eyed Fern's suntanned limbs appreciatively. 'I didn't know you had a niece like that.'

'Oh ay, I've had her for a while,' Todd blurted in confusion.

'I see, well, if I were you I'd lock her up out o' harm's way. The spiteful cailleachs here might no' trust their menfolk wi' a lass who looks like that and would maybe no' think twice about doing her an injury, eh? Eh?'

Clodhopper had a habit of ending his sentences in this enquiring way. He was also wont to laugh at his

267

own wit and this he did now, showing a row of shovel-like teeth in the process, glancing slyly at Fern to ascertain that she had absorbed the full impact of his words.

Fern gritted her teeth and smiled and was relieved when the policeman's attention turned once more to Todd.

'She is still no' working then,' he stated, gazing suspiciously at the Rolls Royce as he spoke.

'No, no, I just keep her looking good till I can gather enough money to have her fixed. It would take a bit o' beer money to get her going again.' Todd blinked, he had said the wrong thing, since any mention of any alcoholic beverage was enough to set Clodhopper on the road to the Portcull Hotel to see if he might be lucky enough to catch a stray drunk or two.

'Well, I'll be getting along,' the policeman glanced at his watch. 'It is nearly lunchtime and I hear that the wife o' the hotelier makes a very tasty steak and kidney pie.'

Touching his cap to Fern he went on his way, leaving Todd to wipe his sweating face and say aggrievedly to Fern, 'What for did you make me say all that about you being my niece? I'm no' a good liar at the best o' times and am next to useless wi' the likes o' big McDuff.'

'Och, come on now, don't be angry.' She smiled up at him and took his arm. 'It was only to save any awkward questions and you know you said you would all look after me.'

Todd immediately melted. 'Oh well, put like that I suppose it did no harm.'

'To be sure it did nothing but good, and surely to goodness you wouldn't mind having a niece like me?'

'I could think o' better uses,' Todd replied with a smirk that deepened to a big grin when she reached up and kissed him on one ruddy red cheek.

Fern took her leave of Todd, her face adopting a brooding expression as she made her way out of the village. The incident with the policeman had upset her more than anyone would ever know, and it was instinct more than anything else that turned her steps in the direction of the lonely shores she had wandered so often since the fates had first brought her to Rhanna.

Chapter Twenty-one

Fern breathed a sigh of relief when Clodhopper took himself off the island after a fruitless hunt for drunks and law-breakers of one sort or another.

'Don't worry about him, lass,' Tina told her reassuringly. 'His visits out here are few and far between and it will be a while before he sets his big feets on Rhanna again.'

Everything else was going well for Fern; she had fitted in well with the general island scene and had a knack of making friends with almost everyone she met.

Elspeth openly adored her and had begun to look upon her as the daughter she had never had, while Kirsteen treated her as an equal and included her in as many family activities as possible. But despite her acceptance of the girl she had once or twice commented to Fergus on the more mysterious aspects of her life and had wondered why she refused to talk in detail about her past.

'Also,' Kirsteen had gone on, 'she's not nearly as happy or as settled as she would have us believe. I've noticed a brooding look on her face when she thinks no one is watching, she gets restless and seems to spend a lot o' time wandering about on the shore in a distracted sort o' way, as if she keeps expecting to find something – or somebody – if she searches hard enough. And I find it strange that she rarely mentions this man that she came here to get away from.'

'Ach, she's probably trying hard to forget about him, that's maybe why she finds it so hard to settle. Besides, she's young, she's bound to get fed up being cooped up here wi' us all the time.' Fergus gave a nonchalant shrug as he spoke, though privately he agreed with Kirsteen and wished that he too could discover more about their young guest.

'I don't think she would ever get fed up with you, Fergie, she looks up to you as if you were a god. I've seen the way her eyes light up whenever you appear.'

'I'm just a father figure to her,' Fergus had answered evasively. 'She's been through a lot and I suppose it's only natural for her to want someone to lean on. She'll soon grow out o' it when she's better able to stand on her own two feet.'

These were uncomfortable moments for Fergus. With the benefit of hindsight he knew now how foolish he'd been to jeopardise his marriage because of the insecurity he'd felt at Kirsteen's absence. Even so, he couldn't forget the dark and dangerous desire he'd felt for Fern, but now that he could stand back from her without being so emotionally involved he was able to get everything into a better perspective, which gave him the chance to get to know her as a person, rather than the exciting young temptress that she had been to him in the beginning.

That wasn't to say that he didn't remain fascinated by her dark wild beauty, her vivacity, her radiance that spread itself like a shining lamp into every dark corner. His infatuation for her was over, though he couldn't help being very aware of her whenever they were alone together.

In her turn she enjoyed provoking him in subtle little ways, with her eyes, and with the sensuous sway of her smoothly tanned limbs, but ever since the return of Kirsteen she had ceased to flirt openly with him and he knew it was because she had a genuine liking and respect for the older woman.

They obviously appreciated one another's company and even managed to remain amicable when they were working together in the kitchen, taking turns to make the meals, swopping recipes, generally enjoying a hundred and one small, shared experiences.

Shona was among the few who managed to remain impervious to Fern's charms, in spite of pressure from Kirsteen to 'come down off her high horse', and some cutting remarks from her father, to the effect that she was being childish and why couldn't she accept Fern like everyone else and take her at face value.

'I am not everyone else!' Shona had retaliated furiously, 'I just know instinctively that she's putting on an act and one day you'll find out I'm right in what I say. You're just soft on her because she's young and attractive and makes you feel twenty again. Don't think I haven't noticed you ogling away at her. All she has to do is bat her eyes and wiggle her bum to make you behave like a little puppy dog waiting for crumbs. Thank God Kirsteen is home, she probably saved you from making a fool o' yourself before it was too late!'

The truth of this was too much for Fergus. He positively bristled with rage at his daughter. One word led to another, which ended in Shona flouncing away and saying she wouldn't be back till he came to his senses.

To make matters worse, nobody else in the family was inclined anymore to agree with her opinions. Initially Ruth had been wary of Fern but now tended to hang on to every word she had to say; Lorn had never had any strong feelings on the matter and refused to take sides with anyone; while Fiona was sympathetic to her sister-in-law's feelings but was too busy with the novelty of discovering that another baby was on the way to get fully involved in much else.

Grant remained as curious and as suspicious of Fern's motives as his sister, though his attitude had weakened once his mother had arrived back on the scene, his view being that Fern would be a fool to try doing anything that might jeopardise her position in the Laigmhor household.

Niall too was not impressed by his wife's views regarding Fern. He listened to her holding forth, then he called her Caillich Ruadh, which meant Red Witch, and told her she was too stubborn for her own good, all of which only served to make her fly into one of her dreaded red-haired tempers and tell him that he was getting complacent in his dotage and that it was high time he got off his backside and took stock of what was going on around him.

Fern, meanwhile, was making some money for herself by helping out with summer work at neighbouring farms, over and above the odd jobs she did at Laig-mhor.

'She must be saving up for something,' decided Kate. 'She works hard and must be earning a bob or two yet she never seems to spend any o' it on herself.'

'She bought herself some things from Elspeth's catalogue,' volunteered Tina knowingly. 'I myself was in the house when the stuff came and it was beautiful just, ethnic skirts and blouses that suited her a treat when she tried them on. I wish I had a figure like hers so that I could wear things like that,' she ended sadly.

'Well, she is certainly earning her keep at Laigmhor now,' Mollie said approvingly.

'She is doing nothing o' the sort,' Behag put in disapprovingly, 'I hear tell she doesn't part wi' a penny for her bed and board. Any other decent body would be only too glad to work for nothing with a free roof over their heads and all the food they want to fill their belly.'

'Ay, she must be saving for something,' Kate affirmed thoughtfully. 'As far as I can see she is by no means a spendthrift yet she is making money hand over fist. Only the other day she took a pound from old Sorcha for going her messages.'

'Terrible just, an old body like that,' Mollie had changed her mind about Fern. 'Anybody else would give Sorcha a pound to buy a wee treat for herself.'

'Ach, but she's a nice lass,' Kate's sudden turnabout brought forth willing nods of agreement, as, in spite of their grumbles about her, nearly all of them were fascinated by Fern and loved any opportunity to meet her.

'And she's young,' nodded Mollie indulgently. 'She's kind in other ways and helped me up the brae wi' my shopping bag only yesterday.'

'It's only natural she should want some money of her own to do with as she likes,' Tina added. 'It's her business what she does wi' it and she seems an honest enough lass. I myself enjoy blethering wi' her, she's got such a sunny nature and she's so bonny too. I just canny help touching that wonderful hair o' hers whenever I get the chance.'

Absently she patted her own hair and down it descended to land round her ears in wispy loops. With a sigh she took her leave of Kate's house, wishing with all her heart that she had been born beautiful.

Whatever anybody else might think of Fern, the McKenzie and the McLachlan children continued to worship her, and in her free time she took them on picnics and other outings, splashing with them in the sea, running with them through the wildflowers on the moors.

Shona didn't take kindly to the idea of her little daughter going off like this with the woman she regarded as an interloper, but hers was just a lone voice in the wilderness.

'I want to go with Aunt Fern!' Ellie Dawn had wailed. 'Lorna is allowed to go so why can't I!'

'Och, let the bairn have her way,' Niall had intervened. 'It canny do any harm, Fern took good care o' Ellie Dawn when she was biding at Laigmhor and it seems unfair to forbid it when Ruth is letting Lorna go. They'll enjoy themselves together.'

So once again Shona had to back down off her high horse, which didn't improve her mood towards Fern in the least. Rather it made her more determined than ever not to allow herself to falter from the stance she had taken, even if nobody else was willing to support her in her lone battle to find out the truth. She was, after all, McKenzie's daughter, and as such she would never let go till she had proved herself to be right.

As for Fern, she had too much else on her mind to worry about the moods and swings of one mule-headed woman. She was living in a temporary world of safety and she knew it, her recent encounter with Clodhopper having brought that home to her very effectively, and as the days of summer moved on something else happened to jolt her out of the illusion of security she had known since coming to Rhanna.

She was busy in the kitchen when a knock came to the door and she was humming a catchy little tune when she went to see who was there.

Stink the Tink stood on the step, rattling his colanders and other wares, a big grin dawning on his smoke-grimed countenance at the opening of the door. It was a hot day, and he was badly needing a bath, but that didn't stop him edging closer to Fern to try and impress her with the quality of his goods.

Beside him was a red-haired, merry-faced woman, displaying a colourful array of ribbons and lace and other bits and baubles on a tray which she quickly and expertly jammed into the open door space. And beside her was a tiny little dwarf woman, whose name was appropriately Tiny, although she was more affectionately known as Little Lady Leprechaun because of

276

her size and her raiments of green, including an oversized hat crammed over her spiky black hair.

Lady Leprechaun was bearing buttons, safety pins and hairgrips, piles and piles of them, reposing in a saucepan with a cheeky face painted on its enamel and the words, *Potty people sell the best, buy my pins and you'll be blessed.*

Fern took one look at the motley trio in front of her and made to close the door but Alaría, Stink's wife, had positioned her tray well, it had lodged itself in the door jamb, and with a shake of her head Alana said, 'Would you look at that now, mavourneen, it is stuck and no mistake and while it's there you might as well take a look at what it has to offer. A nice shiny ribbon perhaps, or a collar of finest Irish lace for your dress? Only a few pennies to you, me dear, and the good Lord will bless you for your kindness.'

'Indeed He will do all o' that, me fine lass,' Stink added his contribution, all the while nodding and beaming and making a great show with his colanders.

Fern made no response, she had turned pale, her eyes were huge and frightened, as she shrank away from Stink who was now staring at her in a most appraising manner.

'Bejabers and bejasus!' he burst out. 'If it isn't young Kathleen Swan from Tipperary! One o' that band o' Irish gypsies you ran away from a year or two back. I mind fine you were the speak o' the place when it became known you had gone off wi' that rogue, Johnny Docherty!'

Alana and Little Lady Leprechaun forgot all about

277

selling their wares as they too looked at Fern with recognition in their eyes.

'Oh, please,' Fern said shakily, 'don't be telling anyone about the things you are saying. I don't mind them knowing that I'm a gypsy but Fern Lee is the name that is on me now, everyone on the island knows me as that. I couldn't use my real name because I came here to get away from Johnny, he wouldn't stop his drinking and sometimes he went crazy altogether, swearing and shouting and hitting me, and so I left him. I just ran and ran, never knowing where I was going till I landed here on this island, safe from Johnny and all the terrible things he did to me.'

Alana shook her head. 'Ah, is that not a sad tale now? Johnny Docherty. A rascal and a rover from the day he drew breath. You're well rid o' him, me lass, and indeed we won't be telling anyone who you were before you got yourself entangled with his like.'

'Ay, you have the travellers' word on that,' Stink promised solemnly, 'I myself wouldn't like any lass to wind up in the clutches o' big Johnny Docherty, so don't you be worrying your head anymore about him, your secret is safe wi' us.'

Fern looked at him quickly. 'What secret?' she asked sharply.

Stink blinked, He looked surprised. 'That you're biding – or should I say hiding – here. If we come across Johnny, we won't say a word o' your whereabouts, you can rely on us.'

Little Lady Leprechaun was growing impatient. In her view there was no need for all these reassurances. They were travelling people, honour was inherent in them; fight as they would among themselves, when it came to troublesome outsiders they closed rank and that was all there was to it.

With that in mind she cocked her head, turned her bright eyes on Fern and said perkily, 'Buy some o' me nice buttons and all the blessings o' Saint Patrick will be upon you. Fern Lee or Kathleen Swan, it doesn't matter what you call yourself, you're as pretty as the heather bells themselves and surely deserve to bedeck yourself in fine buttons and bows.'

Fern laughed; she was about to go inside to get her purse when Shona chose to appear at that inopportune moment, blue eyes glinting curiously as she glanced around at all the faces. 'Quite a cosy little gathering, I see. Would I be right in thinking you all know one another? And which of you is Kathleen Swan? Surely I know you all by name but I've never heard her mentioned before.'

Here she looked pointedly at Fern whose face had turned bright red and who might have given the game away altogether had not Stink leapt to the rescue. 'And you would be right enough in what you say, Shona, mavourneen. We used all to meet up at our gatherings in Ireland. I myself have known Fern Lee since she was just a babe in arms. In those days her mammy and daddy would come in about our camp to join us in our dancing and singing round the fire.' He threw his eyes heavenwards. 'Ah, were they not the finest times I ever knew? At peace with the world and it with us. Now we are chased about from pillar to post and ourselves never knowing from one minute to the next where we are going to lay down our heads for the night.'

'That doesn't explain Kathleen Swan,' Shona probed relentlessly. 'Who she is and why were you talking about her just now.'

It was Alana's turn to wax eloquent. 'Bonny, bonny, Kathleen Swan? It is only natural we should be discussing her. It was a terrible shame that the poor lass had to go and fall sick just as we were setting out on our travels. May the good Saint Patrick bless her and set her to rights for she has the wanderlust in her soul and will maybe die altogether if she has to bide too long in the one place.'

Shona still wasn't satisfied. She gazed long and hard at all the faces but they were wearing an expression of studied innocence and she had to be content with the fact that she now knew a little bit more about Fern's identity, which wasn't much, considering that she had guessed all along that the girl was of gypsy stock.

Stink, never one for letting an opportunity slip by, showed his broken teeth in an apologetic grin and said placatingly, 'There now, mavourneen, you are knowing all there is to be knowing about Fern Lee and Kathleen Swan. And to save us coming to your door, would you be buying something here and now from the fine selection you see here before you? A silk ribbon to tie up that bonny red hair o' yours? Or a few safety pins to hold up your man's breeks? Or how about treating yourself to a nice new set o' pots and pans to brighten up your kitchen? You will never get anything as good or as cheap in the shops for they are just robbers, every one.'

Shona knew when she was beat. She glanced at Fern, who was smiling at her in that oddly winning way of hers, and she smiled back. She couldn't help it, the sun was shining, the world was blue and bright, there was a strong sense of comradeship in the air, and she responded to it in her typically positive way.

'Och, alright, you win,' she conceded with a giggle, raking in her bag for her purse, catching Fern's eye as she did so, knowing that she was drawing close to the girl in spite of herself, in the process feeling utterly glad to shake off the fetters of resentment and jealousy that had beset her ever since she had seen Fern ensconced in *her* bed, wearing *her* clothes, living in *her* childhood home, liaising with her father in a way that had brought out the cat in her and made her most bitter and unhappy.

All that was done with, in just a few moments of a scented summer's day; in common with most other islanders, including old Elspeth, she had capitulated to the charisma of a gypsy girl's sunny smile.

She felt truly happy to have at last buried the hatchet, to feel at rights with the world once more and – most importantly – to know that when next she came face to face with her father she would do so without any of the animosity she had displayed towards him for the last few unhappy weeks.

Stink was as good as his word, not by one whisper did he betray Fern's true identity. The rest of his fellow travellers were also sworn to secrecy, which was as well, since this year they had pitched their camp nearer the village of Portcull, making it impossible for Fern to avoid them even if she had wanted to.

'As long as we remember the new name that is on

281

her,' Stink decreed importantly. 'If Johnny does come to Rhanna he'll be looking for Kathleen Swan, and he'll ask around for a colleen o' that description. As long as we remember she is now Fern Lee all should be well. It might be wise also no' to mention Johnny's name to anyone here, they would maybe connect the two and then the fat would indeed be in the fire.'

Stink, however, did not hold his tongue on other matters concerning Fern's background. Before very long the entire island knew her history.

'She had a hard life as a child,' Stink recounted sadly, holding court at every door he knocked on. 'Her mammy and daddy were heavy drinkers and never cared what happened to their wee one. They went to early graves, pickled in drink, and after that the poor lass ran wild and never seemed to settle herself anywhere.

'I myself lost track o' her for a good long while, then the next I heard she had run away wi' some good-looking rascal or other, the sort young women would lie down and die for. The pair o' them must have gadded about quite a bit because there were sightings of them all over the land, then they just seemed to disappear altogether, and none o' us knew where the lass was. After a while a wee snippet went the rounds, she and he were working in some gentry house, in wi' the bricks it was said, allowed the run o' the place.

'I set off on my travels and heard no more and got the surprise o' my life when I chapped on Fergus McKenzie's door the other day, there was the very lass, straight out the blue, hiding from her rogue o' a man, all hot and bothered in case he should find her and start beating the life out o' her again.'

At this point, Stink would clasp his hands and say sorrowfully, 'Ah, poor, poor lass, when she met that man he must have seemed the answer to her prayers, she likely clung to him for any morsel o' love she could get for she got precious little o' that from her mammy and daddy. It is indeed sad that she picked the kind o' man that she did, but there you are now, there is no accounting for a young girl's tastes, and he wouldny show his true nature to her till it was too late. She'll be alright here, as long as we all watch out for her and do our best to protect her if he comes lookin' for her.'

Stink had done his job well; his story only served to strengthen Fern's position in the community. The islanders closed ranks; as long as she remained on Rhanna she was safe – or so they thought!

Part Three

AUTUMN/WINTER
1968–69

Chapter Twenty-two

Hector the Boat was growing restless. August was moving into September, the mellow days were warm and misty, and he hadn't done any fishing worth mentioning since the day of the Hobgoblin of An Coire.

He was down at the harbour, tinkering with his boat, when Dodie appeared, looming above the steps, spending some minutes gazing fearfully into the green oily water before plucking up the courage to make his way downward, his wellington-clad feet slipping about on the greasy steps which made him ultra cautious till he had reached the bottom.

He had a mission on his mind that day. It had been a long while since he had vowed to go back to Camus nan Uamh to get the 'nice shiny thing' he wanted for Kalak Dubh. It hadn't been for the want of trying; for the past few weeks he had harangued Hector to take him out in his boat, but Hector had shown no inclination to return to Rhanna's eastern shores.

Today Dodie was lucky. The passing of time had dulled Hector's memory of his near encounter with a fabled creature, his fears had diminished, and now he was dying of curiosity regarding further reported sightings of a beautiful mermaid who, it was said, was haunting the Bay of the Caves. He was therefore quite willing to capitulate to Dodie's suggestion that they go out there that morning and it wasn't long before the *Queen o' Scots* was on her way out of the harbour, heading east, cutting steadily through the waves as if she was glad to have her head at last.

As before, Dodie was enthralled with everything he saw as they went along, pointing out all the familiar landmarks, growing so excited Hector had to tell him to, 'Calm down or bail out, before the whole o' the damt island gets out their spyglasses to see what is happening!'

Dodie subsided a little, the idea of stepping out of the boat in the middle of the ocean not appealing to him in the least. He could not, however, contain himself when they rounded a headland and there in front of him was the Bay of the Caves, the great black cliffs shearing up from the tiny sandy cove, the sheltered waters calm and peaceful, the colour of it turquoise and pink where it lapped the shore.

Hector's little marker buoys were still where he had left them, and in a short time he was hauling up his pots to see if they had remained intact in his absence. One or two needed mending, all of them had to be cleaned out and re-baited, and while Hector was absorbed in his task, Dodie got busy with the last pot in the line, scooping out the remains of dead lobsters and bits of debris, his heart in his mouth in case he mightn't find what he had come to seek.

He was overjoyed when he came upon the knobbly little drawstring bag that he had hidden all these weeks ago. It was covered in barnacles and green slime but the contents were all there, duller than he remembered, but he only wanted one of the items, and that he would soon clean up. Extracting it, he smuggled it inside the depths of his jacket and replaced the bag in the pot while Hector's back was still turned.

For the next half hour both men worked in a harmonious silence till the pots had all been cleaned, freshly baited, and returned to the water.

And then they heard it, an angel voice singing in the black depths of An Coire, the most awesome of all the caverns, cathedral-like in its splendour, its great curved arch supported by pillars of black volcanic rock that had piled one on top of the other from some spectacular upheaval of past ages.

The acoustics inside An Coire were unparalleled, and to Dodie and Hector, the sounds that they heard just seemed to grow and grow in volume, echoing all round the bay and the caves, chiming, haunting, magical notes that made them stop and stare in utter wonder into An Coire's yawning mouth.

Dodie was spellbound, he had never known anything so utterly enchanting; and then – his heart missed a beat, for there, in the shadows, was a misty female figure, sitting on a big rock, her hair flowing down her back like a thick dark curtain.

'Kalak Dubh,' he whispered, and again, 'Kalak Dubh.'

That was when he stood up, forgetting everything in his excitement, for he knew, as sure as anything, that the mysterious dark-haired maiden known as Fern Lee, was really a mermaid, one who had come to

Rhanna to live for a short while among its people, until the day she returned to the ocean – forever . . .

The boat rocked, Dodie's foot slipped on the planks, Hector shouted, but before he could lift a finger Dodie had tumbled overboard, straight into the sea, screaming as he went, plunging down, down, into the depths, cold, cold, dark and dreadful, his lungs filling with water as he went under.

It had never entered Hector's head to wear a lifejacket, never mind supply one for any passenger he might be carrying, but he did have a lifebelt, and this he threw as Dodie's head bobbed to the surface.

Blinded by water, half drowned, terrified out of his wits, the old eccentric scrabbled desperately to save himself, but it was useless, his heavy clothing weighed him down like an anchor and once more he disappeared from sight, helplessly floating down through the choking depths to the sandy floor of the bay.

Half unconscious he was hardly aware of being grabbed and lifted, up, up, held in the embrace of some unknown being, breaking surface, coughing, spluttering, Hector's hands reaching out to grab him and haul him unceremoniously aboard the *Queen o' Scots*, before extending his hand once more to Fern Lee to help her out of the water.

'Where did you spring from?' Hector asked in surprise.

'I was in that little dinghy over there,' Fern pointed to a little craft bobbing about in the lee of a rocky outcrop.

'That's Peter Menzies' boat!'

'Ach, to be sure, I know all about that, didn't himself lend it to me whenever I told him I wanted it. He knows how much I like being out alone on the waves.'

Hector didn't doubt it, most of the menfolk of the island wanted to please Fern Lee and Peter, with his brawny good looks, would be one of the first in line when it came to doing her any favours.

Fern had dropped down beside Dodie who was lying on the deck, gasping like a fish out of water, his face a funny blue colour, his limbs twitching violently from shock and cold.

'We'll have to get him home and call the doctor,' Fern decided, shivering a bit herself as she spoke. 'Get something to cover him with, Hector, while I start up the engine.'

Hector wasn't too sure about allowing some slip of a lass to handle his precious boat. Fern Lee, however, soon proved herself to be a capable sailor. In next to no time they were back at the harbour where many willing hands manhandled Dodie ashore and into Tam's truck, after which he was speedily transported home to Croft Beag.

A greatly concerned Mairi was soon on the scene, undressing Dodie, rubbing him down with a big fluffy towel, tucking him into bed to administer hot drinks to him and apply hot bottles to his feet.

When Doctor Megan came she congratulated Mairi on her prompt attention and, after a thorough examination of Dodie, she prescribed a few days' rest in bed for him together with plenty of loving care.

'I'll make sure o' that, doctor,' Mairi said willingly,

'he'll no' want for anything as long as I'm here to see to him.'

But despite Mairi's tender devotion, Dodie developed pneumonia and relapsed into a state of fevered delirium, never knowing what he was saying as he muttered away about the Bay of the Caves and the beautiful mermaid he had seen and heard in the great cave of An Coire.

Doctor Megan and Babbie tended him night and day, Mairi saw to his every comfort, and a regular stream of visitors came and went from Croft Beag, many of them to make mournful and useless comments.

Hector the Boat, ridden by guilt over the accident, could only stare wordlessly at Dodie's blotched countenance, but his sister more than made up for his lack of eloquence.

'Ach, he's a poor soul right enough,' she stated, peering ghoulishly at Dodie to see if he was still breathing. 'I've seen a better looking corpse, and that's a fact.'

'Ay, he's just like a bag o' bones lying there,' supported Winnie Nells, while Canty Tam, her son, leered out of the window to the restless sea lying beyond, and said with conviction, 'It was the Uisge Hags that got him, they're out there now, screeching wi' rage because that lassie pulled him out their clutches. They'll no' rest till they get somebody else in his place, and the next time they'll no' be disappointed.'

'I've never seen Dodie looking so ill,' Isabel commented with a sorrowful shake of her head. 'I hear tell

292

he has the ammonia in his lungs and is having difficulty breathing.'

'No, Isabel, you've got it wrong, it's *pneu*monia,' Mollie corrected her friend.

Isabel frowned; Todd's wife was forever pulling her up about something and this time Isabel couldn't hide her annoyance. 'New or old, it will make no difference to Dodie!' she snorted, and with that she flounced away without uttering another word.

There were other more cheerful visitors of course. Fern had called when Dodie had been at his worst, rambling and raving and never knowing one face from another or what day of the week it was.

This condition lasted for several days, and then one morning, when Babbie had finished giving him his bed bath, he opened his eyes, rubbed his stomach, and declared himself to be 'dying o' hunger'.

After that he recovered rapidly and was soon up on his 'feets', if only for a few hours each day. When he was well and truly on the mend, sitting on a chair by his bed, tucked up nice and cosy with a blanket, Fern came back to see him, bearing gifts of fruit and flowers and a big get-well card, inscribed with all the names of the McKenzie household.

There was also a small card from Fern herself, and when Dodie saw it he very nearly burst into tears and had to hide his anguish by burying his face in the cuff of the smart new dressing-gown that Mairi had wrapped him in.

'Och, come on now, Dodie,' Fern, a lump in her own throat, spoke to him soothingly. 'There is surely no need for tears, you have all your good friends around you, thinking about you and caring about you, so just you be drying your eyes now and I'll make us both a nice hot cup of tea.'

Dodie, in an agony of shyness, was trying in vain to stem his tears but it was useless, they just kept flowing down his sunken cheeks and Fern, near to weeping herself, glanced at the bedside cabinet, hoping to see a box of tissues. Seeing none she hastily wrenched open the drawer . . . and was frozen into complete and utter immobility at the sight that met her eyes.

'Dodie,' she whispered at last, 'what on earth is this – and where did you get it?'

She withdrew her shaking hand. In it she held the plastic wallet, with her own picture staring out at her from under the transparent covering. 'These are my things, Dodie,' she said through pale lips. 'My own personal belongings, birth and marriage certificates, passports . . . surely to goodness you knew they were mine, I've hunted for them high and low ever since I got here.'

'I never looked at any o' these things!' wailed Dodie, guilt and fear making him cry all the harder. 'I canny read anyway and only ever wanted your photy to look at. I knew you would take it away if I told you I had it. I was helping Hector wi' his lobster pots when I found it hooked onto one o' the floats and though I didny know you then I liked your photy and took it home wi' me. I didny do anything bad, don't tell the police on me. I don't want to go to jail.'

'To be sure, they're the last people I would tell,' she said grimly. She looked at his woebegone countenance and putting her arm round his thin shoulders

294

she said soothingly, 'Hush now, Dodie, I'm sorry I was mad at you but it was just the shock of seeing my stuff in your drawer. It's wonderful, you'll never know what it means to me to have everything back again, I only wish I'd known about it sooner, it would have saved me all the bother and worry of looking for it.'

Leaning over she kissed his brow and in utter confusion he shoved his hand into the bedside drawer and withdrew a small package, carefully wrapped in the pink tissue paper from the fruit basket that Kate had brought him.

'Here, take this,' he gabbled. 'I went wi' Hector to the Bay o' the Caves to get it and thought it had lost itself when I was drowning. But it was still in my pocket where I left it and when Mairi wasny lookin' I got it out and gave it a wee rub wi' soapy water. It's for you, nice and shiny, like the stars. I know ladies like shiny things like that.'

With bated breath Fern peeled away the paper and gasped aloud when she beheld the exquisite sapphire and diamond brooch lying sparkling in the palm of her hand.

'Ah, Dodie,' she said softly, 'so you found the jewels as well. You have indeed had a field day to yourself.'

Taking his big rough hand in her little one she went on coaxingly, 'Come on Dodie, you must know where the rest of it is, you've been keeping a lot of wee secrets to yourself, but now the time has come for you to share them with me. I want you to be telling me how to find all the other nice shiny things like this one.'

'In one o' the lobster pots at Camus nan Uamh,' he supplied willingly. 'I found the wee bag when I found the photy, all o' them tied to each other wi' string and caught up together on a marker buoy. I hid the bag because I was feart to take it as well but when you didny want the wooden sign I thought you might like the bonny brooch and went back wi' Hector to get it . . .'

He began to scrub his eyes, 'That was when I saw Kalak Dubh in the cave, the dark maiden who is really a mermaid, and then I fell in the water . . .'

He turned and looked at her and suddenly his strange dreamy eyes were alert and very aware, 'It was you Dodie saw in the cave, sitting on a stone, singing just like the mermaids used to sing to Old Joe when he was at sea in his boat.'

'Ay, it surely was me that you saw, Dodie,' she admitted quietly. Then grasping his arm she said urgently, 'And I want you to come back there with me, back to Camus nan Uamh to show me which lobster pot the wee bag is in.' He shrank away, dread on his face as he remembered the brackish water flooding his lungs, the choking terror of being unable to breathe, the numbing cold . . .

'I canny! I canny go back!' he yelled. 'No' to that place! It's bad luck, Canty Tam said the Uisge Hags will get me the next time! I canny go back.'

'Och, come on now – for me,' she spoke persuasively, all the time holding his hand and gazing into his face. 'I'll be there with you, surely you know you'll be safe with me, I'd never let anything happen to you. You're my friend, Dodie, and if you don't do this for me I'll never be safe for as long as I live, and might even die altogether if I don't get away from here.'

Dodie's heart beat strangely, he couldn't bear the thought of anything happening to Kalak Dubh. She wanted to go home, back to the sea, and she had to take her shiny things with her, so that she could deck herself in all her finery when she sang with a voice like an angel to the fishermen who roamed the oceans and reported sightings of fabulous creatures as they travelled to far distant shores.

He gulped and swallowed back his fears, and his voice was rough with emotion when he said chokingly, 'Ay, I'll go back, I'll show you where I hid the bonny things, just for you, I'll go back, Kalak Dubh.'

'Special man,' she whispered, 'I knew you would do this for me, for Kalak Dubh. Peter Menzies said I could have his boat anytime, it's tied up in Mara Oran Bay, and that is where I will meet you tomorrow morning at eight o'clock, when the tide is on the turn. I need today to get myself ready, but I'll be there in the morning, and remember, you mustn't breathe a word of this to anyone, not even Mairi.'

Dropping a gentle kiss on his cheek she went to the door while Dodie watched, racked by so many strange feelings he couldn't sort out one from the other, only knowing that his enchantment for the beautiful dark maiden would live with him for the rest of his days.

'My photy,' he whispered brokenly, 'can I no' at least have my photy?'

'It's one of the things I need, Dodie, to set me free . . .' She looked at him sitting there, old and bent and thin. A tear caught in her throat, and impulsively she said, 'Och, but I'll give you another, one that Kirsteen took of me with a fancy camera she brought back from Glasgow. She just popped the shutter, a picture rolled out, and a few minutes later it was developed.'

'Ay,' was all he said, softly and sadly. He knew nothing about cameras, all he wanted was a photo of the dark maiden to remember her by, and maybe in this one she would be smiling and happy, the way she had mostly been whenever they had met one another on their lonely rambles around the island.

Chapter Twenty-three

Later that day, Colin and Andrew McKinnon, two brothers of twelve and thirteen, guided their wooden dinghy into the great cavern of An Coire and cut the outboard motor. They had heard all about the elusive being that was reputedly haunting the cave and for weeks they had been daring one another to go there to find out for themselves what all the fuss was about. Knowing full well that a visit to the Bay of the Caves would be forbidden to them, they had told Angus, their grandfather, that they were simply going fishing and could they borrow his boat. Having gained his permission they had set off, bloated with triumph, bolstering themselves up in the way that small boys do when trying to impress one another with their bravado.

But now that they were actually here, in this vast, alien place, their confidence began crumbling a little and they stopped chattering as the silence and the dimness enclosed them. Because it was an overcast day outside, the interior of An Coire was dark; dark and damp and eerie. The green walls dripped slime, phantom shapes loomed in the shadows, and the rocks looked like bent and brooding old men, doomed to spend eternity in the nether regions of a half-world.

Weird and wonderful stalactites hung suspended from the roof, glistening and dripping, gnarled and twisted, fearsome tapering spears that plunged down from nowhere yet at the same time went up and up, growing thicker as they went, on and on into some terrible unknown sphere of blackest space. And miles above, it seemed, was the opening that gave An Coire its name, the blowhole from which the water spumed out when the tides were at their highest, looking tiny from down here, a small gleam of illumination in the dome of An Coire, a ray of unreachable daylight that only served to emphasise the vastness of the cathedral-like cavern where flickering shadows danced on the wet walls and the water sparkled with tiny pinpricks of phosphorescence that came from myriad sea creatures darting hither and thither beneath the green swell of the tide.

It was beautiful, breathtaking, and awe-inspiring, but neither Colin nor Andrew was inclined to any of these feelings. To them the Cave of the Kettle was a world apart from the everyday reality that was normally theirs; each of them longed only to return to that reality, but it wouldn't do to voice such a desire. Instead they tried to act and sound tough and to show one another that it would take more than a smelly old cave to get the better of them.

'Where's the mermaid then?' Colin began in an aggressive voice, as he spoke looking over his shoulder to ascertain just how far in they had come. 'You told me this was where Graeme Donald and the others saw something or somebody sitting on a rock singing.'

'I didn't say they saw it, I said they thought they saw it,' Andrew asserted himself quickly.

'Well, it was all lies,' Colin stated flatly. 'She isn't here and we'd better go home. Dad will skelp our lugs for us if he ever finds out we came here without asking him first.'

He glanced round at the rock sculptures. There was something sinister in the way they were all huddled together, as if they were discussing something of great importance, perhaps deciding the fate of two errant schoolboys who had dared to come here and invade this awful, evil, slimy, world that hád belonged to them from time immemorial.

'I don't like it here.' There was a decided wobble in Colin's voice now. 'I wish we'd never come. You were the one who suggested it in the first place.'

Andrew's lip jutted. 'You're just scared,' he scoffed, jumping a little as a large wave slapped against the boat, making it rock in an alarming fashion.

'No I'm not, I just want to go home, we'll miss our tea if we don't hurry.'

Andrew didn't answer. With eyes that were wide and staring he watched mesmerised as a huge, gleaming wave whooshed in from the sea, catching the dinghy on its breast and lifting it up as if it were made of matchwood.

'The autumnal equinox,' he whispered, then, with a gulp, 'coming in – fast.'

'I want to go home!' wailed Colin. 'Dad said we were never to come to this place on our own.'

'Cry baby!' Andrew jeered, even though he felt like crying himself and would have given anything to be home safe in his own house – on second thoughts, maybe not so safe, their father might tan their hides when all of this came out in the wash.

'Stop blubbering,' he went on in a shaky voice, 'I'll start the engine and we'll get going right away.'

He yanked at the cord, again and again, but the little motor refused to start, and by the time he and his brother had manned the oars the sea was swirling relentlessly into the cave, lifting the dinghy higher and higher.

'We'll never get out now!' yelled Andrew above the roar of the incoming tide. 'We'll have to get onto one o' those ledges and sit it out. Come on, climb up, I'll hold onto the boat.'

Like a young monkey Colin scrambled upwards, a short while later to be joined by his brother who, with great presence of mind, had held onto the dinghy by its rope. Between them the brothers attached the rope to a spur of rock, their fingers numb with cold, their hearts beating fast with shock and exertion. Shivering, they squatted close together, deafened by the thunderous roar of the ocean as it swirled and churned outside An Coire and came rushing in to throw itself out of the spout in the cliffs.

It was a breathtaking spectacle and the boys watched spellbound from their perch, while the water rose higher and higher, covering the heads of the 'old men', insidiously lapping the lower ledges, playing with the boat, making it whirl about and buck alarmingly so that it worried away at the rope, causing it to creak and groan where it rubbed against the rock.

'What if it breaks!' Colin cried in an agony of

suspense. 'We'll never get away from here if it does. Nobody knows where we are, we might die and turn into skeletons or the gulls might eat us . . .'

'Shut up!' snapped Andrew, breaking out in a sweat at his brother's words, his pulse racing as a huge wave spumed into An Coire, making both boys instinctively recoil to the furthest recesses of their rocky retreat.

Colin's fingers touched something wet and icy cold. With a smothered scream he drew his hand away quickly and simply gaped at the sight he saw in the greeny half light reflecting off the water.

It was the remains of a dead body, putrifying and partially eaten away by seabirds, only the clothes giving away the fact that it had once been a man.

Petrified and horror stricken, the boys moved as far away as possible from their gruesome find and clung together, trembling from head to foot, vowing to each other that never again would they venture anywhere without parental permission, nothing was worth this – and they still had to face the outcome of this particularly nasty adventure – if they ever got out of here alive. Hearts like stone in their breasts, exhausted, freezing and hungry, they sat on their ledge, forever it seemed, while the water crashed and foamed amongst the rocks outside before sweeping in to roar out of the blowhole and swell the level ever higher inside the vault.

And then it stopped; gradually but surely the volume of water lessened. Aeons passed, at least so it felt to the boys as they waited for the magical turning of a tide that had brought home to them a lesson that they would never forget.

When at last it was safe for them to leave An Coire they couldn't get into their boat fast enough. Not waiting to try starting the motor they somehow found the strength to man the oars and went shooting away as speedily as they could, away from An Coire and the Bay of the Caves, away from the cold and silent body of a man who was unknown to them but who would remain in their minds for a very long time to come.

'We found a body, Dad!' Colin cried the minute he arrived home, the horror of his discovery overriding all else.

'And it was dead!' supplemented Andrew.

'Oh, ay,' Colin Mor, the boys' father, grinned indulgently. 'Is that a fact now? And I suppose you're going to be telling me next that it sat up and said, "Boo"?'

'No, Dad.' Colin, near to tears, the effects of his experiences showing in the pallor of his face, spoke in a hushed whisper, 'It really was a dead man's body, up on one o' the ledges o' a cave.'

'And where exactly was this cave?' Angus, the boys' grandfather, who had lived with his son ever since the deaths of their respective wives, asked the question in a deeply suspicious voice.

The brothers shuffled their feet and looked at one another, then Andrew, being the eldest, took the great decision to tell the truth. 'It was An Coire.'

'An Coire! The Bay o' the Caves!' Colin Mor's eyes bulged. 'How many times have I told you no' to go there? It's a dangerous place for anybody to be, never mind two lads wi' nothing between their lugs but fresh air!'

'Och, come on now, don't be too hard on them,' Angus intervened. 'They've learned their lesson, the pair o' them look as if they've had the shat scared out o' them good and proper.'

'It was horrible! It was bad enough being trapped on the ledge but when we found the man's body and couldn't get away it was like a really bad dream.' Andrew, responding to the sympathy in his grampa's voice, broke down and burst into a fit of tears which so surprised Colin he too gave way to his feelings and began sobbing into his grazed and grimy hands.

Colin Mor looked uncomfortable. 'Ay, well, it was indeed a terrible adventure for you both, but that body must have been there for a whilie and will keep for a few hours yet. I'll phone the police when I get my breath back, but for now, the pair o' you had better get out o' my sight before I thrash the living. daylights out o' you for disobeying me.'

'Ay, but no' before they've had a good hot bath and a bite o' supper,' Angus decided gently. 'These lads have had a shock to their systems and, as any doctor will tell you, they will need a good bit o' sustenance to help get them back on their feets – as I'm sure you know already, Colin, my lad.'

Colin Mor blinked, 'I didny know any such thing in my day, you're softer wi' these lads than you ever were wi' me.'

'You had a mother, Colin Mor, never forget that. I knew fine that Ethel spoiled you when I wasny lookin' – no matter what I said to the contrary.'

Colin Mor swallowed hard. 'Right enough now,' he said softly, 'I suppose it wouldn't do any harm if I was

305

to make us all a nice hot mug o' cocoa and we gathered ourselves round the fire to drink it.'

'It would do nothing but good,' agreed Angus, nodding in his easy-going way as he slowly and calmly lit his pipe.

Andrew and Colin gazed at him with affection. He hadn't said anything about the white lie they had spun him in order to obtain the loan of his boat, and the gratitude they felt towards him brought fresh tears springing to their eyes. He was the best grampa in the world, they had always known that, but today he was something more, something special, a being apart from all the rest. Going to his chair they perched themselves on either side of him. 'Thanks, Grampa Angus,' they murmured quietly, rather shamefacedly.

His eyes twinkled. 'Next time you go fishing see and catch some fish and no' a body that is dead. I wouldny know what to do wi' one o' these if it was served up to me on a plate.'

The brothers burst into relieved laughter. They couldn't forget their grisly find in the great cave of An Coire but for now it was enough to be here with their father and grandfather, everything else could wait – at least until tomorrow.

That evening, when Fern was sitting with Kirsteen and Fergus round the fire eating supper, she said unexpectedly, 'Will you be listening to me for a minute? Tomorrow I am leaving here – when the steamer sails out of the harbour I will be going with her and I doubt if I'll ever be coming back. I have packed my few bit things, nothing much to be sure,

306

but more than the rags I stood up in when first I came to this island.'

'Tomorrow!' Fergus and Kirsteen cried in unison. 'But why the hurry?' continued the latter. 'You never gave us any indication that you might be leaving!'

Fern lowered her head, an action which caused ringlets of blue-black hair to cascade over her shoulders, partially hiding the flush on her face, the pensive expression in her dark eyes as she gazed solemnly into the fire.

'I knew this would come as a surprise to you both, and I can never begin to tell you how it grieves me to be leaving two people who have done so much for me. There is a lot I have to say to you – and at last I am going to be telling you the truth about myself. The travellers told you some of it when they were here in the summer, I did run away with a man called Johnny Docherty. Together we roamed the highways and byways of Ireland and then we ended up working in a mansion house near the sea. In no time at all the owners came to trust us implicitly, especially Johnny, he was a charmer was Johnny, silver-tongued and good-looking, a man who could twist any woman round his little finger . . .'

She paused and looked at them, sitting together in the ingle, listening intently to everything she had to say. 'Ah, if it could have been for us the way it is for you two, but Johnny couldn't keep away from the drink. He was like my father all over again and I wasn't lying when I said he used to hit me and give me a terrible time. But he was all I had, and when he wasn't drunk he was good to me – in his own way I think he loved me and wanted to look after me.

307

'But I go too fast, there is so much to say. When the owners of the house went away abroad on business for a year they left us there as caretakers. Johnny knew every inch of the place, and it wasn't long before he had cracked the safe and stolen the valuables that were kept there. He told me he was taking me to a new life in America and we got all our things together, passports, papers, everything we would need to start us off when we got to that country.

'The owners kept a motor yacht in the sheltered bay just below the house. The name of it was *Sea Witch* and one night in March we took her from her mooring and set sail for our new life.'

She sighed and shook her head. 'To be sure, it was all like a magical dream, sailing the seas with Johnny in that beautiful boat, the future rosy and bright before us. Then everything started to go wrong, a mist came down, it was night, we couldn't see where we were going and were afraid to use the ship's radio to make a mayday call for help. We knew there could be an emergency at any minute and so we had to act quickly. The jewels, our passports and other documents, were already sealed in waterproof packets and these I attached to my belt. Soon afterwards we foundered on the rocks at Camus nan Uamh and had to abandon ship.

'Ah, my lovely *Sea Witch*, she went down very quickly. There was no way we could even take to the dinghy. It wasn't a rough sea but there was a big swell and the tide carried us right into An Coire. It must have been then that I lost the things from my belt but there was no time to think of anything in those Godforsaken moments. Johnny was badly hurt, I had to hold onto him, and somehow we made it to a safe place high up in the cave.

'There we had to stay for a long time, Johnny drifting in and out of consciousness. I knew I had to get help for him, and as soon as I could I left the cave and made my way over the narrow strip of stony shore towards the village. I was very tired and it took a long time but I knew where I was going. When I was a child, travelling around with the other gypsies, we used to have our summer camps on Rhanna and so I had a good idea where Doctor Lachlan lived. It was to his house I was heading that night but I couldn't make it. I was cold and wet and exhausted and I crept into the nearest barn, meaning to rest for a while. Well, of course, I banged my head on a beam, you found me next morning, Fergus, and for the next two days or so I was laid up, worrying about Johnny and wondering what was happening to him.

'On the second night, when the household was asleep, I got up and went back to the cave to find Johnny dead. He had been delirious when I left him and he had either fallen off the ledge or had somehow gotten down to look for me. I knew I had to hide him, so I waited till the next high tide and – God knows how – I got both of us back up onto that ledge and that was where I had to leave him. It was the worst thing I ever had to do in my life, Johnny was all I had, I loved him but I was always afraid of him. After I got over the shock of him dying I felt a strange sense of relief that it was over. I only had one thing in mind, to make a new life for myself, but I could do nothing without documents or money.'

At that point she gazed directly at Fergus, her dark eyes piercing into his as she went on, 'I had no other option but to try and stay here for as long as I could. I needed a chance to find my papers and also to make some money to start me off. Men have always liked me, my looks were the only assets I ever had, and so I used them to try and win you over, Fergus. It was wrong of me but I was desperate and then Kirsteen came home and I no longer had to rely on your hospitality, she made it easy for me to stay here. The rest of the islanders began to accept me, and I grew to love this place.

'In the beginning I used to meet Dodie and Canty Tam on my travels and they told me all about the myths and legends surrounding Rhanna. That was when I got the idea of using the stories to keep people away from An Coire. I was terrified Johnny's body would be found and I went to the Bay of the Caves as often as I could to search for my things. I was always good in the water, like a little fish Johnny would say. He taught me how to dive and swim underwater, and I did a lot of that in the bay, always hoping I would find the lost wallets.'

She smiled ruefully. 'I didn't bargain for beings like Dodie. All along he held the answer to my prayers and even yet he holds the last key. Tomorrow morning early he is coming with me to the Bay of the Caves where, I hope, he will reveal his final little secrets to me. After that, if all goes well, I will be leaving Rhanna, never to return. With any luck I should be on the other side of the world when all this comes out. As yet, no one suspects anything amiss. When the travellers left here recently I gave Stink a letter to post for me when he got back to Ireland. It was to the people that Johnny and me worked to, assuring them that all was well in their absence.'

'You have certainly thought of everything,' Kirsteen, her voice tight and strange, her blue eyes cold, looked long and hard at the girl she had befriended and trusted for the last few months.

At her words, Fern's golden-skinned face took on a deeper flush. 'Mavourneen, I know you are thinking that I must be a calculating little schemer to have done all this. That isn't the way of it at all, I was weak, I just went along with Johnny in everything he did. Now, if I am to survive, I have to make the best of the consequences. I can't face the thought of imprisonment, I would rather die than have that happen to me. I'm a gypsy, Kirsteen, my dearest friend, it's in my nature to roam free. Please, ah, please, try to understand that. I will never forget you or Fergus, my memories will be of you and your family, especially your darling little grandchildren, Lorna and Ellie Dawn.'

Kirsteen didn't answer. Getting up she left the room without another word, leaving Fergus to shift uncomfortably in his seat as an awkward silence descended over the room. There were a million questions he wanted to ask, a thousand things he felt he had to say, but all of them went unspoken.

His heart was beating strangely, the night had revealed its secrets too well, everything had happened too quickly, and as well as all else he could hardly absorb the fact that after tomorrow he would never see this young girl again. The thought was oddly

311

disturbing and he didn't know how to handle it, let alone try to make sense of it all.

It was Fern who finally broke the spell of unease in the room. 'Fergus,' she murmured, her voice husky and compelling, 'I want you to know that you will always hold a special place in my heart. No matter where I go, no matter how far I may travel, I will never forget you, for as long as I live. Surely to goodness you must know the effect you have on me, so strong a man, so tender under all that toughness. If I hadn't grown to love Kirsteen so much I wouldn't have let go of you, and that is an honest fact, may God forgive me for my sins.'

He couldn't bear it any longer. Getting up he went over to her and stood looking down at her for a very long time. Briefly he touched the petal soft skin of her face, his hand lingering on the burnished tresses of her hair.

Then abruptly he turned on his heel and left her there, alone by the fire, her eyes big and burning in a face that had gone sad and quiet and somehow very lost, like a child who had strayed from the path and was unsure suddenly of which way to turn.

Chapter Twenty-four

Dodie was waiting at Mara Òran Bay, a thin, bent figure, his face grey in the searching light of morning but brightening up when Fern appeared, running towards him, carrying a small travelling bag over her shoulder, her hair caught up and tied in a red ribbon.

'Look, Dodie,' she said as soon as she was near enough, 'I've brought you the photo I promised, it isn't really all that good but at least in this one I'm smiling, not like that other one with my face all dour and sad.'

She was right, she was smiling, a lovely, happy radiant expression, the summer sun lighting her hair, catching the sunburned glow on her skin.

'Lovely photy,' Dodie touched it with one big rough finger, immediately forgetting the other one in his fascinated preoccupation with this new image which, in his opinion, was much, much better, more like the Kalak Dubh he had come to know and admire with such steadfast devotion.

Fern watched him and bit her lip. 'I've got your stone in my bag, Dodie,' she said softly, 'the one you painted with my name on it. I'm going to carry it with me always and think of you whenever I look at it.'

Crimson stained his cheeks. 'Ay,' was all he said as he stared at her, a vision of fresh and youthful beauty against the backdrop of the silvery sea.

'Come on.' She took his hand and led him over to the little boat rocking gently in the shallows. 'Help me to push her out and don't be worrying yourself now, I told you I wouldn't let anything happen to you and I mean it. Just remember – Kalak Dubh will be beside you all the time – the sea doesn't scare me, I've always been at home in the water and today I feel as if it all belongs to me.' She glanced around her, at the great expanse of the ocean, the tiny, far-flung islands, the seabirds gliding in the vast dome of the sky, and she laughed, a bubbly excited laugh that seemed to find its echo in the chuckling wavelets slapping playfully against the sides of the boat.

Dodie swallowed hard. 'Kalak Dubh,' he whispered, a terrible ache inside his chest for this young girl who seemed so pleased to be leaving the earth, and all it meant, far behind her.

Sitting there in the bow, guiding the little craft over the waves, the rising sun spilling its golden rays over her, a catchy tune in her throat, she seemed the epitome of all things mortal and wonderful, and Dodie found it very hard to believe that she wasn't really of the world, that she was glad because she was returning to the element that she knew best. The sea, the endless sea, waiting to take her back into its vast bosom, calling to her in a voice that only a fabulous creature like her would understand.

A fabulous creature! A mermaid! A real, live, mermaid, and he alone had the privilege of going with her to collect the shiny things she needed for her last, long, journey.

Dodie was so busy grappling with his thoughts he forgot all about Canty Tam's gloomy warnings concerning the Uisge Hags and other such fearsome beings, and almost before he knew it they were rounding the cliffs and heading into Camus nan Uamh where all was calm and peaceful in the silence of the September morning.

'Where is it, Dodie?' Fern asked in a breathless voice. 'The pot – the lobster pot with my things inside?'

Dodie couldn't stop trembling as he guided her over to where the marker buoys were bobbing in the water. He wanted very badly to please Kalak Dubh, knew he had to try and stay calm and do everything he could to help her, but the enormity of events was almost too much for him.

'Och, come on now, Dodie, you can do it, I know you can do it.' She spoke encouragingly when she saw how shaken he was. 'Just give me a hand to pull up the pots and before you know where you are it will all be over.'

To Dodie, her words had a dreadful ring of finality, and he remained where he was, frozen to the spot, till she said soothingly, 'Ah, it is a lot I ask of you and you not long risen from your sick bed, poor, gentle, lovely man. But just think Dodie, of all the people on the island of Rhanna, you are the only one who can help to set me free. It is the last thing I will ever ask of you so if you care at all for Kalak Dubh you won't be hesitating any more.'

Her words had the desired effect. Dodie stirred from his seat, then he leaned over the side of the boat, his stomach churning at the sight of the green water so near his face, his imagination carrying him down, down, beneath the waves, silken, cold, terrifying . . .

Then he felt Fern's hand on his arm, reassuring, comforting. He began pulling up the pots and it wasn't long before he was handing her the knobbly little drawstring bag with all her belongings inside.

She took it, her face a picture of delight, her own hands beginning to tremble as she undid the string and peeped inside. 'At last,' she whispered, 'at last, I'm free to go.'

Dodie released a great sigh. He glanced towards the Bay of the Caves, and suddenly he detected a movement near the shore. A boat was tied up there, half hidden among the rocks, one of Ranald McTavish's boats, and out from the great cavern of An Coire came several men, carrying between them a blanket-wrapped bundle.

Fern was so engrossed with the contents of the little canvas bag that she failed to notice anything unusual, and Dodie was so mesmerised by the movements in the bay he was unable to utter one single word.

The men were getting into the boat, gingerly man-handling the bundle aboard, and that was when Fern looked up, her face growing ashen as she stared at the scene in horror.

'Johnny,' she breathed, 'oh, Johnny, they've found you, after all this time, they've found you.'

The sound of an engine split the silence as the boat nosed its way out from the rocks, to rapidly approach the deeper waters of the bay. Ranald was at the helm, Peter Menzies was there too, together with Colin Mor and Grampa Angus. The police had commandeered both the boat and the men for the journey to Camus nan Uamh, leaving their less manoeuvrable launch tied up in Portcull Harbour.

Fern started to her feet, still clutching the bag with the jewels inside. She was trapped, out here, on the ocean. There was nowhere she could run to, not now, now that Johnny's body had been found. It was over. The island that had given her sanctuary was now her prison. No need anymore to flee to a strange new country. This was where it had to end, here in the cold waters of the Atlantic deep.

For a few brief moments she gazed at the sky where the gulls were wheeling and dipping; she glanced above the cliffs to the green sward where the sheep and the cows were peacefully grazing; then she crossed herself and jumped overboard.

Dodie clung to his seat and watched in horrified wonderment as she slipped beneath the waves.

'Goodbye, Kalak Dubh,' he murmured brokenly. 'I'll keep your photy beside me always.'

But Kalak Dubh wasn't gone yet. She emerged some distance away, her dark head bobbing above the silken gleam of the waves, directly in line with the fast approaching boat. There came a shout from the men on board, but there was nothing they could do, no action they could take to avoid hitting the girl in the water.

She went under, the bright red ribbon in her hair lingering momentarily on the surface, then it too was

317

gone, leaving only a swirl of crimson foam as the sea took her and swallowed her up.

The boat's engine throttled back, and everyone began calling Fern's name. There came a splash as Peter Menzies dived overboard; time and again he swam underwater. Then he came up, bearing Fern's body in his strong arms.

Many hands helped him back into the boat. There was a hushed silence as Fern's body was laid carefully on deck, everyone crowded round, those islanders that were present automatically removing their hats as the C.I.D. men knelt to examine her.

'We'd better get Dodie,' Grampa Angus suggested quietly. 'He'll be frightened out there alone and won't know what's happening.'

He was right, Dodie didn't know. As soon as he was aboard the bigger boat he collapsed onto the deck beside Fern to cover his face with his hands and sob out in muffled tones, 'You should have left her, she'll die if you don't allow her to go home, Kalak Dubh will die.'

'She's already dead, Dodie,' Colin Mor said sympathetically, and patted the old man on his stooped and shaking shoulders.

'Why did she do it?' Peter Menzies queried in amazement, his bronzed features a study of stunned dismay.

'She was going back, back to the sea.' Helplessly Dodie shook his head as it began to dawn on him that it was all over, that it was too late for Kalak Dubh to do the things that she had planned. The beautiful mermaid was dead, and nothing that anyone did could

318

bring her to life again. He gazed at her face; it was blue and still, never again would she sing her songs to the fishermen who wandered the oceans, never again would she smile with the joy of living, her eyes crinkling as she looked around in delight at the world she had loved for the short time she had been part of it. Then he saw the little drawstring bag clutched tightly in her slender fingers, and with the tears running down his face he gently extracted it and in one swift movement he tossed it into the sea where he knew it rightly belonged. Other mermaids might find the shiny things and wear them and in that way Kalak Dubh would be remembered as he knew she deserved to be.

'Hey! What was that you threw away?' Clodhopper glared suspiciously at Dodie, who didn't answer but turned away, not deigning to explain his actions to a mere policeman who could never possibly understand anything about the mystical things that went on in the magical lands beneath the waves.

The presence of the police launch in Portcull Harbour had created a great stir of interest among locals and tourists alike, and small groups of sightseers had gathered at the pier to await further developments.

When Ranald's boat was spotted a murmur ran through the gathering; when it tied up and the police came up the steps, bearing the bodies of Fern and Johnny, a ripple of consternation could be audibly heard.

'Come on, make way, everybody!' ordered Clodhopper authoritatively. 'Go back to your homes. You will only get in the way hanging around here.'

But no one had any intention of going home; instead they retreated a short distance and thereafter stood watching the activity in a shocked silence, occasionally murmuring quietly to one another as they wondered what was going on.

Then Fergus came bursting onto the scene, making straight for Clodhopper to demand to know what was happening.

'Get him out of here,' said one of the C.I.D. men sourly, 'This isn't a bloody peepshow. We're the ones who'll be asking the questions later.' But he didn't reckon with those islanders who had been on the spot when Fern had died. In a short while the news went round and this time Fergus wasted no time in preliminaries.

'What have you done wi' her?' he cried, his black eyes snapping in his suddenly white face. 'Tell me this minute or I'll knock the buggering daylights out o' you!'

'Now, now, McKenzie, no need for that kind o' talk,' Clodhopper said warningly, taking a firm hold of Fergus's arm. 'This is none o' your business, just be on your way at once and no more interfering in matters that don't concern you.'

Fergus shook off the policeman's restraining hand. 'None o' my business!' he roared. 'I'll show you what is my bloody business!'

He let fly at Clodhopper but he was too late, a snarling Heinz got there first, and knocking the P.C. to the ground he stood over him, fangs slavering, the rumbles in his throat deepening to fearsome growls that made Clodhopper cringe back, his hand over his face to protect himself.

'Get off, you brute!' One of the other policemen grabbed Heinz by the scruff of his neck to toss him out of the way and the dog landed on the stone flags of the quayside where he lay still, whimpering and crying in pain.

Fergus was immediately on his knees beside his dog, gently lifting the big shaggy head up to his face, fondling and stroking it, whispering words of comfort into the floppy silken ears.

Clodhopper was dusting himself down, glowering at both Fergus and his dog. 'That beast o' yours could have killed me,' he said aggrievedly. 'In fact I've a good mind to put a report in when I get back. A dog like that isn't fit to be among decent people.'

The crowd had thickened, and all at once it seemed to be on top of P.C. George McDuff. 'The cratur' never touched you,' Tam acted as spokesman for everybody. 'We were all here, we are all witnesses, every one.'

There was a general murmur of agreement and much nodding of heads. Clodhopper looked at all the stony faces and took a step backwards.

'Get on with it, McDuff,' his chief growled at him. 'Charge that man later. Right now I want you over here.'

Kirsteen appeared just then, distraught-looking, making straight for Fergus to ask what had happened.

'Fern's dead,' he said briefly, 'and Heinz is hurt. We'll have to get him over to Niall's right away. Be careful how you handle him, his front paw seems to be giving him a lot o' bother.'

A strange expression flitted over Kirsteen's face.

Horrified as she was about Fern she knew that her feelings were nothing compared to those of her husband. He was suffering, she could tell that easily enough, it was all there, in the set of his jaw, the closed look in his black eyes.

She knew him so well, and when he was deeply upset a mask came down, hiding his emotions, making him behave in a stilted fashion. It was his way of shielding himself from the world and the further hurt it might cause him. Well, this was one time she didn't give a damn about all that! In these fraught moments she was more concerned with her own bewilderment to care very much about his.

That morning he had left the house some time after Fern's departure, and she had seen him, cutting across the fields, making for Portcull. She had known then that he had wanted to see Fern off on the steamer. Her last goodbyes hadn't been enough for him, he had needed to give her a personal and private farewell and Kirsteen had fought long and hard with her pride before deciding to follow him.

And now this, everything in confusion, Fern dead, Heinz hurt, a terrible taut atmosphere invading the peace of the harbour. This was neither the time nor the place for disputes between husbands and wives and taking a deep breath Kirsteen followed along behind the menfolk as gently they placed Heinz into the back seat of a readily available car. The dog was then transported to Slochmhor, where Niall diagnosed a strained ligament which was soon bandaged up.

On the way home in Peter Menzies' car, there was

an awkward silence between Kirsteen and Fergus. But as soon as Heinz was comfortably settled on a blanket in front of the fire, with a cushion at his head, Kirsteen turned to Fergus and demanded, 'What exactly did Fern mean to you? She implied things last night, about you and her, when I was away in Glasgow. I want to know the truth Fergus, and don't turn away from me when I'm speaking, I need to see your eyes when you are giving me your answers.'

'Nothing happened Kirsteen, you have my word on that.'

'Nothing! Are you quite sure about that, Fergus?'

He couldn't hold her furious, blue gaze, his voice was barely audible when he said, 'There was – an – attraction between us, I canny deny that. I was tempted, she was a beautiful lass, and young, so young. But though you weren't here you were everywhere, Kirsteen, mo cridhe. I only had to look at your photographs to get the strength I needed. She's dead, let the matter drop . . .' He passed his hand over his eyes. 'I – I need a bit o' time to get over the shock of all this. Please don't talk about it anymore.'

'*You* need time?' Her tones were bitter. 'What about me? I feel such a fool, trusting you the way I did. In your mind you betrayed me and tarnished the love we had for each other. Fern is dead, nothing can bring her back, and I'm sorry such a young life has ended so tragically. But I trusted her too, she was like a daughter to me and – and I can't find it in me yet to forgive her for using my home and my husband for her own ends.'

She gazed at him, her blue eyes dark and big with

emotion. 'I must get away, Fergus, I feel very mixed up at the moment. It will do us both good to have a break from one another. It's as well I'm going away with Phebie . . .'

Chapter Twenty-five

The news of Fern's death rocked the island and when Elspeth heard of it she fell to a storm of weeping. 'Och, my poor, poor, lass,' she cried in anguish, 'why did she have to go and kill herself? I know what she did was wrong but she'd had a hard life and no proper mother to teach her. I could have helped her, she wasny really a bad lassie. If I could have been blessed with such a bonny daughter I wouldny have allowed her to run wild the way her own mother did.'

'There, there, now, lass,' Mac patted her shoulder and folded her into his big comforting embrace. 'It's a terrible tragedy just, but you were like a mother to her in the short wee while you knew her. Fern loved you for that and told me wi' her own bonny lips that you were the best friend she ever had. I know how much women enjoy blethering wi' one another but I'm here now and I'll aye be here for as long as you want me.'

'Och, Isaac, you know fine you're everything to me,' she muttered into his flowing white beard. 'I don't know what in the world I did before you came along.'

She sneezed suddenly, making Mac jump, and after that they kissed and cuddled and cried just a bit for the lassie that might have been Elspeth's – if only.

The rest of the islanders expressed their feelings in a variety of different ways.

'It canny be true!' Kate cried. 'She was so young and full o' life, and her such a lovely lass too.'

'Ay, well, I aye said she was heading for trouble o' one sort or another,' Behag declared emphatically. 'For all her romantic looks and smooth talk, she was, in the end, no more than a common or garden thief. And who's to say that the man they found in the cave died from an accident? She maybe murdered him for all we know, hoping to keep all the stolen jewels for herself.'

'Ach, you would say that,' Kate shook her head sadly. 'The lass has paid sorely for what she did, and I for one canny rightly take in the fact that she's gone.'

'It's Dodie I feel sorry for,' Tam put in. 'He minds me o' thon poor, demented chiel, Quasimodo, in the Hunchback o' Notre Dame, weeping for the lassie who would never be his, only in this case it was her, no' him, that went and died.'

'Never mind him, what about the rest o' us?' Todd said worriedly. 'The police are going to be asking questions and I told Clodhopper the lassie was my niece, they'll be saying that I obstructed the course o' justice and will maybe clap me in jail!'

'We all shielded her,' Tam hazarded uncomfortably. 'The tinks told us who she was and none o' us said a word.'

'Ach, it was the least we could do,' Barra said

reasonably. 'We all thought her man was after her. Other decent folk would have done the same.'

'Anyway, they canny arrest the whole island,' Kate pointed out cheerfully.

'No, but they could arrest one man,' Todd's ruddy face went pale at the idea. 'You know what Clodhopper's like once he gets his teeth into something.'

But his fears were unfounded, he got off with a caution, as did Fergus. Heinz was given a second chance and Kate was right, they couldn't arrest the whole island, though Clodhopper looked as if he might have liked a try at it if he could have had his way.

An official verdict of accidental death in both cases was finally reached and the bodies of Fern and Johnny were released for burial beside their own people in Ireland.

'May the good Lord rest their souls,' the islanders told one another and rather thankfully turned their minds back to the normal events of everyday life now that winter was approaching and the home fires had to be kept burning.

It was the longest two weeks that Fergus had ever spent. The shiny new phone in the hall, installed just before Kirsteen's departure, seemed to mock him every time he had to pass it. The only calls he ever received were local, made regularly by family and friends, all of them anxious to alleviate the loneliness that they knew he was feeling.

Bob, filled with admiration for Heinz's bravery in

tackling Clodhopper, arrived every other day with a large, juicy bone, making Gaffer remain outside in case he might steal both the bone and Heinz's small moments of glory.

Heinz graciously accepted these gastronomic testimonials to his courage, becoming so enamoured with himself that he soon began malingering in a very obvious way, holding up his injured paw for everyone to see, purporting enormous difficulty whenever he had to rouse himself from the fire to obey the calls of nature.

Visitors played up to this amusing little game with many indulgent nods and smiles, and Bob too, once so filled with criticism about the dog's abilities, also thought the whole thing very amusing, going so far as to inform the master of the house that only a creature with brains could dream up such tricks in order to hold onto his comforts for as long as he could.

'Ach, he'd best bide where he is then,' was Fergus's terse verdict. 'For all the good he does when he's supposed to be working he might as well lie in that one spot for the rest o' his days.'

'That's as may be,' Bob said quietly, drawing his hand across his nose as he was wont to do when he was annoyed. 'But he wasny slow to defend you when the need arose, a beast like that would likely die for you if he had to.'

'I know all that,' Fergus returned gruffly, bending to pat Heinz on the head, wishing with all his heart that Kirsteen was home so that he could begin to feel that his life was worth living again.

* * *

328

Phebie came home but Kirsteen didn't come with her, saying that Aunt Minnie needed her and that she would be staying on in Glasgow for a week or so yet.

But the weeks went on and she never appeared. Whenever Fergus talked to her on the phone she was cold and distant and told him she had to have a period of separation away from him. 'I have to become independent again, Fergus,' she said flatly, 'I was too wrapped up in you to be able to function as an individual. I must have my own space for a while. You're strong, you'll manage alright without me, you did it before. In fact I'd go as far as to say that you were glad to have had the opportunity to be alone with Fern in the house. What a fool I was when I think o' it, filled with concern for her when all the while you and she were having a high old time to yourselves.'

'It wasn't like that at all, I told her to leave, I wouldn't do anything that would hurt you, mo cridhe,' he said huskily.

'That wasn't the impression I got when Fern spoke to us the night she informed us she was leaving. When you followed her the next day it just confirmed everything I had suspected. Please don't talk about it anymore. I'll come home when I'm ready and not before. You'll be fine, you have plenty o' women at your beck and call, all o' them only too anxious to see to your every need.'

'You're the only woman I want, you know that full well, you've always known how much I love you.'

'I have to go,' her voice faltered a little, 'give my love to everyone, especially the wee ones, tell them

I'm thinking about them and will write whenever I can.'

Christmas came and went, gifts had been exchanged by post, but still Kirsteen clung to the excuse that Aunt Minnie's dependence on her had become greater than ever and that she couldn't possibly leave her for a while yet.

December moved into January, snow dusted the hilltops, the bitter winds of winter howled over the land, and the sad, lost, lonely bleakness of that month seemed to settle over Fergus like a shroud. He dragged himself through the days, each one much the same as the last, empty, bare. He cursed everything that had ever led up to this critical period in his life. He cursed everyone, Aunt Minnie included.

Then the grand old lady came personally to visit Fergus, head held high, her arrogant, hook-nosed face taut with pride, her blue eyes piercing into his as she said with dignity, 'Will you come and fetch that wife o' yours home? I canny stand another day o' her mooning around looking as if she's sickening for something. She hardly eats a thing, she's become thin and wasted-looking, she's pining away for you, my lad, but is too stubborn to admit it.'

She paused for breath, then rushed on, 'I want my house to myself again. I was aye used to my privacy and all this lass does is nag away at me, telling me to eat all the things I hate because they're supposed to be good for me, to mind wrap up and keep warm, no' to stay up too late because at my age I need my sleep. Nag, nag, nag, from morning till night, I canny stand it another minute!'

Fergus looked at her. He let out a burst of laughter, and to her great surprise he pulled her to him and gave her a resounding kiss on the cheek. 'Aunt Minnie! I love you!' he roared. 'You certainly don't look like one but you're the best tonic I've had in weeks and I'll never be able to thank you enough.'

'Charmed, I'm sure,' she said sourly, dusting herself down, cocking her head to look at him, a twinkle appearing in her eyes. 'Tonight I will be staying with Phebie and Lachlan, tomorrow I will be leaving on the steamer and I want you to come wi' me. Kirsteen thinks I'm biding wi' one o' my cronies and she'll put up a fight when I appear home wi' you beside me. Well, I don't care how you take her away, drag her by the hair if you have to, tie her up and put her in a sack, but home wi' you she's going and that's my last word on the subject.'

Shona came to visit her father that evening, With her came Niall and the children, and they were all there in the kitchen, drinking tea, when the phone jangled from the hall.

'I'll get it,' Shona jumped up, 'it might be Fiona, dying to tell me the latest symptoms of her pregnancy. She's thrilled to bits and can hardly wait for the baby to be born.'

She went out, the murmur of her voice drifting through to the kitchen. In a few minutes she was back, eyes big in her ashen face. 'That was the police, phoning from Glasgow. A woman identified as Kirsteen was in a road accident. She died in hospital, all her things were in her bag, phone

331

numbers, addresses. They tried calling Aunt Minnie but I told them she was here . . .'

There was a crash, as Fergus got to his feet, knocking his chair over in his haste. 'What do you mean – dead?' he demanded harshly. 'She's coming home – tomorrow – I'm going with Aunt Minnie to collect her!'

Niall too got to his feet, going straight to the cupboard to pour a stiff whisky which he bore quickly to Fergus. 'Drink it, all of it,' he ordered. 'I'll phone the hospital and try to find out a bit more, surely there must be a mistake . . .'

'There's no mistake,' Shona spoke through white lips. 'They want us to go there tomorrow – to – to identify the – body.'

She shivered suddenly and the children, seeing all the stunned faces, began to cry, Ellie Dawn sobbing, 'I want to see Gramma, when can I see her? She never came at Christmas.'

Niall gathered his little daughter into his arms, leaving Shona to comfort the twins, Joe and Joy.

'Go home.' Fergus, over by the fire, his elbow on the mantelpiece, staring into the flames, didn't turn as he spoke. 'Take the bairns home, this is no place for them, it's past their bedtime anyway.'

'Niall can take them,' Shona said in a shaky voice. 'I'll stay here with you, Father, you can't be left alone at a time like this.'

'I want to be alone.' He spoke as if to himself, his dark head downbent, everything about him defeated and suddenly very tired. 'Go home, Shona, please, mo cridhe,' he pleaded softly. 'I need to be by myself, try to understand . . .'

His voice broke. Shona looked at Niall and gathering up their little ones they left the house, closing the door softly behind them.

It was seven o'clock the following morning. All night long Fergus had tossed and turned in a torment of grief and self loathing. It was all his fault! Kirsteen had left because of him and this was the result. She had been killed, in a road accident, she who had lived most of her life among the glens and the bens of the islands, more used to flocks of sheep or herds of cows blocking the way than she was to the hustle and bustle of noisy traffic.

He couldn't believe he would never see her again. He thought about all the wonderful years they had shared, his deep and tender love for her, their earlier passions blossoming into something deeper, more beautiful, as time slipped by.

And he had ruined it all. Kirsteen was dead! His Kirsteen, gone, never to return ...

He got up and dressed and went over to the window. January! He had never liked it! Helen, his first wife, had died on a cold, clear, January morning, the snows of the previous night's blizzard sparkling on the hills, the world all clean and new looking.

'It's funny – the way it's always so calm after a storm.'

The last words she had ever spoken came back to him as if it was yesterday; it was so long ago – yet still the month of January brought a bleakness to him that never seemed to diminish.

The two women who had ever meant anything to

333

him were gone from his life – and now it was time for him to go also. He looked up at the hills, silent, dour, shrouded in mist. That was where he had to go to find a solace that would last forever ...

Blinded by tears he turned and stumbled out of the room, down to the kitchen where it was cosy and peaceful, the cats sleepy and warm in their favourite place on top of the oven, Heinz snoring on the rug but opening one questioning eye as his master came into the room.

'Go back to sleep, boy,' Fergus said softly, stooping to fondle the dog's silky ears. 'No need for both o' us to be out there. This journey is for me alone, you'll be well looked after, I have no fear o' that, everybody has a soft spot for you.'

The dog looked up at him, a puzzled expression in his eyes, then with a groan he flopped down on the rug again, though he didn't go back to sleep. Something strange was happening and he needed a few moments to think things through.

Fergus shoved his feet into his boots and seizing his jacket from its hook he let himself out of the house. The freezing blast of the January morning hit him like a blow. Glancing up he saw that the hills had disappeared under blankets of icy sleet, and the sky was heavy with yellow-black snow clouds, great masses of them gathering on the horizon for as far as the eye could see.

He was about to close the door when he heard the phone ringing faintly from the hall and he hesitated, wondering if he should go back indoors to answer it. It would most likely be Shona, anxious to know how he was faring, asking questions which he knew he wouldn't be able to answer rationally.

Shona! His lassie! Could he do this to her? The daughter who had been so close to him since the day she had drawn breath. He felt as if he was being torn in two. Shona, Lorn, Grant, would they ever forgive him for what he was about to do? But they had each other! Partners with whom they could share everything, the love, the laughter, the caring. All he had to look forward to were days and nights filled with emptiness and he couldn't face a future like that, he just couldn't.

He could hear Donald in the byre, clattering the milk churns about, and he strode quickly past the outbuildings, praying that he wouldn't be seen as he cut over the fields and onto the rough track leading over the moors, from there to the foothills of Ben Machrie.

Ice spicules stung his face as he climbed higher and the way became more difficult. But he knew where he was going; as a boy he had trodden these hills with his father, he had played here with his brother Alick when they were children, and as a man he had driven his flocks and his herds up here to their summer grazings, his dogs frisking along beside him.

Onwards he plunged, the sleet and the hail lashing him, the pockets of snow thickening underfoot. He was aware that his hands and feet were growing numb and he welcomed these first signs that his lifeforces were slowing. It was what he wanted, the reason why he had come up here.

Helen, Fern, Kirsteen – they all flashed through his mind, visions of their lovely faces coming to him, radiant with life, alight with the joy of living. Gone, all

335

gone, but he knew they were beckoning to him, they wanted him to cross over, over to that other side where there was no more sorrow or pain. The biting cold was invading his lungs, his heart felt sore in his chest. It was becoming more difficult to breathe, yet still he went on upwards. To reach the pinnacle, that was his aim, to ascend the highest peak where another world awaited him in one of the wildest, most awesome, places of God's creation.

Heinz moved restlessly on his rug. In his haste to leave the house Fergus had left the door ajar and a wicked draught was invading every corner of the kitchen. The dog sat on his haunches for a moment or two, then heaving himself to his feet he went to ease the door open with his nose.

For a few moments he stood there on the step, surveying the winter world, blinking a little as a swirl of snow-laden wind gusted against his face, causing tiny droplets of moisture to adhere to his eyelashes.

He lifted his nose to quest the air, then, tail wagging, still limping a bit, he set off, following a scent that was familiar and dear to him, a faithful black shadow who had rarely left his master's side and who had no intention of doing so now.

It was Shona who set the search party in motion, having arrived at Laigmhor to find her father gone and Donald the only sign of life about the place.

And it was Donald who supplied her with the information she needed, telling her he had seen Fergus going past the byre an hour earlier, to be followed by his dog a short while later.

'I thought he was just taking a bit walk to himself,' Donald said in some bemusement. 'But when neither he nor Heinz came back I began to wonder. At the time I didn't know about Kirsteen or I would have went after him. He was making for the moors – at least it looked like that to me.'

'And God alone knows what he had in his mind,' whispered Shona, gazing up at the black face of the hills where snow clouds were pouring themselves onto the summits.

The men of the village had rallied round willingly to look for Fergus of the Glen, spreading themselves out over the moors and the lower slopes of the great bens above Glen Fallan.

'It is just like that story Ranald was after telling us,' gasped Todd, his ruddy face stung to even greater brilliance by the cold. 'Only this time it's a lad instead o' a lass who is missing.'

'Ay, and we'd better find that lad before he goes and dies on us,' Tam responded grimly. 'If we don't get him before night comes down, the hills will have their way wi' him. The de'il himself bides up yonder disguised as an angel, for when folks are dying wi' cold and hunger that's what they think they are seeing as they are drawing their last breath.'

'Ach, you've been listening to Ranald a mite too much,' Todd said scathingly. Nevertheless he raised his eyes fearfully to the snow-lashed corries and prayed silently for the safety of Fergus McKenzie, the big, dour islander whom everyone had always respected and admired, not only for his unending devotion

337

to the people that he loved, but also for the steadfast loyalty that ran staunch and true in his veins for his beloved island.

The afternoon was darkening, the men had almost given up hope of finding Fergus that day, when Mark James suddenly spotted a dark shape moving down from the snowline on Ben Machrie.

'Up there!' he pointed. 'It looks like Heinz! Pray God all is well with his master.'

It was Heinz, limping a good deal, exhausted, but all in one piece just the same, stopping in his tracks when he saw the rescuers, waiting only a short while to ascertain that they had seen him before giving a short sharp bark of command.

'We're coming, lad!' shouted Grant.

Patiently, Heinz stayed where he was till the men were near enough to follow him, then, with a slight wag of his tail, he turned to brave the elements of the hill once more. He led the men straight to Fergus, who was lying, half buried, half dead, in a treacherous snow-filled hollow, and when he was sure that everything was going to be alright he whimpered and buried his nose in his master's armpit, too close to collapse himself to appreciate fully the plaudits that were raining down upon his soaked and drooping ears.

When Shona saw the approach of the rescue party she burst into tears and running towards the stretcher she threw her arms around her father and hugged him as if she would never let him go.

'Mo cridhe,' he whispered, raising his hand to touch her face. 'I'm sorry I caused you all this grief but – I wanted it to be over. I felt – I couldn't go on.'

His eyes closed, he said no more, and the men who had saved him from a cold and lonely death bore him quickly into the house where there was warmth, and life – and hope.

When Fergus opened his eyes and saw Kirsteen sitting quietly watching him, he thought that he had indeed perished up yonder in the snow-covered wastes of Ben Machrie.

But when he felt the gentle warm pressure of her lips on his he stared at her in wonder, a million questions in eyes that were misted with tears, his lips trembling as he tried to form words that would make sense to her.

'Hush,' she placed a finger on his mouth, 'I'm here, Fergie, and I won't ever go away again. I'm so sorry you suffered as you did. It wasn't me who was involved in that accident, it was the woman who stole my handbag with all my personal things inside. I was out walking in the town at the time, very alone and lonely, thinking of you, wondering how you were. I reported the theft to the police, and this morning they phoned to let me know what had happened. I tried to get through to you but there was no answer and so I just caught the train to Oban – and came home.'

A sob caught in his throat, something cool touched his cheek, and turning his head he saw that she had placed a bunch of snowdrops on his pillow. 'Just to let you see that life still exists, even in January,' she said softly.

A big, black, wet nose suddenly slithered its way up between them, then Heinz's face, tongue flopping, lips drawn back as if he was smiling.

'He made it too,' Kirsteen laughed, 'and he's letting us know he had a hand in all this.'

Fergus glanced towards the window. A soft silvery dawn was spreading its light over the fields; even as he watched it burgeoned and grew brighter till very soon the sea was a sheet of flame and the snow-covered hills were brushed with pink.

And in the sky a lone gull was gliding, its wings glinting golden in the sunlight. To him it was a symbol, encompassing all things free and wonderful as it drifted slowly and peacefully above the tiny jewel in the Hebrides known as the island of Rhanna.